Percy Hetherington Fitzgerald

Life and Adventures of Alexander Dumas

Vol. I

Percy Hetherington Fitzgerald

Life and Adventures of Alexander Dumas
Vol. I

ISBN/EAN: 9783337178161

Printed in Europe, USA, Canada, Australia, Japan

Cover: Foto ©Raphael Reischuk / pixelio.de

More available books at **www.hansebooks.com**

LIFE AND ADVENTURES

OF

ALEXANDER DUMAS.

BY

PERCY FITZGERALD, M.A., F.S.A.,

AUTHOR OF "THE LIVES OF THE KEMBLES," "THE LIFE OF GARRICK," "PRINCIPLES
OF COMEDY," ETC.

IN TWO VOLUMES.

VOL. I.

LONDON:

TINSLEY BROTHERS, 18, CATHERINE ST., STRAND.

1873.

PREFACE.

IT might, perhaps, be thought that the duty of preparing a Memoir of Alexander Dumas should have been left to his own countrymen, and not have been attempted by one labouring under the disadvantage of being a foreigner. To this it may be answered, that for the mere dealing with the more interesting and piquant portions of his life, no national gifts or special citizenship was required. In some respects Dumas was more an Eastern than a Frenchman; and, with a characteristic love of display, he seemed to strive that everything he did or wrote should attract the attention, not of his own countrymen merely, but of all Europe. For the same reason, too, the writer of his life might be tolerably independent of what is almost essential in other cases, viz., family correspondence, and the like. In Dumas's career there was little that could be called private;

and all that was characteristic and really interesting he took care should be found in print. He never scrupled communicating to his " chers lecteurs " matters even of that personal and delicate character which others might scruple entrusting even to a letter. All his essays, prefaces, and " causeries," overflow with confessions of this confidential kind. As Quérard says in that monument of detective industry, the " Superchéries Littéraires "—

" Des mémoires biographiques sur M. Alexandre Dumas seraient un ouvrage très-réjouissant, et rien ne serait facile comme de les lui faire rédiger lui-même à son insu. M. Dumas a, dans presque tous ses ouvrages, parlé avec tant de complaisance de sa personne et de ses moindres actions, qu'en les lisant les ciseaux à la main, on arriverait à en extraire une autobiographie très-curieuse de cet *habile arrangeur de la pensée d'autrui.*"

Further, there might be an advantage in a work of this kind being presented to an English audience by one not a Frenchman. An opportunity is thus gained for dealing with many points of French literary life, which would be accepted as a matter of course by a Frenchman, or passed over as being familiar to all his countrymen.

The Author, too, may be pardoned for saying that having furnished some contributions to the history of the drama, such as " The Life of Garrick," " The Lives of the Kembles," and " Principles of Comedy," he felt tempted to illustrate the same subject still further, by fresh examples drawn from the French stage. The reader will see how intimately the life of Alexander Dumas is connected with this subject.

In conclusion, the Author must express his obligations to M. Philarète-Chasles, who himself a profound English scholar, and perhaps the earliest of his countrymen to recommend and illustrate the study of English literature in France, has aided the work in many important ways. The author also trusts that due allowance will be made for the exceptional difficulties of the task, and that under the circumstances indulgence will be extended to any mistakes in reference to French affairs, and to a few errors of the press which have been overlooked.

London, 37, St. George's Road.
November 20, 1872.

CONTENTS.

CHAPTER I.

THE GENERAL.

1762—1802.

CHAPTER II.

ALEXANDER BORN.

1802—1806.

CHAPTER III.

1806—1814.

CHAPTER IV.

THE WARS.

1814.

CHAPTER V.

FIRST LOVE.

1817.

CHAPTER VI.

FIRST DRAMATIC ATTEMPT.

1819—1823.

CHAPTER VII.

PARIS.

1823.

CHAPTER VIII.

"HENRI III."

1829.

CHAPTER IX.

THE ROMANTIC SCHOOL.

1829.

CHAPTER X.

FAME AND PROFIT.

1829.

CHAPTER XI.

"HERNANI."

1830.

CHAPTER XII.

ADVENTURE AT SOISSONS.

1830.

CHAPTER XIII.

OUT OF FAVOUR.

1830—1831.

CHAPTER XIV.

" ANTONY."

1831.

CHAPTER XV.

DRAMATIC MORALITY.

CHAPTER XVI.

"RICHARD DARLINGTON."

1832.

CHAPTER XVII.

REVUE DES DEUX MONDES.

CHAPTER XVIII.

THE TOWER OF NESLE.

1832.

CHAPTER XIX.

A TOUR.

1832.

LIFE AND ADVENTURES

OF

ALEXANDER DUMAS.

his grandmother's name, assumed by his father when he began the world. On the paternal side, his family was certainly noble, connected by marriage with many good houses, and had its lands, ancestral château, and escutcheon—matters worth recording, since its lively descendant had to suffer a good deal from ill-natured

LIFE AND ADVENTURES

OF

ALEXANDER DUMAS.

CHAPTER I.

THE GENERAL.

1762—1802.

ALEXANDER DUMAS, or ALEXANDER DAVY, MARQUIS DE LA PAILLETERIE, as he claimed to be, dramatist, novelist, traveller, and something even of an adventurer, was born on July 24, 1802, at Villers-Cotterets, a small country town, lying about half-way between Paris and Rheims. It will be surprise to many to hear the vivacious author of "Monte Christo" thus described ; but the more familiar title, Dumas, was his grandmother's name, assumed by his father when he began the world. On the paternal side, his family was certainly noble, connected by marriage with many good houses, and had its lands, ancestral château, and escutcheon—matters worth recording, since its lively descendant had to suffer a good deal from ill-natured and even scandalous stories as to his birth and connections. He himself boldly claimed a marquisate, "created in 1707 by Louis XIV.;" but of this creation I have been able to find no traces.* It must have been one of those agreeable delusions which, with many others, our author persuaded himself into accepting, and as freely offered for acceptance to the public.

This marquis was colonel and commissary-general of artillery. He served with the Duke of Richelieu at Philipsbourg, and was his "friend" in an affair of honour. He was also first gentleman of the chamber to the Prince of Conti. Duly qualified by such a position, he no doubt took his part in the decorous pastimes of the Regency and of the reign that succeeded. However, in the year 1760, when he was some fifty years old, he grew tired of France, sold the ancestral estates, and exiled himself to St. Domingo, where he purchased a large plantation. Almost at once he is said to have married a woman of the island, one Louise-Cessette Dumas, who must have been one

---

* This marquisate is not mentioned in the laborious "Registres" of Hozier, nor in the ponderous folios of Père Aymard, published during the lifetime of De la Pailleterie. Jules Janin, in a recently published monograph on Alexander Dumas, enrols this ancestor among the knights of the Saint Esprit; but I have not been able to find the name in the published lists.

of the pure native blacks, for his son, General Dumas, is represented in the portraits with a complexion almost as dark as a negro's. This swarthy tint was duly transmitted to his son and grandson, lightening, however, with each generation ; but the wiry curly hair and peculiar shape of head and features bespeak their creole descent.*　Long after, when the author of " Monte Christo " was at the height of his reputation, aggressive, vainglorious, extravagant, and even ridiculous, and had assumed the title of Marquis de la Pailleterie, having had a seal engraved with arms and coronet, this assumption of nobility was like a challenge to French scoffers, and his innumerable enemies.　It was asserted that the title had no existence ; that if it had, he was illegitimate ; and finally, that if he were born in wedlock, his father was not.　To this plain-speaking, so characteristic of the pleasant courtesies of French literary life, Alexander replied after his own characteristic fashion : " If I were really illegitimate, I should simply have accepted the bar sinister, as so many celebrated bastards have done.　But what would you have me do ?　I am nothing of the kind, and the public must only resign itself to accepting the fact of my legitimacy, as I must

* *De Mirecourt*, " Maison Alexandre Dumas," p. 7.

do myself." At a club at Corbeil, a person dressed like a gentleman, and, as he was informed, one of the local judges, coolly answered our author, that such was the reason for his not taking his family name. Alexander says that he retorted by calling this gentleman, "what you call persons who make you speeches of the kind." But as this would hardly confute the slanderer, he thought of procuring from Villers-Cotterets the proper certificates. These establish his own legitimacy in the most satisfactory way, as he is described as "the son of General Dumas Davy de la Pailleterie, and of Marie Labouret, *his wife*." His father's marriage is besides attested in due form in the registers, and his legitimacy is supposed to be established by the same documents, which describe him as "*son* of the late Alexander Antony Davy de la Pailleterie, formerly Commissary of Artillery," and which speak of having his "certificate of birth before them." It is hardly worth while discussing this nice question, but it may be said that these certificates are not conclusive. The republic was not very exacting as to the formalities of marriage, and did not accept the theory of "filius nullius;" nor was the notion of a formal marriage between a French nobleman, fresh from Versailles, and a black woman of St. Domingo probable, though, on the other hand, it will be seen that he later contracted a marriage in a rank quite as far below him.

In about twelve years time this lady died, and M. de la Pailleterie, having no one to look after his household or child, grew disgusted with the island, disposed of his establlshment, and, about the year 1780, returned to France.

His son, a youth of eighteen, was a handsome young creole, well made, with small hands and feet, of amazing strength and activity, and one of the best fencers and gymnasts of his day. His strange appearance, joined with his good looks, made him remarkable, and he presently became the hero of various adventures. To figure in such a character is the desire of most Frenchmen ; while the lively imagination of the people is always at hand to invest even ordinary incidents with the true theatrical colour. But this promising career was disturbed by the marriage of his father, then seventy-four years old, with his housekeeper, Maria Retou. The son, a young man of promise, having a proud and gallant spirit, could not bear the mortification of this *mésalliance*. Perhaps he felt he could hardly bear up against the ridicule of such disabilities as a negro mother, and a step-mother from the servants' hall, and he announced to his father that he would go and seek his fortune as a common soldier in the ranks.   His father received the news much as Sir John Chester in the novel would such a declaration from his son ; and coolly stipulated that the family name was not to be dragged through the mire by being borne by a mere private.   The young man proposed taking his mother's name ; the father turned on his heel contemptuously, and the other at once carried his purpose into effect.

Such is the novelist's dramatic account of the adoption by his family of the name of Dumas.   But it must be confessed that a less romantic hypothesis explains it more satisfactorily, and it is hardly conceivable that the legitimate child of a noble family would have been suffered to change his name and be lost in the lower ranks of the army.   His whole career bears out this supposition, and it makes a story of singular interest, full of adventure and dashing gallantry.   This bold spirit perhaps saved him from the guillotine, while it contributed some stirring scenes to Napoleon's history, and inspired the brilliant imagination of his son.   To the St. Domingo blood we owe that unflagging style, the never-failing spirit, and almost tropical luxuriance, the vivid dramatic tone, of the popular novelist, a combination which makes him unique among French writers.   The young man entered the Queen's Dragoons, and though his father died a few days later * persevered in the career he had chosen. He soon rose from the ranks, and made quite a reputation for extraordinary feats of strength and daring exploits. When the soldiers were lost in wonder at the strength of one of their comrades, who was lifting a heavy musket by inserting his finger in the barrel, Dumas would call for four muskets and do the same with four fingers. He could crush a helmet in his hand, and, greater prodigy, stifle a horse between his legs. These feats were supplemented by other extraordinary exploits, such as riding in pursuit of one of his men who was trying to escape down a side street, catching him up by the neck without checking his horse, and as he passed a guard-house flinging his prisoner in at the door, shouting out "Give this rascal forty-eight hours confinement!" He captured thirteen Tyrolese marksmen single-handed, charging suddenly into their midst, and calling on them to surrender. In some skirmish he perceived that a serjeant of the enemy was aiming at him from only a few paces distance, when, without a second's hesitation, he discharged his pistol with such amazing precision that he actually pierced the musket-

* The "Act" of death of the old De la Pailleterie does not style him "marquis."

barrel through and through.* Many more such astonishing deeds are recorded by his son, who, with filial reverence, has pursued the dashing soldier's career through all the wars of the Revolution. The specimens just given of personal strength and gymnastic prowess were supported by deeds in the field quite as astonishing. Such, for instance, was his capture of thirteen Tyrolean chasseurs single-handed, who were so confounded by his sudden onset that they surrendered to him without attempting resistance.

He became a general in 1793, and was named Commander of the Army of the Western Pyrenees the same year, an appointment that did not give satisfaction to the local revolutionary junta. He was later given the command of the Army of the Alps, but somehow through all his dealings either with the revolutionary chiefs, or later with Bonaparte himself, he seems to have worked inharmoniously.

"You may dispute," says his son, "my title to the name of Davy de la Pailleterie, but you can't dispute that I am the child of a man, who won the name of '*Horatius Cocles*' before the enemy, and of '*Mr.*

---

* After a brilliant charge he was able to secure this remarkable fire-arm, which his son long kept as a souvenir of the feat. He justly describes it as "a miracle of accurate aim." The reader will probably agree with him.

Humanity' before the scaffold." The last of these sobriquets was earned by the General closing his shutters when the guillotine was at work under his windows, the mob yelling, " Come to the window *Mr. Humanity*." The former was one of the complimentary revolutionary titles given to him in the despatches on account of a daring feat in the Tyrol.

Some of his deeds were worthy of a Paladin, and all had an unvarying character of reckless dash and brilliancy. The general orders always contained mention of some signal exploit. After Inspruck, Joubert said, " The brave Dumas was the terror of the Austrian cavalry ; his horse was shot under him, and he only regrets a pair of pistols which had been presented to him by the Directory." His scaling the Mont Cenis during a night attack was a feat as successful as it was daring ; but it is completely eclipsed by the heroic and dashing achievement which supplied him with the title of the " Cocles of the Tyrol." When he was in service in the Tyrol, during the Italian campaign, he saw that a detachment of the enemy would succeed in reaching a bridge at Brixen before his own men. Without a moment's hesitation he spurred his horse forward, and succeeded in reaching the bridge first. He defended the approach single-handed, killing three men, wounding others, and receiving no less than three wounds himself. But he succeeded in holding the ground until his men came up.[*]

He was not without a rude spirit of drollery, as when, on a sudden instinct, he threatened a prisoner coarsely that he would have him cut open to find a letter that he swallowed. This was a mere random shot, but the man turned pale. He had swallowed his despatches, which were made up in a ball of wax.

He next set out with Napoleon on his Egyptian expedition; but his vehement temper and want of restraint did not suit the temper of the chief, who took a dislike to him. It is stated that he was favoured by the good graces of Josephine; but this may be only an insinuation of his son's, well meant, no doubt, and illustrative of the incurable propensity

---

[*] This story of his exploits and adventures, as told by his son, was considered to be a creditable work of imagination. It professes, however, to be founded on family papers and letters, and copies of letters, which, it is probable enough, the General treasured up. But on turning to one of the numerous "Galleries of Contemporaries," published about 1822, we find a simple record of these wonderful services, with a bitter complaint that the man who had performed them had been left unhonoured even with the cheap ribbon of the Legion, while an ungrateful country allowed his widow to keep a tobacco shop in a poor country town. He had left a daughter and a son, "*who promises one day to be worthy of his father.*" At the time this compliment was written, Alexander was obscure and unknown, and he owned it to Arnault, the academician, one of the editors of "The Gallery."

of most Frenchmen to colour up the smallest feminine attention into a genuine *bonne fortune.*

In Egypt he performed some of his most sensational exploits, claiming to have crushed an insurrection at Cairo almost single-handed, and to have sent to Napoleon treasure worth £80,000 which the General found in his own house.* But he was too rough and independent to suit the temper of the conqueror, who accused him of being seditious, and once actually threatened to have him shot. He even condescended to wrangle with him, and interchange undignified personalities. The truth was the General was a Republican, and a rude one, and with some of his friends had begun to detect the designs of their chief. A rupture soon took place which ended in the General asking leave to return to France. He sold his effects, and laid out the money in four thousand pounds of Mocha coffee and twelve Arabian horses, with which he freighted a small bark and set sale. This rather ungallant desertion of the army, in the midst of a serious campaign, might fairly justify Napoleon's

---

* Napoleon ordered a picture to be painted by Girodet, representing the Capture of the Mosque at Cairo, and declared that Dumas should be the principal figure. A blonde-looking hussar now occupies the place, and Alexander has been ridiculed for maintaining that this substitution was owing to the vindictiveness of Napoleon. Whether this be true or not, it is quite in keeping with known exhibitions of the Emperor's undignified petty malice.

subsequent treatment of him. They set sail, and after a tempestuous voyage, were obliged to put in at Tarentum, where they were thrown into a dungeon by the Neapolitans. Here an extraordinary adventure befel him, which his son makes him recount in his own words. Several deliberate attempts were made to poison him, which, though not ending fatally, brought on apoplexy, destroyed his hearing and his stomach.* Suspecting that a visit from a band of armed men, headed by the Marquis Della Schiave, was a prelude to a more violent attack, he seized his cane, which had a heavy gold knob on the top, and fell on them with such fury that they fled in terror. Soon after an accommodation was proposed, and he was exchanged for the well known incapable General Mack.

This was in the year 1801. When he returned to his own country, an aggrieved and disappointed man, he was placed on the retired list. The Emperor was not likely to forgive those who had ventured to oppose his views, or to show even a want of sympathy with his plans; and, in spite of all remonstrances and appeals, the General found his military career was

---

* This account is given most graphically, and reads like an incident in his "Monte Christo." Allowing some margin for the excitable character of the General, it seems probable enough, especially after the revelations of Casanova.

closed. Thenceforth, mortified and chafing against what he considered unworthy treatment, he was to present the always piteous spectacle of the old officer with a grievance. Unlike the other Imperial generals, he had not enriched himself in his campaigns; and, in addition to his sense of mortification, he had to struggle on in an obscure little country town—in an obscurity and inactivity that must have been torture to one of his tastes and habits.* Indeed, the whole sketch of this old officer given by his son is natural and unaffected, and, apart from a little touching and colouring which so inveterate a story-teller could not keep clear of, may be accepted as a truthful and interesting little piece of biography.

* He is not to be confounded with another General Dumas, who figured in Napoleon's later campaigns, nor with the Count Dumas, who has left memoirs.

CHAPTER II.

ALEXANDER BORN.

1802—1806.

WHEN Thomas Alexander Dumas was quartered at Amiens, being then lieutenant-colonel of a newly raised regiment, the " Hussars of Liberty and Fraternity," he made acquaintance with a young girl of Villers-Cotterets. She was the daughter of one Labouret, proprietor of the Crown Inn, *Hôtel de l'Ecu*, who was also colonel of the National Guard of the place, and had formerly been maître d'hôtel to the father of " Egalité " Orleans. His eldest daughter's name was Maria-Louisa, and with her the young colonel, then only thirty years old, fell in love. After a short courtship, the marriage took place, at Villers-Cotterets, on Thursday, Nov. 28, 1792, in presence of two brother officers, who came from Cambray, of the bridegroom's stepmother, of Deviolane, a notary and commissary of the town, and of the bridegroom's stepmother, the former housekeeper, who travelled from St. Germain for the ceremony.* The bridegroom had soon to depart for the wars, and, after nearly ten years of such service as we have described, found himself once more at home in Villers-Cotterets, comparatively disgraced. Then began his appeals to the War Office, to old friends and comrades in arms—to Brune, Foy, and others. To Bonaparte himself he wrote a really pathetic letter, asking some small arrears of pay, and imploring that he might not at his age—he was only thirty-six—be compelled to live in dishonourable idleness.† No attention was paid to the earnest appeals of the veteran, and even his old comrades, now marshals and generals, were cold, and dared not show sympathy for one whom their chief disliked. Hopeless and fretting, he had to settle down in that obscure

* The "Act" is given in the "Mémoires," page 2, édition Lévy, and professes to be extracted from the registers of the town.

† To the Minister of War he gives a little *resumé* of his services. "The affair of Mont Cenis, of Mount St. Bernard, the desperate defence of Mantua, where I had two horses killed under me, the passage of the Weiss, *for which Generals Baraguay D'Hilliers and Delmas obtained all the credit;* the feat of Horatius Cocles revived in the Tyrol, and which brought me the honour of being presented to the Directory under that very title, and the Cairo insurrection crushed by me in your absence." He added that "he had never been beaten, and was the oldest general of his class." These claims, and the impatient style in which they are advanced, give an excellent idea of this brave and impetuous soldier. There was something grotesque in that sobriquet of the "Horatius Cocles of the Tyrol," and which extorted the loud laughter of the wits of a later day, when his son first described his father's services, but it was no more ridiculous than the other Roman and classical titles, like Aristides and Brutus, which were in vogue during the Revolution.

little town, where his wife was presently to be confined of a son. This was Alexander Dumas, the hero of our narrative. He himself describes the event to us with a characteristic particularity. "I was born," he says, " at Villers-Cotterets, a little town in the department of the Aisne, on the Paris road, about two hundred paces from the Rue de la Noue, where Demoustiers died, two leagues from La Ferté-Milon, *where Racine was born*, and seven leagues from Château-Thierry, where *La Fontaine first saw the light*. I was born on July 24, 1802, at half-past five in the morning, in the Rue de Lormet, in a house which now belongs to my friend Cartier, who would gladly sell it to me any day, so that I may be able to die in the very room where I was born." *

The soldier was enchanted at this arrival, and wrote the next day to his friend, General Brune, announcing with great simplicity and pride what was the weight and size of the infant—nine pounds, and

* Jules Janin has recently visited the house, which was no more than a poor sort of cottage, and, moreover, a "maison sombre." No one lived in it, and in times of plenty it was made use of as a barn. The proprietor said that Alexander was always bidding him take care of it for him. " It would have been his long ago," the owner added, "if it had been only worth 300,000 francs." There is something highly characteristic in this speech. He could build a great "Folly" at Paris, but could not purchase this little cabin. The reason probably was that the first need not be paid for; the latter required ready money. He was a French Brinsley Sheridan.

eighteen inches. He reckoned on the General coming to stand godfather. He was longing to see him. The General wrote back excuses that must have fallen coldly on the heart of his poor friend. He was unlucky in such offices, he said, no less than five of his godchildren having died; he liked his friend too well to be the cause of any misfortune, so they must excuse him. Probably he wished to avoid having to return to Paris burdened with the old grievances. He had, however, to agree to a middle course; he was to be godfather by deputy, the father taking his place.

Though the General lived but four years after Alexander's birth, the child recalled with an affectionate admiration the gallant figure of his father, and some characteristic traits. He saw him plunge into a pond to save some foolhardy bathers, and the infant mind was delighted by the finely moulded figure and its graceful motions in the water, contrasting it with the mean and ordinary limbs of a servant, who was helping in the work. But he also noted the dejection and disappointment, and the progress of a disease which was hurrying his father to the grave. The old officer took his wife and boy with him on an expedition to Paris, to consult an eminent physician, which left the impression of some dusky scenes that were never to be forgotten.* One was that of a stately hotel, with servants in scarlet liveries, a long suite of sumptuous rooms, and a majestic old lady on a sofa, who put out her hand to be saluted respectfully by the visitor. The little boy, sitting on a stool at his father's feet, listened wondering, as they talked for half an hour. The old lady was Madame Montesson, widow of the Duke of Orleans, and the General waited on her, as belonging to the great Orleans family of Villers-Cotterets, and perhaps to urge the old grievance. He then went to the physician, who tried to give some hopes of recovery, but somehow left him with an impression that his case was hopeless. He found out his old friends, Murat and Brune, now marshals of the Empire, and asked them to breakfast with him. He found the former changed and grown very cold, but Brune was still true. The broken-down soldier was not going to trouble them with the old story of injustice and of his wrongs, which it was now too late to redress ; he simply asked them to try and

* " This visit," he writes, " how well I recall it, though the journey is not present to me, and I see myself all at once in Paris. It was about August or September. We put up in the Rue Thiroux, with a man called Dolle, a friend of my father's. He was a little old man, in a grey overcoat, velvet breeches, cotton stockings, and shoe-buckles ; he had a grotesque wig, and a little queue tied up with a ribbon, and ending in a white tuft, while the collar of his coat twisted up in the air." These little details are characteristic, and are mentioned, he says, to show how vivid was the impression left of these days.

do something for his poor wife and children, who would be left without anything in case of his death. Both gave him a promise. He had tried to interest them in the boy, by making him ride round the room, mounted on Brune's sword, and wearing Murat's plumed hat, bidding him never forget that he had enjoyed this honour. Long after both marshals had died violent deaths, Alexander visited the scene, and gathered up the different accounts of the catastrophe, which he related in his most graphic style.* His father made a last attempt to see the Emperor, but was refused, and then returned home to die.

Yet one more of these dreamy scenes flits before the son's eyes—a visit to another stately castle, close by Villers-Cotterets, a procession through its long chambers, with servants in green, and a vision of a beautiful lady, who made his father sit down at her feet, and whose dainty slippers seemed like those of Cinderella. As they talked, sounds of hunting horns were heard, and the child gazed in wonder as he saw his father carry the lady over to the window to see the hunters go by. The beautiful woman, he was told, was Pauline Buonaparte, widow of General Leclerc, and then wife of Prince Borghese. The house was the château of Montgobert.

* In his *Impressions de Voyage.*

After this there remained but a few months of life for the disappointed officer. Gradually the sports in which he delighted were given up, the riding was over; he could hardly leave his room, where he would take his boy upon his knee, and talk to him sadly. Even at the end was to come one last mortification. He had applied for a license to shoot in the Crown forests. This was in the department of Berthier, "the Grand Huntsman," but who was his old enemy. The license was dated from September, but was not forwarded until the end of February, when it had but twelve days more to run. His old sensitiveness naturally imputed this delay to design, though it is probable the Grand Huntsman was too much engrossed to bestow a thought on such a matter. He threw it on the table without a word; then, with a desperate resolution, called for his horse and mounted. It was to be his last ride, and he had to return after a few minutes, utterly exhausted, and take to his bed. His bold spirit gave way. "Heavens!" he murmured, " is a general who, when only thirty-five, commanded three armies in the field, to die in his bed in this way, like a coward!" The next evening—which was February 26, 1806—he sent for the Abbé Grégoire. As midnight struck, he turned to his wife, and looking fixedly on her gentle face, expired.

An hour or so before, Alexander had been sent away to a neighbour, an honest locksmith, in the Rue de Soissons, where a little bed was made up for him. He thinks that they did not let him take leave of his father. He always delighted in the forge ; the semi-darkness, the blowing of the flame, the clinking of the hammers, had for him an inexhaustible charm, and this evening he spent among its attractions. At eight o'clock he was sent to the little bed, improvised on two chairs. Every room in this house was vividly present to his recollection, and forty years later he could draw for his readers an exact plan of the house and its gardens. At midnight he was roused by a violent knocking at the gate ; a night-lamp was burning, and, as he sat up, he remembered seeing his cousin rise with a frightened air. The little boy got up and went to the door, half dreaming, half troubled by the solemn mysteriousness of some coming event. When his cousin called to him to stop, he answered cheerfully, " I am going to open the door for papa, *who has come to say good-bye.*" "The poor girl jumped up, caught me in her arms, and brought me back to my bed again. As I struggled with her, I called out, as loud as I could, " Good-bye, good-bye, papa ! " It seemed to me that something like a soft breath passed over my face, and made me quiet. Then I dropped .

off to sleep again, but with tears in my eyes, and a something choking in my throat."

The next morning he was told in the usual solemn way, "My poor child, the father who loved you so much is dead." Like children of his age, he had no clear idea of what this meant. The only notion that at all approached it was gathered from the death of a big dog whom he was fond of, and the insensible bather whom his father had rescued from the pond. He could not understand such a thing in connection with the grand figure of his father; "especially," he adds, with a happy touch, "as I had seen him go out to ride only a day or two before." * That image of his dear father was always present during the course of his life. He thought always, with a sort of longing affection and wonder, of that " Herculean framework and enormous strength ;" he could recall his infantine pride and delight in the gold-embroidered uniform, the tricoloured cockade and the huge sabre which he could hardly stir. All this filial retrospect is natural, genuine, tender, heightened with delicate touches worthy of Lamb or Dickens, and shows

---

* He spoils this natural and pathetic picture of childish bereavement by clumsily fitting on to it an old story. He was told that " the Bon Dieu had taken his father." He describes himself being surprised on the stairs with his father's double-barrelled gun in his hand. He was "going to kill the Bon Dieu who had killed papa."

that the much abused Dumas had an affectionate heart.

The widow and child were left almost destitute, and with little to look to, but that visionary chance, the successful prosecution of " claims against the Government." There were arrears of some two years' pay, amounting to about a thousand pounds, and a share in an indemnity of 20,000*l.*, the compensation due by the Neapolitan Government for their imprisonment of French subjects. Brune and Murat pressed these claims,—the latter feebly. Other old friends of the deceased officer, Augereau, Lannes, Jourdan, exerted themselves to obtain even a small pension for the widow. But Napoleon was obdurate, and at last angrily forbade Brune " to mention that man's name to him." Nothing is more probable ; he had never forgiven the display of republican opposition and the disapproval of his own personal schemes.* She was then advised to go up to Paris, and appeal personally to his Majesty ; and the poor widow actually undertook the journey. But the great man was implacable, and refused her an audience. This outlay was, therefore, only a fresh and useless waste of her slender resources.

* The refusal, indeed, was justified on the ground of the law sanctioning such pensions in the case of those only whose husbands had died in the field, or of their wounds. But the Emperor could dispense with all such restraints if he chose to do so.

CHAPTER III.

SCHOOL DAYS.

1806—1814.

ALEXANDER had been born in a small house, which Jules Janin, who long after went to see it, describes as being little more than a cabin. But his father had been obliged to leave this humble dwelling, and died under the roof of the " Crown Hotel," which had changed its name to that of "The Sword," where his wife's father, no longer proprietor, had retained some rooms. There he died, and there the widow and her two children—for a girl had been born before Alexander—remained, waiting till something could be done for them. In addition to their fruitless claims, they had a little property, unluckily burdened with an annuitant, who, with the perverseness of all annuitants, lived to draw the value of the property many times over. They had to remain at "The Sword Inn," living in the very room where the General lived, perhaps glad to secure such a shelter ; though this place must have brought her husband perpetually before her eyes. The widow made a pious pilgrimage every evening to the grave of her lost General.

While she was oppressed with anxiety for the future, her boy, with the happy unconsciousness of childhood, was noting all the persons and scenes about him—the beautiful gardens, the noble hunting forests, the grim figure of Deviolaine, his mother's relative and adviser. This gentleman was the most important personage in the place, being the Inspector of the Forest. Every widow's child recalls some such austere patron, whom the anxious mother consults timorously, and who is regarded as a stern and reproving monitor. The little Alexander revelled in this garden, filled with fruits, flowers, and running water, where he was allowed to play about, and in the noble park into which it opened. The house, with its great courts and stables, seemed a palace to him, after the straitened rooms in which he had lived.

The figure of the inspector was always present to him in these childish days—a tall, strongly-built man, roughly dressed, with shaggy eyebrows, from under which glared little black piercing eyes. He had been married twice, and had a large family—a son and two girls by his first wife, a son and two girls by his second. He was nearly always in a savage temper,

and on the days he was known to be in one of his
" wild boar " fits, the whole family, sons, women, and
servants, fled in terror as he was heard leaving his
study.   He was scarcely ever known to speak without
oaths.   Once, when a swarm of bees had settled on a
tree in the garden, he went out in a hurry, his shirt
open, to collect them himself.   The little boy and the
rest of the family were waiting anxiously at the
kitchen-door, when, to their amazement, they saw
him coming towards them smiling sweetly, speaking
softly in the most engaging tones, and waving his
hands.   They heard him murmuring, " Go away, my
little dears ; fly away."   They thought that he was mad.
The swarm had settled on his bare chest !   His soothing
treatment had the happiest effect.   But when the last
bee had flown away, and he saw the anxious faces of
his family before him, he burst into his old torrent of
imprecations, and it was a week before his fury abated.
This little picture is highly dramatic, a piece of
true comedy, and shows the nicety of Alexander's
touch.   It was noticed, however, that this humour of
the inspector's did not go beyond words, that in these
fits he had never even given so much as a kick to a
dog.   With all this violence, though Alexander stood
terribly in awe of him, he was the man he regarded
and respected the most, now that his father was gone.

Another house which Alexander recalled was that of a M. Collard, who had married a daughter of the famous Madame De Genlis. Madame De Montesson, the old Duke of Orleans's widow, was aunt to Madame De Genlis, and Collard had been appointed one of Alexander's guardians. Thus there was a sort of distant connection with the great family of Orleans, or with its patronage, which was later turned to profit. Enchanted as he was with the inspector's house and forest, he recalled with more delight the charming grounds, with its winding brook and flowers, of his guardian. Above all, there was a splendid illustrated Bible, whose pictures he was allowed to turn over, and which left as deep an impression as the ponderous "Stackhouse" which Charles Lamb's incautious fingers tore. This volume, with an illustrated Buffon which he found at another house, and was privileged to pore over, was an inexhaustible entertainment. One day, while deep in the great Bible at M. Collard's, a carriage was heard to drive up, which was attended by some commotion and cries, proceeding from the hall. All started up and ran to the door, where the little boy was terrified by the sight of a wild-looking old witch dressed in black, without a bonnet, whose false hair had tumbled off and left her own original grizzled locks to fall about her shoulders. Utterly scared, he fled from the room to his bed, where he drew the clothes tight over his head. This apparition turned out to be the famous Madame De Genlis herself, who had lost her way in the forest, and seized with a sudden panic at the idea of ghosts, had fled in this disorder. All his childhood was full of dreamy visions of these great ladies, in old-fashioned costumes of the Revolution and Empire, who flitted past him, with a background of charming gardens, of disused convents, down whose deserted cloisters he was privileged to scamper, and of the old Orleans château, built by Francis I. and Henry II., now or till lately, a poor-house. It will now be seen, as his recollections grow fuller, what a good picture of the old simple country town life in France he can bring before us. Those of this generation who have spent a few months of their childhood in the country will feel the old and curious flavour coming back, and see the scorched roads, across which the lamps swing on cords, the green shutters, the white houses, and the almost eccentric costumes of the figures, rising before them.

The relations were friendly, and the lad was always welcome to stay at one or other of their houses. Though but five or six years old, he had learnt to read, chiefly through the aid of such books as the great Bible, the copy of Buffon, and a "Mythology," which last he devoured. There was not " a god, a goddess, a demigod, a faun, or a dryad whose parentage I did not know. Hercules and his twelve labours, Jupiter and his twenty transformations, Vulcan and his thirty-six accidents, all these I had at my fingers' ends, and, strange to say, have them still." The relations were interested in the shrewd little creole who was so free and quaint. One morning, after breakfast, the guests were speculating as to the latest news, when the awful Deviolaine rang the bell and ordered a newspaper to be sent for. The little boy, with his hands joined behind his back, said eagerly, " Cousin, don't give yourself the trouble. I looked through them this morning, and there was nothing worth reading, except the debate in Parliament ! " The churlish inspector gave him a sound kick for his freedom ; and, indignant at such humiliation, Alexander did not return for three months. This interest in the Parliament was owing to his having lately seen his friend Collard dressed up in gold lace, and, on his asking " *if he was a general like papa,*" was told that it was the dress of a member. From that day he read all the reports, " *to see what M. Collard said,*" but never could find anything.* This is a

* In this case it is easy to separate the true from the invented recollections. Thus there next follows a sketch of an old Mademoiselle Pivert

genuine little trait, and has the air of having happened. All sorts of curious figures were about him. One was that of Hiraux, the old music master, who seemed taken out of a page of Hoffmann's, with his lanky nervous figure, his morone-coloured coat, and curious periwig, which flew off when he made a low bow. It was for this reason kept for state days and holidays, as being too inconvenient for professional work; and then he appeared in a tight silk skull-cap, which seemed to Alexander "a part of his skin." As he played his fiddle his lean figure quivered, his muscles started, and his thin horny fingers danced over the strings. This creature, attached to whom were endless odd stories, gave lessons in his art, for which he received payment in kind, according to the means of his pupils: sugar and tea from the grocer, clothes from the tailor. But he could make nothing of Alexander.

The author remembered another figure, that of Labouret, the old proprietor of the Crown Hotel, where his mother had been married—an old man, always seen with a pipe in his mouth, having a grave "innkeeper walk," and always playing his game of dominoes at a particular café. Every night, at ten

to whom he lent a volume of the Arabian Nights, which she read through and returned, only to receive the same volume, which she read through again as a new one, without discovering any difference. This is an old story, which our ingenious author has turned to account.

o'clock precisely, his dog would come and scratch at the café door, carrying a lantern, like his predecessor of Montargis, when there was no moonlight. For ten years he was never known to have made a mistake in this duty, or even to have broken his lantern. But a night came when the dog was to have no journey, and Alexander was again taken away to a friend's house. Such a removal is often the child's notice of a death in the family. Four relations had died within four years; but Alexander frankly confessed that, except in the case of his father, these losses seemed associated with nothing more serious than daily walks to the churchyard. To this he imputes his curious interest in all old graveyards, with their meagre shrubs, frail and decayed black crosses, painted with white inscriptions, and shattered tombstones.

Though this death brought them a small patrimony of land, it had been already mortgaged to its full value. They had then to leave their room at "The Sword," and seek a new abode. He found in these constantly shifting scenes of his childhood the source of all the more developed ideas of his manhood, exactly as in the case of Lamb and Dickens, the sensitiveness of whose childish instincts and vivid power of observation during the same period, furnished a whole storehouse which was to supply them abundantly in their maturer years. These different houses and scenes—the " Fosses," Antilly, the little room in the inn, the ruins of the old castle, the forest inspector's house and garden, the St. Rémy cloisters, Collard's château, the great park of Francis the First, and the little churchyard—each had some distinct influence on the character of his various writings. " I have always," he handsomely admitted, " had a great respect for sacred things, great faith in Providence, and *a true love of God;*" and this vague sense of religion he no doubt owed to his mother's daily little pilgrimages to the grave of his father, and to the spectacle of her pious grief.

When ten years old, he had begun to learn fencing from a noted " character," an old fencing-master who had received " a lunge " in his palate, which rendered his oral teaching rather unintelligible. This professor was an inmate of the poor-house. Alexander had always the Frenchman's taste for arms, though he owns that physically he was something of a coward. He never could look down from a height. His cousins, the Deviolaines, particularly a fine girl, Cecilia, who " romped " like a boy, delighted in leading him into traps, up to lofts, whence the only descent was by a ladder, enjoying his agonies, and screaming with laughter as he began to descend. Once this bold girl, while challenging him from the top of an enormous haycock, lost her footing, and came rolling down, nearly breaking, not her own, but *his* neck. Once when playing at "King and Queen," at some little festival, he fell into the garden pond. They all screamed out "that Dumas was drowning," but left him to get out by himself. He then made his first "mot "—" Stupid ! you ought to say, 'There, the king drinks.'" Miss Cecilia, however, contemptuously pronounced that "he would never be good for anything but a divinity student." The greatest agony of terror he experienced, in perhaps his whole life, was when he happened to be struggling with a companion at the door of a grocer's shop, where the owner was engaged in mixing chocolate with a sort of chopper-knife. In the contest Alexander received a push which sent him backwards into a tub of honey displayed at the door. With a loud cry he got out and fled, pursued by the grocer, chopper in hand, the sticky honey seriously impeding his progress. He felt the grocer gaining on him, in an agony of terror saw the open mouth and fierce eyes over him, and was at last caught half fainting. He really believed that he would be sacrificed on the spot. The grocer clapped him on his knee face downwards, the victim being almost unconscious, and having carefully scraped the back of the boy's trousers with his chopper, set him down again unharmed and went his way.

As he was now ten years old it was time to think of sending him to school. Admission to the Lyceums and colleges—nearly always given gratuitously to the children of the higher officers of the army—had been begged, implored, and refused. Another cousin, an Abbé Conseil, who had been "governor of the pages" at the old court, and once held rich benefices under Louis XV. and Louis XVI., had just died, and left a "Bourse," or free admission, for one of his relations at the seminary at Soissons. This was intended for Alexander, who used to be taken to see so influential a person twice a year, but received only a dry reception. The admission involved his going into the Church, to which the lad had the greatest repugnance, a good deal owing to the pleasant railleries of Miss Cecilia Deviolaine on that subject. But the entreaties and tears of his mother, and a promise that he should be taken away if he did not like the place, at last prevailed. On the day of his departure he went to buy an ink bottle, and in the shop met the sarcastic young lady, who wickedly wished him joy, and promised that as soon as he was ordained she would make him her spiritual director. Inexpressibly mortified at this raillery, he suddenly declared that now nothing would get him to go, and instead he ran away from home for three days to the woods, where he spent the nights snaring birds with a ravenous old poacher, who had the reputation of having once eaten a whole calf. His good mother was too overjoyed to receive him back to think of forcing him to leave her, and it was determined that he should go to a day-school in the town, known as the " College," which was kept by the Abbé Gregoire.

The abbé was a severe but just instructor, and was assisted by a meagre, humpbacked sister, who worshipped him. His new scholar was a free, rather insolent lad, who "thought a good deal" of himself, and gave a great deal of trouble. His light-coloured hair which fell over his shoulders, his great blue eyes, his thick rosy lips, and his startling white complexion, which he says did not turn swarthy till he was about fifteen, must have made him a most remarkable-looking boy.

The first day of going to this school was a most important occasion. A new suit had been ordered, made out of a riding-coat of his father's, which was of a *"café au lait"* colour. He expected that it would produce a remarkable effect; and thus attired proceeded at eight o'clock one Monday morning to make his first visit. The anxious mother had fitted him out with school books, also new—the *Epitome Historiæ Sacræ* and others—those little primers half-bound in dark marbled papers, familiar to all who have had their schooling in France. He had entered the court through the large archway, when the door was suddenly closed behind him, and he found himself among a noisy mob of school boys, who at once proceeded to make him go through the new boy's probation of practical joking of a very rash kind. He was hustled, deluged with water, and played other tricks, which had the effect of destroying all his new finery. Utterly mortified at this reception, he could only sit down and cry bitterly.

Presently entered the abbé, having come from saying mass. He found all his pupils gathered round the new boy, who was sitting crying on the steps, and asking each other with an appearance of genuine wonder and interest what could be the matter with him. The abbé pushed through the ring of little hypocrites, and fixing his glass in his eye, bent down over the sobbing child, to ask what ailed him. Alexander looked up, and was about to tell, when he suddenly saw a whole range of menacing fists threatening him from behind the master, and checked himself with an abrupt cry. The abbé turned round sharply and found them all smiling. "Tell me what it is all about," he said. " We can't make out," they said; "he has been crying in that way ever since he came." Indignant at this misrepresentation, Alexander then blurted out the whole story of his treatment, and appealed to the state of his new clothes in proof. "Very well," said the abbé, "I shall punish you all for this; you shall have no recreation to-day, and plenty of ferules too." These were at once administered, amid groans of suffering; but there were fierce glances directed at the new boy, while muttered denunciations of "Informer," "Spy," came to his ears, and began to alarm him. There was no mistaking these symptoms : a heavy reckoning would have to be paid for his indiscreet revelation. Four o'clock came and the end of school; the abbé said a short prayer and dismissed the class. Alexander for a moment thought he would invoke his protection, or get the humpbacked sister to take him home; but he felt that this would only be a temporary aid—the abbé or the sister could not *always* see him home. The school poured out into the street. With a beating heart he gathered up his books as slowly as he could, in the faint hope that they might have gone away home before him, and then descended into the court.

He found the whole school gathered on the steps

in a sort of semicircle or council, evidently waiting for him, while a young champion, named Bligny, to whom had been deputed the duty of avenging the school, was standing at the steps, coat off, and sleeves ready turned up. At this alarming spectacle the new boy was seen to falter and stop short, on which a yell of execration burst forth. He felt himself ready to drop, and a cold sweat burst out on his forehead. The situation was, however, desperate ; there was no escape. With a sudden impulse he recovered himself. Cowardice often finds bravery its most effectual resort, and in many of his duels, when he was grown up, Alexander behaved courageously from much the same motive. He descended the steps, addressing his enemy,—

"So that's the way it is ? "

" Yes, that's the way it is," said the other sneeringly, who was son of a clothseller in the town.

"And so you want to fight ?"

" Yes, I do."

" Oh, you do, do you ? "

" Yes, I do."

" Well then—*there !* "

He had got to the bottom of the steps ; in a second he had laid down his books, stripped off his jacket, and had fallen on his enemy.

"Ah, so you would, would you—take that, and that! and that, and that!"

Surprised and taken aback at this readiness, where he had expected to find "shirking," the clothseller's son was staggered, overwhelmed, and finally borne down, receiving a blow in the eye, and another in the mouth. The day was gained, and the victor characteristically saluted by his lately hostile companions with shouts of applause. As they respectfully made way for him to pass out, they heard him muttering "When I'm—when I'm——" which they interpreted significantly. He was never persecuted again.

A cousin of his going to keep house for her uncle, an Abbé Fortier, who lived some five leagues off, was allowed to bring Alexander with her for a little holiday excursion. This furnishes another pleasant picture. They set off together mounted on a donkey, which was driven by a friendly villager. After seven or eight hours' march, during which Alexander gazed with wonder at the huge mountains and towers, and was enchanted with all he saw, they reached Béthisy, and the charming little tenement of the abbé, which seemed a bower of grapes and peaches, whose harvest was just at hand. The owner was a tall clergyman, "built like a Hercules, carrying his body straight, his head high, giving a short stamp with his right foot every minute, like a fencing-master on guard." (This last is a graphic touch.) He had the bearing of a dragoon officer, great sporting tastes—keeping his dogs, and going out to shoot after he had said mass. There was no more excellent priest, or one more respected and esteemed. He was known to have exhibited what is called "muscular christianity," and had soundly thrashed a peasant who, from some old grudge, assaulted him on the road, as he was going to visit the sick. Such a man won the heart of the boy, who felt that this description of clergyman would almost reconcile him to going to the seminary. He might, however, congratulate himself on not having gone, as only a short time before some powder blew up near the college, which was blown into ruins. Some eight or ten of the inmates were killed, and had Dumas been there the world might never have read "Monte Christo."

CHAPTER IV.

THE WARS.

1814.

IT was now the beginning of the year 1814, and some very important matters disturbed the peace of the little town, and interrupted the Abbé Gregoire's lessons. Napoleon had been falling rapidly, and even the dullest quidnunc of the place, who accepted all that he read out of the *Moniteur*, because it was in print, had been confounded by the rapidity of his disasters. After the battle of Leipsic, the possibility of the "sacred soil of France being profaned,"—one of the many ridiculous national phrases—by the tread of the enemy, began to come home to many. News soon arrived that the enemy *was on* the sacred soil; and, finally, it was reported that they were drawing near to the little town of Villers-Cotterets. Now they were at Château Thierry; now at Nogent; but when it was known that Laon, not very far away, was actually occupied by the enemy, Villers-Cotterets

fluttered in a perfect panic. In those days such agitation was very different from what it would be now,
when the telegraph can be used to appease anxiety or
furnish actual details. Then, after the news was
brought in, and a weary interval of perhaps days had
followed, during which nothing could be learned, the
words "*The Cossacks are coming!*" flew from mouth
to mouth, and every one was busy hiding their valuables. In the garden of the Dumas family was a
little cellar, in which his mother hid away carefully
all her linen and other property, and buried in a
marked spot a leather case in which were some thirty
old pieces of gold, her little hoard.

But one day, a dusty, shattered party of three or
four gendarmes came riding in at full speed. Soissons
had just been taken ; and they had barely got away,
though some half dozen of their party had been shot
down. These warnings were coming fast, and yet
faster. The good Madame Dumas sorrowfully found it
was time to prepare a great dish of haricot, which,
with sundry bottles of Soissons wine, was to be left
for the terrible Cossacks, to keep them in good
humour. Outside the town, in the plain, were mysterious catacombs or caves, whose depths were im-
penetrable, from whence issued a dull roaring, like
that of a shell held to the ear. To this retreat some

five or six hundred of the scared inhabitants brought their bedding and valuables, each choosing his own corner, while a ladder was kept ready. These terrors were not so unreasonable, as dreadful rumours had gone before of the excesses committed by these savage horsemen.

Three days passed by and no Cossacks. Suddenly there appeared scattered soldiers, but they were French, the corps of Marshal Mortier, which was charged with the defence of the forest. There was great joy in the place at this welcome apparition; every one felt secure, and Madame Dumas's haricot had to be eaten by French mouths. Alexander saw M. Deviolaine obsequiously leading the marshal through the forest, but was struck by the latter's bent and dispirited-looking figure. The widow ran to detach the old tricolor cockade from the carefully-treasured hat of her loved general, and presented it to the inspector, who fixed it in his own hat. That evening the inspector gave a grand dinner in honour of the marshal, and bethought him that the son of a general would be found interesting, so Alexander was brought in, and questioned about his father, whom the marshal had known. But there was a weight over the whole party, and the marshal withdrew early. In the middle of the night the town was roused by the sound of shots. They learned in the morning that the enemy had surprised the French in the forest, and that the marshal had barely time to escape, half-dressed, to M. Deviolaine's house. They had disappeared, but had carried off nine pieces of cannon. Even there was the same carelessness as to outposts, and ignorance of the enemy's movements, which has helped to bring about the ruin and recent disgrace of French armies. The marshal, with his army, hurried off that day, and left the little town in quite a fevered state, and Alexander's mother had again to get her haricot ready.

At times a paroxysm of terror invaded them, and as a crowd of frightened mothers and children flew screaming through the street, windows were thrown open to be shut fast again by trembling fingers, every-one being now certain that " the Cossacks at last had come." The good Abbé Gregoire was, however, always composed, and went about comforting the people, assuring them that the Cossacks would do no harm if they were not harmed. Five days had gone by ; they were obliged to eat their haricot once more. Madame Dumas was busy with her third, when one morning, at the end of February, again rose the cry of " The Cossacks ! the Cossacks ! the Cossacks ! " The trampling of horses was heard, the cloud of dust opened, and down the Soissons road came cantering a small group of strange-looking horsemen—men with long beards, long lances, and dark dresses. They came on at full speed, dashed through the street, turned back at the end of the town, every window and door being hurriedly closed as they repassed, and were gone as they came. Only the sound of a single shot was heard as they disappeared. The inhabitants were in the street in a moment, and Alexander recollected seeing a wretched woman tossing her arms wildly in a doorway. A capmaker, named Ducoudray, looking out from curiosity, had hurriedly closed his door, and one of the Cossacks, as he flew by, had wantonly discharged his pistol at the closing door. The ball passed through and broke the neck of the unfortunate man, who was now lying dead, his head supported on the knees of his distracted wife.*

On this fatal overture everyone fled to the caves, and as they hurried out, they could see the band of Cossacks in the distance—tiny figures—galloping up a great hill called Dampleux, far beyond the town. The ladder was drawn, and the whole population remained for twenty-four hours not daring to put out their heads.

* These scenes, simply and most graphically told, really anticipated the dramatic pictures of the authors of the " Conscript " and the " Blockade of Phalsbourg."

But for Madame Dumas this agitation became unendurable, and, returning to dig up her little treasure, she set out, with her son, with an old lady who was also flying, scarcely knowing where she was to go, and, after some journeying, halted at Mesnil, where they began to discover that they were no safer than in the town they had just left. There they heard of a grand review that was to take place on the 25th of March, which the old lady became curious to see. As Paris was such a short way off, Alexander was taken on this little expedition, and he remembered the dazzling scene in the Court of the Tuileries, when, amid braying trumpets and the shouts of fifty thousand men, a little blonde child, its hair all curled, was lifted up and shown to the people.

As they were returning, they learned that the Cossacks had been again at Villers-Cotterets, had discovered the cave, and were reported to have committed all manner of atrocities. The allies were closing in on Paris, so they took refuge at the little town of Crépy, which was out of the beaten track, and therefore likely to be safe. There one day they saw a small party of Prussian cavalry ride in, dressed in blue frock coats and grey trousers, with a flat peaked cap. Alexander was struck by their handsome blonde faces and distinguished air. Suddenly, they returned, pursued though the streets by some French cavalry; the ground trembled under the horses' hoofs, the windows clattered; both parties fired pistols and used their sabres as they rode. Suddenly the Prussians turned at bay, and as though from the boxes at a circus, the inhabitants could see the whole skirmish. Five or six Prussians dropped from their horses, the rest turned, and both parties swept away past the windows, out of sight.

Many such scenes passed before his eyes. Months rolled by and the Bourbons were restored. Even in Villers-Cotterets were found the two parties into which France is to be eternally divided, and the exulting faction was only too glad to brand the widow and her son as " Bonapartists." They felt it not a little hard that this reproach should be applied to them, who had so little reason to be partisans of the conqueror; and Alexander had many a conflict with the street boys, who pursued him with this epithet. Good friends were at the same time working for them, and their relation Collard had gone up to Paris, to use his royalist influence to obtain for the widow that most coveted of privileges, a license to sell tobacco and salt.* He describes amusingly how when he would

* Alexander describes a theatrical scene, in which it was solemnly put to him at this time whether he would assume the family name, the

enter with a black eye or a bleeding nose, after one of these street rencontres, how his mother would have an additional cause of trouble, from the fear that this was imperilling the chance of the tobacco privilege. It was, however, obtained to their great joy. It seems strange that a general officer's wife should obtain nothing better than this miserable provision, now given chiefly to the widows of non-commissioned officers ; but at that time the privilege was probably much more valuable, and the depôts not so numerous. On this they moved into another house, and opened a regular shop.

Soon things settled down into the old routine. Alexander recommencing his lessons under his various masters. An odd M. Oblet taught him mathematics and writing, who himself excelled in flourishes, and was able to develop hearts and darts, with Adam and Eve, and the portrait of Louis XVIII., in marvellously flowing scrolls. He was an ardent loyalist, and always spoke gravely of that " M. Bonaparty," whose defeats he imputed to his illegibly written orders. Presently the pupil was to make his first communion, for which he was duly prepared. His religion was always

Marquis Davy de la Pailleterie, which would secure him honours and a place at Court, or remain Dumas and be content with the tobacco privilege. He says he spurned the first proposal. Here he is writing a portion of one of his romances.

of the most elementary kind, though he did not want for a self-complacent righteousness. He tells us he always had an infinite reverence for consecrated things, and though he never entered a church after he grew up, and that it would require an angel to drag him in by the hair of the head, churches were for him such sacred spots, that "he could not bear to profane them by entering in the way many do, to satisfy curiosity or religious caprice."* For this important occasion an entirely new suit was ordered from the local tailor—nankeen trousers, a blue coat and metal buttons, and a white cravat. He was profoundly affected, and owned that, on this day at least, he seemed to have glimpses of the heavens. (He explains this phenomenon by his "religious worship of all that is grand.") His tears and agitation were so great that he became ill. The good Abbé came to see him, and when the boy burst into tears remarked with much sagacity: "My dear child, I would prefer that all this was not so violent, and that it would last."

---

* When he was drawn into a church by the proper motive, his behaviour was no less characteristic. He would kneel down, "generally at a pillar, against which he could lay his head," and there would think of God. "I could find not a word to address to Him, or a prayer to put up. What could *you say to God*, what was the use of praying? &c." This poor stuff is, however, characteristic of the man, for he deals with religion in the same free and careless style in which he does every moral subject.

By this time too he had taken up that passion for shooting, or rather for having and carrying fire-arms, which is found in so many Frenchmen. This he inherited from his father, and it was of course strengthened by the neighbourhood of the noble forest in which he might be said to have been reared, and which abounded in wild boars and partridges, and all kinds of game, carefully preserved. As he naïvely says in a charming passage—and his remarks on the spirit of all the great scenes of nature are always charming, and show a true instinct : "A great forest has very much the effect that the sea produces. Sailors and keepers, as each find themselves on their own element, become silent and thoughtful, because observant." In Alexander's case this forest gave a special open air and even adventurous tone to all his writings. When a boy he was longing to have a gun, and his father's favourite fowling-piece was promised to him "*when he should be big enough*"—words which being so indefinite gradually became a positive torture to him. The local gun-maker who had the charge of this piece was forbidden by the anxious mother to let it out of his keeping ; but he good-naturedly lent the boy a small " walking-stick " gun, the breech of which could be carried in the pocket, and the barrel used as a cane. There was a band of keepers patrolling the forest who were now and again startled by the sound of a stray shot, but could never detect the poacher; for when they came up they only saw the mischievous·lad with his stick. At last he was caught in the very act, and the dreadful consequences rose before him—a fine of two pounds, which would come upon his poor mother's scanty earnings, with possibly imprisonment. When on the evening of this dark day the grim figure of M. Deviolaine was seen approaching to pay an accustomed visit, he knew that his fate was sealed, and fled from the house. He was saved, however, by the arrival of the startling news of Napoleon's landing. All his recollections of the forest are most agreeable— the *battues*—the hair-breadth escapes, often comic as tragic, from the tusks of the boars, his own misadventures, related with a pleasant candour, the figures of the keepers—have all the true local flavour, are well drawn, and are described with singular vivacity and little exaggeration.

Associated with this crisis were some curious scenes. Everything was in agitation and alarm, and the women of the place exhibited a sort of savage royalism. The owner of the tobacco-shop and her son were again pointed at and screamed after as " Bonapartists " and " reactionaries." It was known that the two Lallemands, who had tried to tamper with the soldiers and had failed, were hiding somewhere in the neighbourhood, and one evening the expectant town witnessed the spectacle of three carriages driven in, each filled with gendarmes sitting beside their prisoners. The unfortunate officers had been captured, and were being taken to Soissons for summary trial and execution. The crowd behaved as a French crowd would on such an occasion, and a woman frantic with rage climbed on the step of the carriage and spat in one of the officers' face.* Later on came the news of the Emperor's arrival at Paris ; later again a rumour that he would pass through Villers-Cotterets on his way to the army. At six in the evening Alexander was at the Post-house, and saw the carriage dash up to change horses, and caught a glimpse of the ivory face.

After an interval of a few days, on June 20th, a rumour went round the little town that some strange men had come into the town with news that the French army was destroyed, and that the enemy was marching on Paris. Every one ran to the Town Hall, and there found a crowd gathered round a dozen men, some of whom were on horseback. · They gave themselves out to be Poles, were bleeding, and covered

---

* A very dramatic adventure is told, in which Alexander was conveyed into the prison to furnish them with pistols and the means of escape ; but it is omitted here, as being too much in the style of D'Artagnan's exploits.

with mud and dust, and it was scarcely possible to understand them; but an old officer came and questioned them in German, and to him they gave a detailed account of the disaster at Waterloo. At five o'clock the English had been beaten, but the Prussians had come up, and turned the scale. The French army was not routed, but annihilated. This news was, as might be expected, received with scorn, and the relators were carried off to prison as spies, or, at the best, liars. The men said they had ridden from Planchenoit in forty-eight hours.

As soon as the crowd had seen them in custody for " bringing false news," it dispersed, every one to tell his neighbour of the disaster, which was accepted as true. This characteristic national trait was often exhibited during the last war. Alexander and his mother ran to the Post-office, where news was always certain to be obtained. At seven o'clock a courier galloped up, splashed all over, his horse ready to fall with fatigue, who ordered four horses to be ready for a carriage that was to arrive presently. He was, eagerly questioned, but could tell nothing. The horses were brought out and harnessed. Presently a clatter of hoofs was heard, a carriage and four came tearing round the corner, and drew up. Alexander saw the face, and, pulling the wondering postmaster by the skirt, asked, " It's he, isn't it—the Emperor ?" It was his ivory face, paler, and more sunk upon the chest. He was seen to look round vacantly—" What place is this ?" " Villers-Cotterets, Sire." " Good ; then we are only eighteen leagues from Paris. Drive on !" and the carriage was whirled away out of sight.

All this is picturesque enough. The French children of our own day will have many such scenes to think of, which will come back upon them when their heads are grey, and bent over the winter fire.

CHAPTER V.

FIRST LOVE.

1817.

ALEXANDER was now fifteen, and his mother determined to fit him with some profession. There was a young notary in the place, named Mennesson, a gay and pleasantly-sarcastic official, who went up to Paris pretty often, and who agreed to take him into his office; though, from the known character of the youth, it was believed he would turn out what was called, in the slang of the place, as "a brook-skipper" —*i. e.* a mere amateur. He was employed to copy, and see to the due signature of "acts." With this promotion begins the second stage of his life.

At Villers-Cotterets, as at many other French towns, was held a charming annual fête, which took place about Pentecost. The villagers from all the neighbouring districts poured in. For fifteen days before, every place was taken in the diligences, and, as these failed, all sorts of vehicles were put in requisition.

The great park of Francis I., then in all its bloom, presented the gayest appearance, crowded with natives and strangers.   For this festival there had arrived from Paris, on a visit to Alexander's old tutor, the Abbé Grégoire, two young ladies—one a niece, named Laurence, or Laura, the other a Spaniard, a friend of hers, called Victoria.   The Abbé officially informed his pupil that he would expect him to be attentive, and to take on him the charge of amusing the guests.   Alexander was a little nervous at this responsibility.   He was no more than a rough country lad, of the kind Parisian humorists are so fond of ridiculing on the stage and in caricatures, who are *gauche*, and stand in awe of ladies from the great cities.   Such a one was his *Ange Pitou*, who, in the main, he says, represents his own character at this era; for, like every good and popular writer of romance, Dumas has found that his own experiences and feelings have furnished him with the most effective and natural passages.[*]
Our own great English novelists, from Fielding and Smollett to Dickens, have been supplied by the workings of their own character with materials for dealing with the workings of the characters of others.

The young fellow's first thought was as to his costume ; but an investigation showed that he had

[*] Compare *Ange Pitou*, chap. "Bucoliques," vol. i.

nothing to fall back upon but the suit he had worn on the occasion of his first communion—the nankeens, the blue coat and gilt buttons. These had providentially been made with a margin to allow for growing. He now found that he had outgrown these garments very slightly. He then thought of the old wardrobe in which his mother had carefully stored away his father's clothes, and to these he paid a stolen visit, carefully locking the door of the room. All the old uniforms and other suits had been carefully folded and put away with camphor. But he decided on his own blue coat and nankeens.*

The young ladies arrived. The niece, Laura, was a tall, handsome girl, with a grace and "style" that came of living in Paris, and was in remarkable contrast to that of the rustic belles of the place. Her friend, Victoria, was a pale Spanish girl, with dangerous eyes, but was slightly marked with the small-pox. He presented himself, not without agitation, and took them into the public places, where the party was re-

---

* He also found here a copy of *Faublas,* and he describes in one of those disagreeable confessions, with which French writers too often destroy their most charming and simple situations, how he carried these volumes off to the Park for study, in order to *fit himself for paying his court to the young ladies.* With all his dramatic and romantic power, Dumas is one of the worst offenders in this respect, though such matter is introduced with a naïveté and simplicity that is either affected or, more probably, genuine.

garded with extraordinary curiosity. He felt not a
little uneasy about his dress, which had grown
decidedly old-fashioned—"an anachronism," in fact—
and which, from its connection with his father's
apparel, as well as from its imperfect fit, was more
that of an old, than of a young, man. He found himself blushing as he passed by, with the cold, calm, and
even haughty young Parisian on his arm. The
Spaniard was following with the little humpbacked
sister of the Abbé. Neither seemed to notice or to
care for the curiosity they excited. Their cavalier felt
growing more and more awkward. He could not
talk; his awe and confusion was increasing every
moment.

A young man passed them named Miaud, who had
come from Paris two or three years before, and who
was dressed more according to the mode. Laura
asked who he was. Alexander told her a little maliciously, that he was "only one of the clerks at the
poor-house."

"How curious," she said, carelessly; "from his
dress I should have taken him for a Parisian."

This was a little bit of comedy; for the truth was, the
young man did come from Paris. He was dressed in
a high-collared brown coat, with a chamois waistcoat,
gold buttons, and coffee-coloured trousers—the mode

in 1818. The indirect stroke at his own garments overwhelmed our hero. In desperation, he brought the ladies to a great ditch in the park, over which he proposed " to jump," to redeem himself in their eyes.

" You see this tremendous ha-ha," he said ; " I can clear it at a bound."

" Really ! " they said, indifferently; " it seems very wide."

" It is fourteen feet ! Miaud couldn't do it, I can tell you."

" But why *should* he ? " Laura asked, in a sort of wondering way. " What would be the object ? "

He was again taken aback by this answer; for the feat had been the admiration of the whole place. He fancied that they did not believe him : so taking a run he cleared it. But a new misfortune followed ; the nankeens, meant only for gala occasions, were unequal to the strain. He felt, as he landed with bent knees, that they had given way ; there was " a sense of cold air." He dared not explain, and without a word, or turning back, he set off home at full speed, leaving the wondering Parisians on the other side of the ditch. The friendly needle of his mother repaired the damage, and he soon returned, only to find that he was late, and that they had already gone to the dance.

On entering the ball-room, he saw his fair friends

already dancing—the Spaniard with one of his fellow-clerks, Laura with the odious Miaud, who seemed to be his rock ahead. They laughed gaily, and every laugh made him sure that he was the subject of their merriment. They were charming, both for their dress and elegance of style.

He was determined to redeem himself, and asked Laura to dance.

"We were afraid," was her first remark, "that you had met with some accident."

The best style of rustic dancing at this period, as at the present, was founded on a series of gymnastic bounds, and he determined to dazzle them by such a display. He fancied that he excelled himself. But still nothing would do. He could see by their significant glances at each other that they still considered him only a *gauche* country lad ; and when he innocently told Victoria, who complimented him on his waltzing, that his skill was the more surprising as he had hitherto "only waltzed with chairs," the Abbé having forbidden him to waltz with girls, her amazement knew no bounds. "You really are very funny," she said.

The visit of these young ladies was his first introduction to what is called the gentle passion. He was determined to make an impression, and imputing his failure to his grotesque dress, he implored his good-natured mother to let him order a becoming suit from the village tailor, exactly on the model of the odious Miaud's. Dress-boots, too, were necessary, being articles which the Parisians regarded critically. Their little resources were strained enough already, but when he told his mother that he wished "to pay his court and make a figure with the rest," she consented to sanction the expense. For without *her* security and guarantee of payment the local bootmaker refused the order in the most mortifying way. A fortnight went by, but he seemed to make no advance. He prepared speeches and compliments to be "let off," the young ladies offered him all sorts of openings, and were, indeed, anxious to encourage him ; but in their presence he found his voice faltering and his face growing hot : he could say nothing, and only became more *gauche* than ever. Still he looked forward to his appearance in the new suit, and imputed his failure to the old grotesque garments. At last the ladies grew disgusted, and on the very day the boots and clothes came home he received an ironical letter from Miss Laura, jestingly dismissing him from the office of being their cavalier, recommending him to join his companions at their games, and announcing that for the future, in public, M. Miaud's arm would be preferred.

This cruel mortification was the talk of the place. He took to his bed, and did not quit it till the young ladies had returned to Paris. It was, however, a good and wholesome lesson, and opened his eyes to his own deficiencies.

With such distractions his education was not advancing. He made little progress in arithmetic, though he had had three masters, had learned but little Latin, and had tried poetry, but with indifferent success.* On the other hand, he was becoming a famous shot, and could mount any horse.

The visit of the Parisian young ladies awakened in him what had not yet made itself felt sensibly—viz., *love*. All round him were a body of charming girls of different ranks, on whom he had never yet turned his eyes. Most, however, were provided with official admirers, and these young people—*chacun avec sa chacune*—rambled about the park of summer evenings, or all met together at the house of a friendly chaperon. Alexander naïvely admits that until now this sort of amusement had no charms; but it discovered to him that he had an inflammable heart, and a young rustic belle, named Adela Dalvin, became the object of his adoration.

Even at this early age, and with all his *gaucherie*,

* See his preface to *Antony*.

he had the art of attaching friends who were in a rank higher than his own. One of these was Adolphe Ribbing de Leuven, a handsome young man, son of the Swedish Count Ribbing, who was concerned in the assassination of Gustavus III. The family had incurred the displeasure of the Bourbons, and were living quietly down at Villers-Cotterets, where they were unnoticed. They were now staying with the Collards, at their château of Villers-Hellon, and Alexander was asked out for a few days to join the party. There he formed a warm friendship with this young De Leuven, afterwards to turn out a clever man of letters. One of the young ladies of the house had married the Baron Capelle, and was staying there with her little child three years old, who was destined to grow up to be the notorious Madame Lafarge. The young girls of the house were full of spirits, and played practical jokes upon the gentlemen, putting frogs in the bed of one and hiding a cock in the room of another, who woke him up at midnight. De Leuven was in love with one of these frolicsome young ladies, and amazed Alexander by showing him a sonnet he had written to her. This seemed to be a new revelation to the future writer, who now understood being in love, but knew nothing of urging a passion by means of poetry. He had always associated poetry with printed books, but to

see a real living being who could write it confounded
him. At this house he spent some delightful days,
which he looked back to fondly.

It is extraordinary with what freedom he relates the
most intimate family details, exceeding the usual French
licence.   Thus of one of the young ladies, Mademoiselle
Louise Collard, he tells an odd adventure.   When
De Leuven, who was her admirer, discovered that he
had made a geographical blunder in his verse, putting
Iberia for Siberia, he was in despair, and tried hard to
get back her album in which he had written them.
There were so many difficulties in the way that he
actually stole into her bedroom at night, and was
carrying off the book, when he knocked down some
ornament. The young lady raised an alarm, and her
father, rushing out of the next room, seized him. His
story and the fact of the album being in his hand
saved him, in a very awkward situation.*

* Dumas furnished the fullest details, by which the young ladies could
be identified by the public. One became the Baroness de Martens ; and
the heroine of the album, Madame Garat, wife of a financier. The agreeable Alexander seemed to be privileged, and to have got into no trouble
from his indiscreet revelations. Possibly it was thought a hopeless task
to deal with so incorrigible a gossip.

CHAPTER VI.

FIRST DRAMATIC ATTEMPT.

1819—23.

HE had now begun to apply himself with some seriousness to study, and a friend named Ponce induced him to learn Italian, which he mastered without much trouble. But a short expedition to Soissons seems to have had a more direct effect on his future taste. A corps of country actors happened to be performing at the theatre of the place. The play happened to be "Hamlet," in the singular version of Ducis, where Shakspeare is frizzed out, and trimmed, and "mauled," according to certain correct but hideous canons of French art. Yet, even in this maimed and distorted shape, it filled his whole soul, and left the profoundest impression on him, in which even the detestable player who performed the chief character had his share.* Another work that

* When Dumas, later, in his egotistical fashion, complimented Shakspeare with being the inspirer of his own particular muse, there was much

affected him strongly was Bürger's ballad of " Leonora,"
the rough and nervous thoughts in which seemed an
amazing contrast to the trim conceits of his favourite
native authors, Bertin and Perny, or even to Demoustier,
the popular sonneteer of the town.

At this time, which was about the year 1819, Paris
was in a state of political ferment, which had
already begun to manifest itself after a turbulent
fashion in the regions of art and literature. The in-
subordination which dared not manifest itself in the
face of despotic laws and prosecutions, could be exhibited with more safety in theatres, where some dull
lines were made to apply with rapturous effect to
the government or to political events. Thus all
France was hearing of the prodigious success of a new
piece, " The Sicilian Vespers," by Casimir Delavigne ;
how there was crushing at the doors for three hours
before the play began : how the " auditorium " of the
Odeon was crammed to suffocation, and rang with
frantic applause. All the journals and reviews praised
the brilliant author to the skies. Alexander sent
up to Paris for a copy of the play, and in a fit of

"hilarity" at this complacent coupling of two such intellects together.
But Alexander was perfectly sincere in his declaration, for it was the
situations in "Hamlet" that struck him so forcibly, and the strange attitude of the leading figure. When he saw the English players on their
visit to Paris, in a whole series of Shakspeare's dramas, this impression
was renewed even more vividly.

enthusiasm insisted that all his young friends should hear it read aloud. Never was there found so dull a production; they struggled on to the second act; but neither reader nor audience ever proposed to go further. Its success with the public, it was said, was entirely owing to some lines :—

> " Must we stand by and see
> A Minister attack our liberty, &c."

This, affording an opening for a frantic political demonstration, made the audience enchanted with the play itself. Ten or twelve years later Dumas and his friends were often to enjoy this curious kind of success.

Young Adolphe de Leuven had now returned from Paris, bringing with him sketches of quite a new world for Alexander. During this visit he had been admitted within that charmed inner circle where actors and poets and dramatists revolve. At Arnault's house, where he had been staying, he had seen and heard, and even touched, all the leading figures of that *coterie*, including Scribe, then beginning to be famous; while he had the honour of being introduced to authors of dreary, behelmeted tragedies, such as " Sylla," " Regulus," and " Leonidas." He was even gratified with the *entrée* to the fairy-land " behind the scenes," " the dullest thing in earth for those who enjoy the privilege," says Dumas; "but the seventh heaven to those who do not." For De Leuven it was a feeling of enchantment, and he inspired his friend with a longing for the same privilege. In their long walks together all these recollections were poured out, the listener eagerly putting his questions; "And Talma?" "and Madlle. Mars?" and the rest. But, above all, he had actually been allowed to present a piece at the Gymnase, which had been read and, of course, rejected; but still this was so much encouragement, and he now seriously proposed to his friend they should do as clever writers did at Paris, join their wits and write a piece together. This plan was solemnly debated, and finally agreed upon.

At this time Dumas frankly owned that he was almost uneducated. He had learned but little of his notary business, and saw that he was not likely to make anything of it: while the neighbours harassed his poor mother with such prophecies as; "depend upon it he will never do any good!" He had read but few works of amusement, not even such popular books as "Don Quixote" or "Gil Blas," but had devoured the scandalous stories of Pigault Le Brun. Thus qualified, he set to work on his first production, whose progress he relates with that pleasant candour which gives a charm to anything he says. They determined that this little vaudeville should be called THE STRASBURG MAJOR. Though why he enjoyed that rank, or was made to belong to that city rather than to another no reason could be given. At these seasons the memory of defeat and disaster had begun to wane, and with prosperity the French began to talk of glory and vengeance, and to dwell with pride and martial enthusiasm on former victories, just as at the present time the astonished stranger travelling in France will hear only of the glories of Buzenval, Champigny, and other triumphs.* Hence at all the theatres " gloire " was duly rhymed to " victoire," and " succès " to " Français," and songs celebrating past, or prophesying future glories were rapturously received.

Our young authors entered into this spirit, and conceived the idea of a retired Strasburg major, at his little cottage door in the country, thinking over the

---

* This amazing feature in the French character can be well illustrated by Dumas's own view of the battle of Waterloo. " Singular defeat ! where, in spite of a terrible catastrophe, the glory of the conquered suffered no loss, and that of the conquerer received no increase. The memory of the one will survive this repulse; that of the other will, perhaps, be sunk for ever in that victory. No, sire," addressing Napoleon, " *your* glory has not been diminished, for you struggled against destiny. Those victors, with the names of Wellington, Bulow, Blücher, were mere human masks, spirits sent by the Most High to worst you." According to the same authority, the sole cause of the loss of the battle was a peculiar form of illness which enfeebled the powers of the great commander.

past with dire bitterness, and dreaming of "la revanche." Two strangers, "the Count" and "Julien," observe him from a distance with curiosity.

"*Julien.*—What can he be reading ?

"*The Count.*—No doubt some tale of battle and of strife.

"*Julien.*—'Tis the ' Victories of France.'

"*The Count.*—I *knew it !*

"(*Song.   Julien.*)

" His heart flies back to the German plains,
He sees the gallant French prevail ;
Father ! he reads of our last campaigns,
And tears roll down his cheeks so pale."

This stirring passage was entirely Dumas's work. His collaborateur was enchanted with it, and found it would "go" to a popular martial song. It was repeated to good judges, who pronounced that it would certainly bring down the house. They encored the words :

" Father ! he reads of our last campaigns,
And tears roll down his cheeks so pale."

There the true chord would be touched, and the house roused to enthusiasm.

"Every one knows," says Dumas, candidly, "that my weak point is vanity ; so under this warm encouragement it positively grew and developed out of the vessel in which it had been shut up, like the giant in the fairy tale."   Every one had a certain instinct that this verse alone showed future dramatic instinct and power ; and it was resolved that the gifted young author should set seriously to work, and prepare several pieces, which Adolphe should carry up to Paris, and dispose of to the metropolitan managers. The new dramatist worked hard, and at the end of the year had ready a light farce called " A Friendly Little Dinner," "The Abencerages," a more ambitious drama, on a subject dear to beginners, and of course " The Strasburg Major."   With these wares De Leuven set off to Paris about the year 1821.

During his absence there was a prodigious anxiety, and every post was anxiously watched for. The first letter arrived, and it seemed that the Paris directors were not quite as forward in competing for the new works as might be expected. Still there was great hope. A month went by, and then came a second letter. It seemed that "The Friendly Little Dinner," was too weak in the plot; "The Abencerages," had already made their appearance at a good many theatres, while " The Strasburg Major," turned out to have a most extraordinary resemblance to another piece then actually playing with enormous success. However, as some comfort, De Leuven was already working with clever men like Soulié in various new pieces, and when he had obtained a regular footing he could then introduce his friend.

The friend was quite dispirited by this failure, and turned back in disgust to business. The severe Deviolaine had recently been appointed Inspector General of all the Orleans Forests, and had been moved to the chief office in Paris. The faithful mother here saw a chance for her son, and pressed the grim official to do something for him. The reply was, " Your beggar of a son, ma'am, will never do any good. I wouldn't trust him." But the good woman persisted, and at last extorted a sort of gruff promise that after a time " he would see what could be done."

Alexander now received the offer of a clerk's place in a notary's office at Crêpy, about three leagues away. His mother was growing poorer and poorer every day, and he himself had no resources ; and so with a heavy heart she agreed to a separation, which would lighten the strain on her slender resources.

M. Lefèvre, his new employer, was a dramatic character in his way, a good-looking man of about five and thirty, and of stately manners, who believed in his own attractions. He carried on his business a good deal *by manner*, made regular journeys to Paris for amusement, and to " keep off the rust," receiving his clients in lofty and gracious style, with courtly speeches, meant to convey that he was thrown away in such a place, and was paying them a compliment by residing among them. Even the fashion in which he took his Paris journeys was imposing. There was no vulgar securing of a place in the diligence, but his chariot and post-horses were ordered for a particular hour. The postilion in those days still wore the powdered queue and enormous boots. A little crowd would assemble. Then the notary appeared wrapped in a flowing cloak, and throwing himself back in his vehicle, gave the word and was whirled away.

During one of these absences, Alexander and a friend planned a secret expedition to Paris for a couple of days. They could only muster a few francs between them and a horse, so they arranged to walk and ride alternately all the way. In the same manner, and nearly a hundred years before, did Garrick and Johnson make their way to London, a fashion that was common enough for needy travellers, and called "ride and tie." As Dumas was such a good shot, they resolved that he should support them with his gun ; and if a keeper came in view, the sportsman was to mount and ride off with the game shot and the gun, leaving the pedestrian to encounter the danger and difficulty. This was carried out so cleverly that they reached Paris with a good bag. They put up at an old-fashioned little inn in the Rue des Vieux Augustins, where the landlord agreed, in return for the four hares and twelve partridges they brought, to board and lodge them comfortably for two days and two nights.

This was Alexander's first regular introduction to the great city, where he was later to figure so conspicuously. He had but two days before him, but he made the most of his opportunity. He was enchanted, bewildered by all he saw. He set off to call on his friends, and passed by the majestic Théâtre Français. He saw " Sylla " announced, with Talma in the leading part, and was seized with an overpowering longing to see the great tragedian. He made out his friend De Leuven, who actually took him to see Talma. They found the great actor dressing and bathing his chest. He received them most kindly, and wrote two orders for " Sylla." The provincial saw with astonishment that his Parisian friend took the matter very quietly, and in fact did not know the name of the piece that was to be played that night.*

---

* In his own characteristic way, Dumas describes this meeting. " Our hands touched. O Talma, had you been but twenty years younger, or I twenty years older ! All this honour was for me. I knew your past, *but you could not know my future.* Could any one have told you at that moment that the hand your hand had just touched would write *some sixty or eighty plays, in each of which you would have found a cha-*

He had settled to meet his friend that evening at the Café du Roi, where he was amused at seeing some of the odd literary men of Paris. One was writing a comedy in verse on one of the little marble tables, regardless of the noise about him. Then they proceeded to the theatre, which was crammed, as it is to-day, on nights whenever old pieces are represented. The great actor affected him with all the grandeur and magnificence of his acting, though the play was one of the usual interminable pieces in verse on the Racine model, of which the French are to this hour so respectfully enamoured. At the close, Alexander was taken round to Talma's dressing-room, where they found a bevy of dramatists, and where the great actor was receiving their compliments.*

racter to have dazzled the world with, you would not have let me leave you as you did. But *how could you have seen* what was within me, since I did not see it myself?" This passage, as a specimen of delightful complacency, is perhaps unique.

* Our hero, when he had an interview with any important personage, had always a propensity for dressing out imaginary conversations, which he threw into the shape of dramatic dialogue. The following strange remarks passed between him and Talma on this occasion. He told the actor that he blushed to say he was only a country clerk. "Bah," said the other, " we must not despair ; *Corneille* was a clerk. Gentlemen, let me introduce a future Corneille." " Then touch my forehead, sir," said Alexander, " it will bring me luck." The other did so. "There ! " he said, " I baptize you poet in the name of Shakspeare, Corneille, and Schiller.—That lad has enthusiasm," he added, " and will do something yet." Dumas was delighted with this association of his name with the great poet ; but he little dreamed that when the august names were next coupled, he would receive one of the happiest reproofs ever given in a

They returned to Crêpy next day, but to their alarm found that the notary had returned the night before. The latter, however, appeared all bland and smiling. He made no remark until after dinner, when he detained Alexander for a private interview. Then in his grandest and smoothest style, he proceeded to compare each clerk in his establishment to the wheel of a carriage, which should take its share "in the general movement" of the vehicle. He would merely give him warning that he could never allow one of his wheels to stop. But Alexander was completely unhinged by what he had seen in Paris, and the notary work had become odious. So he seized the opportunity and haughtily took leave of the stately notary, who seemed a little taken back at this result.

Here was a fresh trial for his mother, who was really at the end of her slender resources. She was now obliged to sell her little patrimony to pay the debts with which she had become burdened, and when these were discharged a couple of hundred francs was all that remained for them to live on. Alexander felt

court of justice. The story is well known. He was summoned as a witness at Rouen, and was asked his profession. " I would call myself a dramatist, were I not in the city of Corneille." " Sir, there are degrees in everything," said the president, good-naturedly. This was true wit. To this official might be addressed Johnson's hearty praise : " Sir, say no more ; rest your conversational reputation on that."

himself every hour more and more drawn to the metropolis, where he had an instinct that he was certain to succeed, and found himself turning over the letters of his father's old comrades in arms. He thought of one Dauré, who lived some miles away, and who would recommend him to General Foy. A happy chance brought him a few napoleons. Gradually the scheme began to take shape, and his mother reluctantly gave her consent.* He took leave of his friends, especially of his old master, the Abbé Grégoire, who gently reproached him with having never come near the church since the happy day of his first communion.† He paid a last visit, with his mother, to the cemetery of his father, and set off to seek the fortune, he was destined to find, at Paris.

* A fortune-teller had predicted to her, he gravely tells us, that her son was to have a commanding position. "Your son belongs to that class of men who are destined to be RULERS of their fellows."

† His pupil gravely defended himself, and read him a lecture on the true meaning of real devotion at church. "One must not," he said, "grow too familiar *with sacred things.* How do you know but that one of these days I may not want the church for some signal consolation, just as one might want bleeding?" We pass by some ridiculous devices in which, he says, he secured a free journey to Paris, and which belongs to his romances, namely, by winning "six hundred glasses of absinthe" from the postmaster at billiards, who was glad to compound for a seat in the diligence!

CHAPTER VII.

PARIS.

1823.

HE arrived in the great city at five o'clock on a
Sunday morning, was set down at No. 9 in the Rue
du Bouloi, and from this place carried his parcel to
his old hotel in the Rue des Vieux Augustins. Such
was the modest entrance of the future owner of the
splendid "Folly" at St. Germain, the builder of the
great Théâtre Historique, and the world-renowned
literary "conjuror," to whom thousands owe a heavy
debt for many a weary hour beguiled.

Almost his first proceeding was to look over the
list of the ministers, and he found that Victor, the
Duke of Belluno, was Minister of War. His port-
folio furnished him with an old letter of the marshal's
to his father, thanking the general for some service.
He sat down and prepared a modest application
founded on this document. But he had even a better
card to play. There was Jourdan, whose letters gave

evidence of a friendship as warm as that of Damon for Pythias, to say nothing of Sebastiani, whose letter showed that he actually owed a command to the intercession of the general. There is some worldly knowledge to be gathered from this passage in Dumas's life, and not to be disdained by the reader, viz., that such weighty obligations are often a hindrance rather than a recommendation to the obtaining of favours from the great.

He first went boldly to call on Jourdan, and sent up his name. He was admitted at once. But he saw a look of surprise on the marshal's face, who had some dim idea that this might be his old friend. He had never heard of his having a son, or did not choose to run the risk of being deceived. All the young man could say would not convince him, and he was dismissed coolly. Alexander, not a little discouraged, then passed to Sebastiani's hotel, whom he found in his cabinet, dictating to several secretaries as he walked about the room, each of whom as this chief came near, offered a gold snuff-box, out of which the general took a pinch. With such a busy man he was not likely to have success. Much disheartened he then thought of an old General Verdier, whom he found out in a little room higher up, near the roof, engaged in painting. This veteran received him cordially, but was himself in disgrace. He, however, was very kind, and asked his young friend to dine at a cheap café. He bade him not lose hope, told him frankly that he need not expect *anything* from the people who were in power, and bade him go and present his letter to Foy, for there there was some chance. Dumas followed this advice, called on the general in the Rue Mont Blanc, and found him writing his History of the Peninsular War. He was received in the kindest manner, was questioned as to his qualifications, which were found sadly deficient, but was dismissed with hope.

"I dine to-day," he said, "at the Palais-Royal, and will speak to the Duke of Orleans about you. Come to me to-morrow morning." The young man retired full of hope. When he got home he found an official letter from the Minister of War, to the effect that there was no time to receive him, but bidding him put in writing what he had to say, which was, in effect, the usual circular.

His last chance, therefore, was Foy, and the next morning he waited on him with a beating heart. The general received him with a smiling face. There was good news; it was all settled. He was to have a small place in the secretary's office at the Palais-Royal. It was scarcely worth fifty pounds a year, but still it was a beginning. A beginning! it was a fortune! The young man was enchanted, as well he might be. He flew to his friends the De Leuvens, who wished to celebrate his good fortune by keeping him to dinner; but his first thought was to return without a moment's delay to Villers-Cotterets, and announce the good news in person to his dear mother.

He started at once. It was past midnight when he arrived at the little town. His mother was in bed, but he rushed in to her room, crying "Victory, dear mother, victory!" The good woman thus aroused, was frightened out of her wits, but was soon listening to the delightful story. He told her everything, heightening the failures to make the success more welcome. The affectionate parent made him tell the story again and again, and indeed she might feel some pride in the unfriended country lad, who, by his own exertions, had done so much. Not till morning broke did he leave her to enjoy that most delightful of slumbers—the one that succeeds to some welcome change of fortune.

The next day all Villers-Cotterets had the news—everyone was talking of it and congratulating him. He was attended to the door of the good Abbé Grégoire, on whom he waited, by quite an escort. Everyone was enchanted. "They had never doubted a moment," says Alexander; "they had always *said* I would do something yet. They had prophesied it to my mother, these being the very persons who had been predicting that I would never do any good." Then came plans for the future. She must give up the tobacco business and come with him to Paris. She was frightened at the idea, but it was impossible not to have confidence in one who had already done so well. So she agreed. Finally, having arranged everything, he set off back to Paris.

On the very day that he arrived, he went to look for a lodging, and after ascending and .descending innumerable flights, found a little room with an alcove on the fourth story of a house in a block of houses known as the Paté des Italiens. This he secured at the modest charge of about five pounds a year. He then went to *flaner* it on the Boulevards, and in the evening repaired to the Porte St. Martin, where they were playing " The Vampire," a truly sensational piece then drawing crowds. He relates his first experiences of a Paris play-house, which were not a little unfortunate, owing to his rustic simplicity. These and other recollections of the same kind in other hands would be trifling, and scarcely worth recording ; but Dumas had such an unrivalled dramatic instinct, and such a command of dramatic dialogue, that he could extract the true spirit of comedy out of his adventures, and al-

most put them in stage shape. While he was gazing
hopelessly at the enormous *queue* which stretched
away from the doors, some one good-naturedly offered
to sell him his place for two francs. After a little
hesitation he accepted the offer, fancying that he was
thus secured admission to the theatre. When he was
required to take his ticket at the office he expostulated,
and tried to explain the matter. He said he had already
paid, but the impatient queue behind him would not
wait, and insisted on his either giving place to others
or passing on. Indignant at this unfair treatment of a
stranger, he was obliged to take a ticket, and passed
into the pit. There he was astonished to find a crowd
already seated, which seemed incomprehensible, as he
had been one of the first admitted. As he walked
across the benches, this group looked round and set
up a loud laugh, evidently at his expense. The truth
was, he was dressed not a little absurdly in a coat
that descended nearly to his heels, while his hair was
ridiculously long. This might have been the fashion
at Villers-Cotterets, but it was strange to Paris. When
one of the scoffers went so far as to call out, " Lord,
what a head ! " the young provincial singled him out,
and gave him a hearty cuff. Instantly rose the cry,
which is so characteristic of that hounding or hunting-
down spirit which at times seizes on Frenchmen, " *À*

la porte!" "Turn him out!" He laughed at them.
"That *is* a good joke," he said sarcastically. "Turn
me out, after paying twice over for my place,—once at
the door and once at the office!" But the cry swelled,
fists were shaken at him, fingers pointed him out;
everyone was standing up on the benches, or looking
down from the boxes. Even those who knew nothing
of the case joined in the shouting, on the ground that
there would be thus a place to spare. Suddenly a
gentlemanly man advanced, and with a motion of his
hand required him to follow. The young man re-
monstrated, and asked why. "You are disturbing
the performance." "Why, it has not commenced!"
"Well, you are disturbing the audience. Follow me
at once." He had to do so amid the loud applause of
the crowd, who, like all crowds, seemed delighted at
justice being thus vindicated. His guide led him
through various dark passages until they came to a
door, when Dumas found himself in the street. "There,"
said the agent, "now don't try that sort of thing
again," and left him. Bewildered and indignant at
such treatment, Alexander determined not to be de-
frauded of his place and money, and after some hesitation boldly presented himself at the wicket. "Ticket?"
said the official. He explained that he had given it
already. Well, his pass-out? They had not given

him one. Then he could not be admitted. Furious at this treatment, he said that it was a shame, after his paying twice over, once at the queue and another at the office. The official smiled. "You are a joker," he said. But it won't do here." "A shame," said Alexander furiously, "do you take me for a swindler?" "I take you for a disorderly fellow, that has been put out for making a disturbance in the house, and if you don't keep quiet, you may find yourself not in the street, but in the police-office." Still more bewildered at this turn, Alexander felt that he was overpowered, and saying, "You are the strongest," retired.

Still he did not like to lose the performance, and determined to take a better place, which he was allowed to do. His night's pleasure thus became rather expensive. He found himself seated by a curious sort of old antiquary, who he later discovered was Charles Nodier.* The chief part in the piece was taken by the famous Madame Dorval, soon to be his intimate friend, and the actress of his own heroines.

On the Monday morning he presented himself for the first time at the Palais-Royal. He felt not a little nervous. The place was not yet open, but after waiting a little two young men arrived, who greeted him

---

* We pass by, as fanciful, the minutely reported conversation on Elzevirs and other subjects which he had with his companion.

cordially. These were Ernest and Lassagne, his fellow clerks. A more serious ordeal was his interview with the head of the office, M. Oudard, a hard, cold, ambitious man, with piercing black eyes, who sent him off to see his relative, M. Deviolaine, who was installed under the same roof. The latter, received him in his favourite style, and asked after his good mother, saying, in his elegant fashion, he wondered how a fellow like Alexander could have been brought into the world by her. However, this official, like Johnson, had no more of the bear about him but the skin ; for it turned out that he had aided in getting the place for his relative, and now asked him to come and dine whenever he could. Another of the heads of the office was an old M. de Broval, who explained to him that there were different ways of sealing a letter, according to the rank of the person addressed. After a little time he began to give satisfaction, and, being discovered to write a very good hand, was sent for to assist the Duke himself in his private cabinet. The future King was then a man of about fifty, still good-looking, but inclined to be stout, with a quick eye, which, however, did not exhibit much depth or brilliancy. He was always engaged in business, looking after his estates and money matters, he himself drawing up the facts and instructions for his agents. Alexander acquitted himself so satisfactorily on this occasion, that he was fixed upon the establishment, for hitherto he had been merely on probation. Nine months later, in January, 1824, his salary was raised to sixty pounds a year.

He now thought it high time to send for his mother, who at last arrived with a little furniture and eighty pounds in money. He was obliged to look out for another lodging, for his own little rooms would not be sufficient, to say nothing of new responsibilities that obliged him to take this step.* After much trouble he found rooms in the Faubourg St. Denis, No. 53, on the second floor, next door to the " Silver Lion." For three rooms and a kitchen he was to pay fourteen pounds a year, an amazingly small sum compared with current prices in Paris, but rather a heavy charge on sixty pounds a year. Mother and son were enchanted at the meeting, and after a few days she grew quite accustomed to the change of life. Even still they were soon to find out that that rent was too high for their resources. A lodger on the same floor was dying of consumption, and, when they were complaining,

---

* " On the 29th July, 1824," he tells us, in his own odd fashion, " while the Duke of Montpensier was coming into the world at the Palais-Royal, *there was born for me a Duke of Chartres* at the Place des Italiens, No. 1." This was the future author of the *Dame aux Camellias.* It is amusing to contrast the carelessness with which he discloses the character of his son's birth, and the sensitiveness with which he vindicates his own legitimacy. In this sort of selfishness he rivals Sheridan.

said good-naturedly, "Only wait a little and you can have my rooms." These were only nine pounds a year. In six weeks they became vacant as he had predicted, and they moved into them.

Louis XVIII. was now dead, and Charles X. on the throne. Alexander was to lose his old patron General Foy, whose death affected him deeply. It inspired his first production, an "Ode," which he printed at his own cost, and which, of course, produced him nothing.[*] Indeed their fortunes soon begun to wear a very unpromising aspect; their slender resources were fast wasting away, and in a year and half they found they had spent about a hundred and sixty pounds, which was some eighty pounds more than they were entitled to do. The emoluments of his post were utterly insufficient to support them; and as ruin and poverty was staring them in the face, it was absolutely necessary that he should find some way of earning money. In vain had he and his friend De Leuven worked together at plays. No one would accept them. De Leuven had tried with Soulié and other friends, but with the same result. Pressed by necessity, they determined to abate their pride and take into partnership a common hand, of inferior talents, who had a fair

* "A mes frais, bien entendu." But he quietly adds, that his mother supplied the money from her little hoard.

connection with the theatres, his own pieces being accepted. This artist bore the classical name of Rousseau, and was one of those souls who could do nothing unless the bottle and glasses were on the table. He was always drunk, and well known to the police, but, like the story of Sheridan and "Wilberforce," in his deepest fits of inebriation he could always recall the name of a friendly commissary. Thus when he was picked out of the gutter, he always astonished his captors by an inarticulate demand to be led before the favourite officer, who knew his failings. He delighted in those practical " jests," which confound even the victim by the laborious politeness with which they are carried out.

Once, seeing a shop with the sign of " The Two Apes," he entered it late at night, when the proprietor was in bed, and insisted on being conducted to his room on business of the last importance. The owner was roused up and the joker introduced. He made a thousand apologies, and said it was to his partner that he wished to speak. " I have no partner," said the other. " Then why put it on your sign ?" expostulated the other, gravely. " Observe 'The *Two* Apes.' It is taking in the public." Of his drunkenness there were numerous characteristic stories. A friend was struggling hard to get him home one night, and finding him impracticable, set him down among the cabbages at a greengrocer's door; then buying a small lantern, lit it, and placing it beside him, went his way. Rousseau slept through the night, and in the morning found some halfpence in his hand, given by the charitable.

They accordingly consulted this worthy assistant, and put their various pieces into his hands. A day was fixed when his report was to be given, and his attendance was secured by the promise of champagne. He arrived, and declared that none of the pieces would do. They were convinced that he had not read a word of them, though probably he was correct enough in his judgment. Comforted by this idea they proceeded with their supper. Alexander told stories of his shooting experiences. Their friend listened, and in his rough way called out suddenly, "Why, there you go borrowing and cribbing melodramas from Florian and other fellows; and yet I can see in what you have just told us a capital little piece called 'Love and Sport.'" They at once drank a bottle to the idea; pens and paper were procured, and the plan forthwith sketched out. Each was to complete a portion, and all were to meet again in a week, when the whole was to be complete. On the day appointed they met, and, as a matter of course, Rousseau had not written a line.

Alexander had worked out the idea of a comic sportsman from Paris, which was pronounced a complete
success. The piece when finished was taken by
Rousseau to the Gymnase, for, as an *acted* author, he
had the right of demanding a reading. After an
anxious delay came back the news of its rejection,
and the three partners were in despair. The worst
was, that the failure was ascribed by the judge to the
vulgarity of Alexander's cockney sportsman.

They met again in council. "Nothing," says
Dumas, "is more dismal than these meetings of
rejected authors." It was resolved to try a theatre of
humbler rank, and the piece was dispatched to the
Ambigu Comique, where the reading was fixed for the
Saturday following. Alexander and his mother saw
the day approach with something like terror, for
matters were growing almost desperate with them,
though they had pinched themselves in every conceivable way. When he was sitting in his office overwhelmed with anxiety the door opened, and he saw
joyful news in the faces of his visitors. The piece had
been received, and, strange to say, what delighted the
judges most of all was the cockney sportsman !

This is an epoch in Alexander's life, and his perseverance and spirit deserved all success. His foot
was already on the first step of the great ladder, to

the top of which he was soon to climb in a few bounds.

The next point to be ascertained was the pecuniary value of this success, and he found that *his* share of the author's rights would be the magnificent sum of four francs per night, with the right to two seats. Here it is that Dumas' recollections become particularly interesting as throwing light on the curious life and shifts of writers for the stage in Paris. His friend Rousseau presently put him in the way of discounting these privileges by introducing to him one Porcher, a kind of humble speculator about the theatres, but also the creator of a great system.* Formerly authors and writers gave away to friends the tickets to which they were entitled. This, it seemed to him, was so much waste, so he proposed to purchase these tickets and dispose of them himself at reduced prices. The actors, as may be conceived, were delighted. He was always friendly and gracious to young and rising talent. He agreed to give two pounds for Dumas's tickets ; not much, he owned, but the piece might fail the very first night. Alexander accepted with joy, and promised, moreover, to deal with him exclusively. Most welcome

---

* For an amusing account of this official and his system, see Texier, *Récits et Critiques.* Many an author waited on him with his play, as on a bill discounter, Porcher making as many objections as a bill discounter ; the state of the weather would prejudice the receipts, &c.

is the first money thus earned, and Alexander, enchanted as he was with what he had gained, could never have dreamed that these were to be the first few drops of that heavy golden shower which, within a few years, was to stream down upon him.   Was he ever to become acquainted with Boswell's "Johnson"—a book of whose existence he probably never heard—he would have appreciated "the potentiality of becoming rich beyond the dreams of avarice."

"Love and Sport" (*La Chasse et L'Amour*) was played on September 22nd, 1825, and received with much favour, an actor named Du Vourjal taking the principal character.   Indeed, so successful was its first representation, that the worthy speculator advanced him twenty pounds more on his tickets.   Thus early did our hero prove himself faithful to a practice he never gave over, that of being always *in advance*. From this hour everything was forestalled.   This money, however, he wanted for a literary venture. He wished to publish a volume of short tales, which he had taken round to all the booksellers, not one of whom would "touch" it.   "Get yourself a name," said one to him, "and then I'll publish your books."*

---

* "I don't believe," says Dumas, "in talent ignored, or neglected genius."   Where true genius or talent has failed to be recognised, there will always be some fault or misconduct to account for the failure.

He however found an opening; and his history is instructive, as showing how he turned to profit every chance. He was a favourite with a printer's wife, who read and admired his verses, and she got her husband to print them, on condition of Alexander finding twelve pounds or half the cost. This was done, and the book appeared under the title of "Tales of the Day" (*Nouvelles Contemporaines*), and with his name on the title. Of "Tales of the Day" four copies, he candidly tells us, were sold, and the printer, of course, lost his money.

Still, these little efforts were not without effect; and a bookseller, who was bringing out a series of engravings of the Duke of Orleans' pictures, applied to him for illustrative rhymes, which he furnished. He then proceeded, with one of his office friends, to write another piece, founded on a story in the Fairy Tales, of a shipwrecked sailor who had married in a savage country, where was a custom that on the death of a husband or wife the survivor should be interred with him. The choice of this subject—which contains the elements of real comedy—proves that Dumas thus early was showing dramatic instinct, for the subject has shown genuine vitality, and has been treated many times since.* It was called

---

* In England this piece of Dumas's was translated as " The Illustrious

" Married and Buried," and was produced with great success on November 21st, 1826.   He and his mother sat in the orchestra looking on joyfully, though his conceit was not a little taken down when he heard a neighbour say, as he rose to go away, " This sort of stuff won't keep the theatre going."   " I believe he was right," adds Dumas.   Still, the piece " ran," and he received his four francs nightly, a very acceptable little pittance, though already mortgaged.*

But this very success was to expose him to serious dangers.   The austere heads of the office soon learned that their clerks were engaged in hanging about stage doors and writing plays.   They had an utter dislike to these frivolities, not on the ground that they might interfere with work, but based on simple bureaucratic contempt.   He was sent for by the chief, and solemnly warned.   The office would tolerate no play-writing.   The young man pleaded the miserable pittance on which he and his mother had to live, and was told, if he must write, to write respectably, like Casimir Delavigne, not things like " Love and Sport,"

Stranger,"—a piece of genuine fun, beside which our modern farces seem tame and pointless.

* Though the " *droits d'auteur* " in France are often contrasted with the English system, the result is probably the same.   As we have seen, these profits are generally mortgaged by needy authors, and otherwise speculatively disposed of, for much less than their proper value.

or " Married and Buried." Much hurt at this depre-
ciation, he was imprudent to answer, that if he was
not to look forward to producing better things than
M. Delavigne, he was content never to write another
line! This heresy and self-sufficiency so amazed the
official that he could say nothing, and for days nothing
was heard of but Dumas's ludicrous conceit.* This
boldness, though it amused his superiors, did not injure
him, and a place falling vacant just at this time, he
asked for it and obtained it. He had now seventy
pounds a year, though he confesses the office into
which he was moved, that of the Almoner's, was of a
lower rank than the one he had quitted. But it
brought him greater pay and more liberty for seeing
actors, and visiting the theatres.

* He seems to think that, at the date of his writing, he had more than
justified his prophecy. Delavigne was librarian to the Duke.

CHAPTER VIII.

" HENRI III."

1829.

THERE now occurred an event which produced the profoundest impression on his mind and general current of his thoughts. This was his witnessing some English acting for the first time.

The wholesale dependence of English dramatists on translations from the French during the last twenty or thirty years, has been often dwelt on with severity; but it should not be forgotten that against this is to be set off some serious French depredations. It was curious that the vehement revival of letters after the Restoration should have turned the thoughts of young and ardent spirits in the direction of England. It would be an interesting inquiry to consider the meaning of this fashion, the more so as there was a similar taste exhibited during the days of conceded licence that preceded the First Revolution. It is at least complimentary to this country, that the first uses of a new found liberty should be associated with our literature and tastes; and it is not improbable that a similar tendency may set in, should the nation now receive its full intellectual liberty after twenty years of imperial repression. Shakespeare had been translated by M. Guizot, abundant dramas had been shaped out of "Othello," "Richard the Third," "Macbeth," and "Romeo and Juliet"; while Byron, Walter Scott, and strange to say Cooper, were read and talked of *à folie*. The taste for Shakespeare and Byron was simply an affectation, the true power of the former being more or less unintelligible, and to this hour, a sealed book to the French mind; the latter being in favour on account of a morbid interest in his personal history, which was supposed to be reflected in "Manfred" and "Childe Harold." The strangest thing was to find Cooper and his "Leatherstocking" placed on the same level; but this was, beyond doubt, more the personal partiality of Dumas himself, with whom the American was a favourite. But the English writer that enjoyed the heartiest popularity, and who was read with delight and interest, was Walter Scott; and though Dumas, like his countrymen, disdained to acknowledge obligation, historical romances like "Ivanhoe" and "Quentin Durward" suggested the romantic historical drama which Dumas and Victor Hugo were

presently to introduce; nay, the dashing spirit of
" Monte Christo " and of the " Three Musketeers " is
to be found in the same illustrious models. Here,
again, it would seem the French have shown their
appreciation of English matters in the wrong direction;
as it is stories like " Ivanhoe " and the " Talisman,"
which in England are not considered the best works of
the writer, have enjoyed the highest popularity. It
will be seen, too, that in the instance of the " Divine Wil-
liams," only the familiar *situations*—Macbeth with the
witches, Hamlet and his father's ghost, the love of
Desdemona for a black—are what have taken hold of
the French mind. As for Dumas's own unbounded
worship of Shakespeare, he was merely struck by the
effective dramatic situations, and having acquired a
superficial knowledge of the great bard, he afterwards
felt a complacent pride in associating the names of
Dumas and Shakespeare in a handsome partnership.

It was when a company of English actors came to
play in Paris during September, 1827, that Dumas
owns that a new light as to dramatic treatment and
representation broke not only on him, but upon the
eager band of young men who were later to become
teachers of the country. The troop consisted of
Abbott, Charles Kemble, Miss Smithson, and " a comic
actor named Liston." They acted " Hamlet," " Romeo

and Juliet," "Othello," and many of the popular English pieces. It was a new revelation. Even for those who did not understand the language, the freedom and animation and spirit, the nature, especially in *tragic situations,* was perfectly intelligible, and they could not help contrasting it with the stiff and regulated motions in which the native player interpreted similar situations. Dumas, with a frankness rare in a Frenchman, owns his obligation to the English stage, though he will only condescend to admit the direct inspiration of Shakespeare. "It was the first time," he says, " that I saw on the stage real passions, warming men and women made of flesh and blood." This is probable enough ; but it seems ludicrous to compliment Shakespeare with the extravagant inspiration of " Antony " and " Richard Darlington ;" and this again illustrates the hopeless incapacity of the French for understanding the true meaning of English ideas. As we have said, they could see nothing more in Shakespeare's plays than the " business " which their translators and adapters set before them, without attempting to convey the wonderful " spirit " and philosophy and poetry which is behind. " Hamlet " they were specially pleased with, looking on him as a sort of Byron ; but the action and incidents seemed to be the work of some disorderly and rather "barbarous" genius.[*]

Dumas was enchanted with Miss Smithson and Kemble, in the rapturous balcony scene of "Romeo and Juliet," where the chivalrous bearing of Kemble must have contrasted curiously with the rhymed and declaimed love-making of French actors dressed in Roman and Turkish dresses, to which he was accustomed.

Abbott attracted him a good deal from his graceful and vivacious style. It is some proof of the influence of the English players that Miss Smithson should have captivated the young composer Berlioz, whose works reflected a new and romantic style in music, and drew their Shakespearian inspiration from her acting. English playgoers were not a little amused at the *fureur* excited by one whom they considered to be an ordinary actress ; though old playgoers of judgment have pronounced that there was a strange charm in her acting. The history of Berlioz's passion for her is a most romantic episode. The lady rejected his frantic advances, which were more calculated to inspire terror than love ; and to

---

[*] It is amusing to read French contemporary criticism, in the *Débats*, for instance, of 1825 and 1826, where, for their own credit's sake, they are compelled to praise, but, at the same time, are hopelessly bewildered by the extravagance of "le grand Shakspeare."

console him, a friend mentioned to him an actress at one of the theatres who had an extraordinary likeness to Smithson, and to whom he might "make love in effigy." This plan was carried out, and with soothing effect. The very titles of his works exhibit the genuine influence of this English inspiration—"The Tempest," "Death of Sardanapalus," "Wawerly,"* "Romeo and Juliet," "Harold." The "effigy" actually proved faithless, and married another—a trying and highly ludicrous situation; the lover hurried from Rome with *three pistols*, one for the husband, one for the lady, and one for himself. He was diverted, however, from this bloodthirsty purpose. The original object of his passion relented, and they were duly married, only to be separated in a short time. Suitable *finale* to such a history!

Other actors came over later—Macready, Kean, and Young. "Then I witnessed," says Dumas, "the spectacle of players forgetting that they were on a stage; their artificial life seemed to become part of the daily life about us." Thus inspired, and being filled with an irresistible ardour for writing for the stage something that should express these new sensations, a small basso relievo at one of the exhibitions suggested a subject. This was the murder or execu-

* Sic, in *De Mirecourt's* Les Contemporains.

tion of Monaldeschi by Queen Christina at Fontainebleau. No sooner had he found the subject than he
set to work impetuously. But he first prepared himself by an arduous course of study of the works of
Shakespeare, Molière, Corneille, Calderon, Goethe, and
Schiller (!), and from this rather miscellaneous reading
was to derive a profit more practical than simple inspiration, and which unfriendly pens were to expose
many years later.*

But while thus engaged, he received notice that there
was no work for him in the Almoner's office, and that
he must pass into the department of the forests, where
was his relative Deviolaine. Nothing can be better
than his sketches of the characters he met in these
bureaux—that of the old official who took a fancy to
his handwriting, " because it was so like Piron's," who
at one time had been in the office ; or that old Parseval
de Grandmaison, who was so absent that he would
forget his own name.† He saw at once that with a
man of this temper, with whom he had never agreed,
it was hopeless to think of getting on ; and almost on
the first day his hot temper betrayed him into a dis-

---

* These were, of course, in the shape of those prose versions of poetry
to which the French were partial, and which gave so false an idea of the
original. Scott's " Marmion," " Lady of the Lake," &c., were all presented in this diluted prose shape.

† All these traits are, no doubt, coloured up ; but they are, beyond a
doubt, developments of real experience.

pute, about a room to which he conceived he was entitled, and which raised up enemies.

Meanwhile he was working night and day at his play, which he called " Christine," and at which he laboured with such enthusiasm, that he was speedily at what he calls. " the famous last verse :"

> " There ! I can have have pity on him now.
> Dispatch him !"

But when the play was finished, and finished to his satisfaction, what he was to do with it ? — he, an obscure young clerk, an atom in mighty Paris ! He was actually looking wistfully to the first house in the kingdom—the august French Theatre—which was fenced round with ranks of Academicians, and the pedantic admirers of the grand style. He had no friends, and it really seemed ludicrous that so obscure a youth should dream of getting even to the threshold of the great house in the Rue de Richelieu. It is instructive to see from his example what resources are within the reach of the most obscure, provided they have energy and versatility. He cast about for every aid that could procure him an introduction. A messenger from the theatre brought tickets for the Duke of Orleans's establishment, and from him he learned that Baron Taylor, the king's commissary, was all powerful in securing the reception of pieces. But how was he to reach Baron Taylor ? After asking friends a curious opening soon suggested itself. Some one mentioned that Charles Nodier had great influence; and then Dumas recalled the Bibliomaniac beside whom he sat on the unlucky night when he had been turned out of the theatre. There was something so odd in this temporary acquaintance, and something so quaint in the man himself, that he was induced to write, begging an introduction to Baron Taylor. From Nodier he received no reply, which was, indeed, only what he expected. But to his wonder and delight came a letter from Baron Taylor himself, offering to hear him read his play. This was in itself an enormous advantage for a work of real merit : thus securing it a fair hearing.

The reception of pieces at the French Theatre was managed after a sort of republican system, and the acceptance of pieces lay with the players assembled in council, who heard the play read. This might seem eminently a fair system, as securing a fair chance for every one ; but it is obvious that, with such encouragement, the year would be far too short to dispose of the vast numbers that would be sent in, and that a certain power of selection would be necessary, so as to stem the flood of pieces that were certain to arrive. In short this system of free acceptance, whether on the stage or in literature, has been found impossible to work, as it would amount to the reception of works from about the whole community. It seems probable that the reception of works from "one of the staff," as it were, secures better work than this system of open competition.

Taylor at this time lived in the Rue de Bondy, and was so busy that he could only receive Dumas at seven in the morning. The latter arrived with his manuscript, but found another author before him.[*]

This seemed a fatal prologue for "Christine," especially as a five-act "Epaminondas" was to follow. But the Baron was good-natured, and, going to bed, courageously bade the young dramatist begin his play. He was really pleased with the first act, asked for the second, listened to the others with interest, and at the end was actually enthusiastic. He promised that it should be read at the theatre within a few days. Dumas exulted in this triumph of perseverance and address, and, it might be added, of the power of talent and genius. It was, indeed, enough to make Paris wonder. Here was an obscure clerk in an office, without education, and with but little reading—a Provincial but a short time arrived from the country—

---

[*] Dumas here gives a picture of the Baron in his bath, compelled to listen to a *Hecuba* of a pitiless writer, and groaning as each of the five acts were read. This is a little too farcical for sober truth.

who had passed in the race Academicians, pedants and poets, the regular purveyors of the theatre. This was a phenomenon of the most extraordinary kind. And so Dumas himself would have us believe.

But there were some practical, not to say spiteful, natures, who could furnish a solution of a simpler kind. The young man was a clerk indeed, but a clerk in the employment of the Duke of Orleans, to whom he often acted as confidential secretary. The Duke was the landlord of the actors, their theatre being on his ground, and, possibly, his property. The wish of such a patron was a law. The very change to the Almonry was, it is stated,* an act of good nature on the Duke's part, to secure him leisure to write this play. The whole indeed is the beginning, not only of Alexander's success, but also of a chapter of ingratitude, which forms an unpleasant episode in his life.

On the Thursday following he found himself in the stately salons of the great theatre, surrounded by the players, all in full dress—a fashion that used to obtain at English theatres, in compliment to an important piece. It was listened to with much approbation, and when the votes were taken, was received " unanimously," subject to a revision by one of the advisers

* " Fabrique de Romans," p. 15.

of the house.* He left the theatre enchanted, scarcely knowing what he was doing—"proud as on the day when his first mistress said to him, 'I love you!'" He flew towards the Rue St. Denis, and felt tempted to call out to every one he met, "*You haven't written a 'Christine'! you haven't been received at the French Theatre!*" He dashed across the road among the carriages and horses, careless of danger, and found on reaching his mother's house that he had dropped his manuscript out of his pocket. It was all in his head, however, so it was only a question of labour. He burst into the room.

"Received by acclamation, mother!" he shouted, and began to sing and dance round the room. She thought he was mad.

"*But what will they say at the office?*" she said, with a naturalness that recalls Mrs. Shandy.

"Let them say what they like : they may all go hang!"

"My poor child, it is *you* that will go hang; you will be turned out."

"So much the better, mother ; I shall have more time for the rehearsals."

---

* The piece was not what it became later ; and though of a romantic kind—that is to say, the characters acted on the impulses of ordinary men and women—was still classical in adhering to the unities.

"But if your piece fails, and you lose your place, what in the world is to become of us ? "

All this is truth and nature—the son looking only to the chances of success, the mother seeing only the dangers of failure.

This great day was April 30, 1828. He spent the whole evening and night in writing out his play again. But the next morning, when he repaired to his office, there was a fresh delight in store for him : he was greeted maliciously by one of the heads of the office, "So you have been writing a tragedy ? " The newspaper was then shown, and there was actually a paragraph announcing that " The French Theatre had received a new piece by a young man who has as yet not written, but who was powerfully supported by the interest of the Duke of Orleans, in whose establishment he was." Dumas says this was but the inauguration of that tissue of wilful blunders as to his affairs, into which the newspapers were hereafter to fall. "All distorted as it was " (he refers to the passage about the Duke's interest) " there was some foundation for the statement." He never forgave Louis-Philippe for neglecting him ; and this bitter hostility made him conceal, and even deny, his obligation to the Duke of Orleans.

Everyone in the place had the news ; and he received both ironical as well as sincere compliments. His chief, Deviolaine, full of spite and bitterness, sent for him.

"So there you are, you mountebank," he said; "and you did not see that the actors were only laughing at you!"

"Still," said the other, "they have accepted my play."

"All very fine, but will they act it, or will the public listen to it?—All stuff and nonsense! I shan't be alive when it is played."

At this one of the officials interrupted them, and in a mysterious manner announced that there was *a play actor* below looking for M. Dumas—one Firmin.

"Oh, yes," said Alexander carelessly; "*he* plays Monaldeschi."

Deviolaine was aghast. "*Firmin* play in your piece!"

When he heard that not only Firmin, but Madlle. Mars was to play, he lost all control over himself, and threw up his hands over his head.

But everything was not to go so smoothly as this, and Dumas frankly tells us his failures as well as his successes. The next step was the waiting on a little humpback, with large hands and piercing eyes, who was the adviser chosen by the actors. He was one Picard, and he received the manuscript with an affected humility, fearing that his poor judgment was incapable of judging properly these " grand romantic affairs," from being so accustomed to the old-fashioned classical pieces. This did not augur well. Dumas returned in a week, and had his play put into his hand, neatly tied up, with a question, " had he any regular means of support ? " When he answered yes, he was told smilingly, " Then get back to your office —take my advice, get back to your office."

In despair he went to his friend Taylor, who soon got this verdict set aside. But the piece had again to be read before the actors, and to be submitted to a second judge named Samson, whose tastes were not so utterly opposed to the new style, and whose suggestions led to a complete remodelling of the piece. Everything seemed to be going well, but the young author was now to make acquaintance with the singular uncertainty that attends all stage arrangements.

By one of those coincidences from which dramatic writers often suffer more than others, the idea of " Christine and the Execution at Fontainebleau " had taken possession of no less than two other minds.*

---

* Many instances could be given of this taste for a particular subject acting on various minds like an epidemic. Within ten years, a little before this date, the subject of Charles VI. had been treated no less than five times for the stage.

This was specially unlucky for the beginner. Soulié
had sent in *his* " Christine " to the Odéon—while a
certain old Prefect named Brault, who enjoyed the
patronage of Decazes the minister, had succeeded in
getting his received at the Français. The actress for
whom the leading part was intended was the " dear
friend " of the editor of an important newspaper, and
it was found impossible to resist the pressure of
minister and editor. It is thus curious to see how
an institution, supposed to be as independent as pension and State recognition could make it, should have
become a mere nest of intrigue and " jobbing ;" while
it shows an utter indifference to the interests of the
theatre that two plays should have been received
on the same subject.* Again, the actors had grown
cold—had begun to feel alarm as to the " risky "
character of the parts they were to play. Indeed his
hopes now began to fall as rapidly as they had
mounted. There was then to come a fresh obstacle.
The author of the second " Christine " was dying, and
his son made an appeal *ad misericordiam,* for his
father, that could not be resisted. He would die in peace
did he but know that his play was in hand. Dumas
had to give way, though he knew that a year must

* Farther on the reader will find this interesting question discussed
more fully.

elapse before his own piece could be thought of.
This good nature was at once rewarded by a paragraph in the papers, to the effect that the Committee
of the theatre having found that there was more
merit in Brault's play, had postponed M. Alexandre
Dumas's indefinitely. It is probable that he saw there
was no choice in the matter, and that he had best
yield gracefully. But his enemies were not justified
in giving the matter the turn they did, viz., that he
withdrew it from one theatre only to dispose of it in
another. This he indeed did, but not till long after
M. Brault's "Christine" had failed and had been
forgotten.

His mother was good-naturedly told this news by
friends! Indeed the poor soul must have often looked
back wistfully to the simple pastoral days at Villers-
Cottcrets, now exchanged for these anxieties.

But he was presently to be indemnified for this
self-sacrifice. He soon rallied under this bitter disappointment. One day, when in the library at the
Palais-Royal, his eye fell upon a paragraph in a
volume of Anquetil, relative to the Duke and Duchess
of Guise, that seemed to have the germ of something
dramatic. It quite took possession of him. He looked
into other French memoirs, for what would supply
the rest of the story, and in two months the tragedy

of " Henri III." was written. He wrote with enthusiasm, and was full of the subject. As his habit was, he had the whole plan arranged and prefected before writing down a word. He was fond of relating a story to friends, something additional always occurring to him on each repetition. " And by this method," he says, " one fine morning I find the piece complete."*

It was proposed that there should be a reading of the new piece before friends and good judges, of whom Béranger was to be one. Everyone that heard it was carried away by a sort of enthusiasm ; and, indeed, this is the charm of the play—its great spirit, colour, and interest. Béranger was pleased, like the rest, and this was the beginning of their intimacy. " This friendship of his was often satirical and even bitter," Alexander confesses ; " for Béranger was never wholly that sort of simple 'good creature' that he was supposed to be." Some of the actors, who were delighted with the romantic nature of the characters, secured its reception at the theatre. Thus he had once more got his foot on the ladder whence he had been thrust so rudely down a short time before. But, though he owed this success directly to himself, a

---

* He wrote most of his dramas in bed, which, he says, will account for much of " the vigorous and even brutal force " with which his subjects are handled.

certain element must not be left out, namely, the desire of the administrators of the theatre to do what might be complimentary to the Duke of Orleans. As they complacently "stretched a point" to please ministers and journalists, they were naturally eager to please one in so high a position.

At this time he was treated with harshness at the office, and was one morning actually required by De Broval, his chief, to choose between the desk and the theatre. He was allowed to retain an honorary position in his Highness's establishment, but was to receive no pay. This sacrifice to the drama, he tells us, he paid cheerfully; but the probability is that his theatrical connections, his attendance on readings, rehearsals, &c., had made him neglect his duties, and though these were almost a sinecure, still, as he received pay, the compliment of his presence might at least be considered necessary. He had certainly contrived to offend his patron, who under his own hand directed that an annual gratification, always distributed among the *employés*, should not be given to Dumas. The latter's dislike and even hatred of the Duke was so inflamed at the time he was writing his memoirs that it is hard to know how much truth is contained in the statement. But it seems highly probable that the impetuous Alexander should have failed to appreciate the favour hitherto shown him, or have grown so conceited as to affect to be independent of the Duke.

Thus, with a boldness that it is impossible not to admire, he had staked all on his talents. He went further. Without salary—without the " gratification " on which his mother had been counting for their little household expenses, there was nothing for them now to turn to. But he ventured on a bold step. Using the influence of Béranger with Lafitte, he presented himself at the Bank, his tragedy in his hand, stated his hopes and prospects, and was allowed, on that security, to draw a bill for £120. " I would tell an untruth," he says, " if I were to say that Lafitte was very eager or gracious in the matter ; but the fact is, he did so accommodate me."

When the piece was in preparation, the usual difficulties behind the scenes set in. Madlle. Mars objected to a young and pretty woman playing the part of the page, and insisted on its being given to another very clever but plain and elderly person. The great tragedy-queen also wished that an actor named Armand should play Henri III., but who seemed to the author too good-looking for the part. He was courageous enough to refuse, and with due benefit to his play. Every thing then went on well until it

came to a day or two of the performance, when, just
as he was leaving the theatre, a servant of M. Deviolaine's came running to him with a sad piece of news.
His mother, on leaving her relative's house, had been
seized with a fit on the stairs, and was lying unconscious. She had been paying them a visit, and the
poor, suffering woman had been obliged to listen to a
long tirade on the behaviour of her son. He was
" going to the bad : " " would disgrace them all." He
had repaid the goodness of the Orleans family, *their*
patrons, with ingratitude. His piece would fail to a
certainty : he would not be able to pay the money that
he owed, and then there would be nothing but ruin
for him and those dependent on him. This picture
affected her terribly ; she was greatly agitated ; and
on going away was seized with a fit. · Doctors
were sent for ; but her state was very critical. The
Deviolaines lived in a house at the corner of the Rue
de Richelieu, and it was fortunately discovered that
there was a room to let on one of the upper stories.
Her son, who, to do him justice, was affectionate, took
it at once, blessing the happy chance that had
helped him to secure the loan, which would find the
charges necessary for a long illness. With all his
anxieties, he seems never to have failed in that filial
duty for which the French (bating the little theatrical

exaggeration of "ma mère!") are so conspicuous. It had always been a festival when both set out on some little expedition. "I fear," he says, in a charming passage, "I had latterly not been so attentive to her. So long as the guardian angel that we call mother is living, we leave her carelessly for all the light whims and follies of youth, until there comes a moment— always unexpected and fatal—when she must leave us! Then we think, with tears and remorse, of this foolish neglect, and for what we have so often left her who has now left us for ever."

Yet he was now obliged to quit her, and spent his time rushing from her bedside to the theatre and back again. His play, indeed, seemed so bizarre to those who were to interpret it, that the presence of its author became indispensable at every stage. Nothing could exceed the kindness of his friends. All showed sympathy, and one sent him a purse with twenty louis in it, not knowing that he was "as rich as Ali Baba." The money he returned, but he kept the purse as a souvenir.

At last it came to the day before the performance, when he ventured on a bold *coup*, which he had re- served for the last. He asked for an audience with the Duke, and was received with some graciousness. He submitted an humble request that his Royal

Highness would honour the performance to-morrow night by attending it. The Duke was not a little astonished by this demand. But it was impossible for him to comply : he had a large party to dinner, some twenty or thirty persons of the highest rank, including princes. The young author was not discouraged by this difficulty. With surprising readiness and boldness, he suggested that his Highness should bring the whole party on to the theatre! The Duke was not displeased, and merely suggested another difficulty. His dinner was to be at six, while the play began at seven. The petitioner had another suggestion ready : the play could be put an hour later, and the dinner an hour earlier! Strange to say, the Duke inclined to the idea. But would the theatre agree; and where was such a party to be placed? The theatre *would* agree, and the author had already reserved the grand gallery, hoping that the Duke might consent. The latter smiled, and agreed. Again, it may be said, this young man deserved to succeed.*

The night now arrived, February 11th, 1829. The house was crowded to the roof. The grand

---

* These and many similar scenes were, of course, set to the account of Alexander's fertile imagination ; but, on consulting the *Debats* of the day following the performances, it is recorded that the Duke of Orleans and a large party of friends filled the grand gallery. The Duke ordinarily occupied his own private box at the side.

gallery was filled with princes and nobles with orders ; the boxes with ladies glittering with diamonds. De Vigny, Victor Hugo, and all the wits and writers of Paris, his friends and old office companions mustered in force. Every place had been taken for a week before, and at the last moment a box found a purchaser at twenty napoleons. At a quarter to eight he embraced his mother, who had not yet recovered her full intelligence, and knew nothing of the critical struggle that was to begin in a few minutes. He met the grim Deviolaine in the corridor, who even at such a moment encouraged him in his usual friendly style : "So you have got here at last," he said. "I told you I would," was the reply. "Well, now, we shall see what the public will think of you!"

It was an exciting moment when the play began. The first act passed off well, though there was a good deal of explanatory matter, and its highly dramatic conclusion, where the Duke of Guise, discovering the intrigue of his wife, says roughly, " Find me the men who assassinated Dugast!" brought down the curtain to a tumult of excitement. The third, where the Duke forces his wife to write to the lover, and fix a meeting, which is to be an ambuscade, was felt to be the most dangerous, and, at the same time, would make the success of the piece if it passed unchallenged.

But though there were " cries of terror," there was also thunders of applause.   Between the acts he hurried away for a moment to see his mother.   From that time to the end it was a triumph—a tempest of applauding hands—the women all in tears, and scarcely able to contain their emotions—while Malibran was seen hanging out of one of the upper boxes, clapping hands with all her might.   At the end, when the actor came out to announce the author's name, the Duke of Orleans was observed to stand up in homage. He must, indeed, have felt proud of his clever clerk ; and all through the night had shown the deepest and most ostentatious interest.   And, in truth, there was no need for any simulated attention ; for it would be impossible even to read the play without feeling the most absorbing interest in its romantic and dramatic situations.

Yet this exciting night was not to close without a little piece of satisfaction, which must have made him smile.   He found a letter in his room from the Baron de Broval, the official who had so haughtily and cruelly required him to choose between play-writing and the office.   The Baron could not lie down without offering his congratulations. He shared in this triumph of perseverance and filial duty.   He was certain that crowns of glory, &c., &c.   This, on what was perhaps the happiest night of his life, was perhaps the most satisfactory proof of the success of his piece. What would they say at Villers-Cotterets would be another gratifying thought. That night began a career of extraordinary brilliancy. There was more in this than the delighted reception of a new play. It was the opening of a struggle which has revolutionised the stage, and the effects of which are seen to this hour. The battle of the ROMANTIC school had begun. This, then, would seem to be the place to glance at the condition of the French stage, on which the work of a young and untried man had produced so remarkable an effect.

CHAPTER IX.

THE ROMANTIC SCHOOL.

THE sudden revolution that took place on the French stage about this time, some forty-four years ago, is certainly one of the most remarkable phenomena of social history. The heat and violence with which it was opposed and carried out, at least proves the firm hold that the drama has upon a nation like the French. For a couple of centuries, Romans and Greeks, Phœnicians, and other nations of antiquity, had held possession of the stage ; who in helmets and togas had made speeches of inordinate length in rhymed verse. The reputation of Racine and Corneille established this peculiar form, " the grand style," on a permanent footing ; and henceforth barbarous kings and heroes, with all the heroes and heroines of the classic poets, strode over the boards, and delivered rhymed exhortations. The unities were rigorously enforced : one scene, one time, one action. No act of violence, no " deed " involving physical motion was tolerated ; and when such were required by the story, a minute and elaborate narrative explained how the transaction took place.   There can be no doubt that the observance of such rules belongs to the drama in its highest state, that is, where it deals with display of human passion and emotion ; and the interest of the story is found in the working of passion and character on other passions and cha-. racters.   Combats, murders, death scenes, escapes, fires, "burnings of Joan of Arc," and the like, are strictly outside the dramatic boundary.*   Even in a play of the modern school, where a story will bear this unity of time, place, and emotion, the effect is enormously increased.   The less the feeling of illusion is strained the better.   Where there are intervals of years "supposed to have elapsed," or of countries that have to be traversed, the whole begins to fall into the character of a show.   We cannot change from scene to scene without suffering a loss of interest.   This direct singleness of purpose and emotion helped to impart to the

* A single combat on the stage belongs to the department of *exhibition.* There is never anything to excite in such displays—the crossing of swords, the passes, &c.   The play is really stopped while this goes on. So with dying agonies, which, even under the best conditions, have always an unreal air.   Interest in a person's story is not increased by the mere act of *seeing* him die ; if there *be* interest in the character, it is owing to the emotional proceedings up to the time of death, and could not be impaired by having the news of the death communicated.

incidents of the Greek drama that concentration which made them seem like terrible events of reality.

This grand style has been common to all the theatres of the world. It obtained on the English stage in the heroics of the poets contemporary with Racine; but what was more extraordinary, audiences at the most brilliant era of the stage, when Garrick and the finest company of actors ever seen at Drury Lane were delighting the town with gay comedies and perfect acting, a series of stilted, vapid dramas, heavy solemnities, with Roman generals and Eastern matrons and Turkish sultans for characters, were trailed tediously across the boards, and received with complacent acceptance. It is inconceivable how such a long series of these pieces, " Ægis," " Boadicea," " Vitellia," " Virginius," "Irene," "Siege of Damascus," "The Fall of Aquileia," and a host more, could have been endured from 1745 to about 1780. And this brings us to the question, how could a public that relished "The Clandestine Marriage" or the "Suspicious Husband," or a public that enjoyed Molière and Marivaux, tolerate a species of entertainment that seemed so tedious, uninteresting, and remote from all sympathy? How should intelligence, and an instinct for wit exist with a relish for monotony, sluggard motion, and a wearisome baldness of plot and treatment? The answer would seem to be that

with the "grand style" there was found a grand style
of playing—a lofty chaunting, a bearing that was inexpressibly dignified, both of which seemed to raise the
listener, through a sort of fascination, to the level of the
kings and heroes who were declaiming. The "tragedy
queens" of Mrs. Bellamy, Mrs. Cibber, and Mrs.
Pritchard, by the melody of their voices, their noble
presence and costume, are described as irresistibly
fascinating; while the high-pitched emotions of love
or hatred, chivalry and sacrifice, which in the mouths
of inferior actors would sound irresistibly like burlesque, with them became ennobled, and "purified the
passions by means of pity and terror" in the most
effectual way. These emotions, being removed from
the familiarity of every day events, and founded on
what was *general* and common to all mankind, exhibited
a dignity which commanded respect and interest, and
with really great players, gave opportunities for noble
elocution, splendid gestures, and the finest acting.

On the French stage pieces of this class were chiefly
presented at the great national theatre, the Français,
where traditions, elegance, decorum, and a native
dignity in the actors, that came from feeling that they
were public servants, recognised as such by government and people, lifted the whole performance into the
ranks of some august ceremonial. Even nowadays it

is impossible to "assist" at one of the performances in the Rue de Richelieu without being thus impressed. Between the masterpieces of Racine and Corneille, and stiff modern tragedies, there is nothing in common but the form; but these old pieces, in spite of their antiquated declamations, are fresher and newer, because founded on a truer view of human nature, than all the hastily-written productions of the modern day.* This accounts for the successful stand which these masterpieces have made, and by being presented with becoming dignity and state, as they are at the chief French theatres, they have escaped those burlesque associations of indifferent acting which have unfortunately become associated with our own Shaksperean drama.†

During the days of the Empire and Restoration, a tyrannous censorship had controlled it. This did not merely affect political allusions or expressions that might have the air of political allusions, but went so far as to control the whole tone of the piece. There was one

* Vide "Physiologie du Théâtre," tom. i. p. 217, by Hippolyte Auger, a temperate and sensible review of the stage and its true principles.

† This is shown even in the comparatively minor department of the scenery, which is handsome, mellow, and tasteful in its tones, of a surpassing richness, and yet of the simplest and most elementary kind. There are no elaborate "sets," mimicries of houses and streets, and yet the illusion is infinitely more perfect. It is curious to think that the more laboriously perfect the imitation of natural objects on the stage becomes, in the same proportion the sense of illusion is lessened.

instance where the dictator tolerated the play on the condition that the scene should be shifted to another country, and the names of the characters changed. Under such conditions all inspiration became impossible, and anything like nature or spirit was excluded.

The supply of pieces fell into the hands of some stilted academical " pundits," who wrote according to rule, and who recal very forcibly those old members of the Royal Academy in England, who, while contributing nothing that was above contempt to painting, contrived by their pedantic rules and obstructive arts, to stifle all wholesome progress. Corresponding to these men were the Jouys and Arnaults, in France who, with their series of lifeless "Syllas," "Marius at Minturnæ," &c., had reduced the drama to a lifeless state. Supported by the authority and the honoured name of the French Academy, these writers enjoyed a monopoly which was accepted complacently; and, while their productions, if unentertaining, commanded respect, Talma and Mdlle. Georges condescended to galvanize those solemn bits of declamation with their talents ; and the presence of such great players may, after all, have diverted attention from the meagre pieces used to set off their gifts. But it should be remembered that the sovereignty of a single great actor, either at one theatre or at a particular era, is almost invariably a sign of decay, and the temptation to write what shall set off his special gifts can only be yielded to at the expense of the drama. Thus the Arnaults and Jouys believed that his success was a proof of theirs, and that they were fairly entitled to a portion of the credit. "Sylla" and "Marius at Minturnæ" now seem unreadable. There is no local colour, no ancient character about them: the so-called Romans are Frenchmen in their most pedantic humour, dressed up in helmets and togas, and without a particle of the emotion or spirit of Frenchmen.*

The young men, who had been trained like their elders to relish this buckram school, were fretted by the tedious style, which at last they began to find intolerable. They were full of ardour and aspiration, and were burning to see reflected on the stage those longings for freedom which were in their own hearts. As we have seen, the writings of Scott, and, in a less degree, of Byron, were before them, presenting the treatment of romantic adventure and passion, after a highly dramatic fashion: works to which there was only wanting scenery and technical stage treatment.

* The names alone of a few of the pieces produced under the reign of Napoleon are significant of this character—*Omasis, or Joseph in Egypt, The Templars, Telemachus, Cato, Mucius Scævola, Artaxerxes,* and *Ninus II.* by Briffaut—the new shape of the piece which Napoleon had ordered to be changed.

Another kind of drama paved the way for the change from the inanimate "grand" to the romantic style. This was the ordinary French melodrama, which indeed was romantic itself, only that it dealt with incidents and characters of the day, which thus lent it a familiarity, and even coarseness, that was highly effective. Of this an excellent specimen was the "Thirty Years of a Gambler's Life," often reproduced on the English stage, and which had an almost painful interest. All Paris had crowded to see it. In pieces of this sort, presented at theatres of the second rank, was found what might be called raw and brutal conflicts of the various passions; such as were developed by incidents in Paris life, or took their rise from human nature in a vulgar state of debasement. Such are of a lower order, and have an interest limited to the classes familiar with such things, or to the country where the scenes take place. The spectacle too is more or less unhealthy, and instead of elevating, deteriorates the mind.

Dumas and his friends were ambitious enough to wish to secure the classical audience of the "Français," and at the same time kindle the dry bones into true life. With this view they thought that an historical subject should be chosen from their own history, that life and warmth could be supplied from the

numerous memoirs existing, and that the introduction
of natural melodramatic elements would create a
further sympathy. The nobility of the subject, and
remoteness of date, would furnish dignity. This combination was the drama of Dumas and Victor Hugo
and Casimir Delavigne; the latter, however, retaining
much of the old leaven of stiltedness. Hugo, though
he chose subjects of a royal and historical character,
took care to select such episodes as would bear a
human and romantic treatment. All this, it will be
seen, must have been refreshing to those who were
accustomed to listen to the prosy platitudes of
Romanised Frenchmen, or, as was more often the case,
of the Frenchified Romans.* There was, however, one
feature which was to distinguish all his plays, and those
plays which his example encouraged, and which was a
sign of weakness. It has indeed since become such an
accepted point, that remarking it will seem matter
for surprise. This is the undue prominence given to
one motive, viz. love, which has developed into a
violent, raging passion, bursting all the bounds of law
and decency, and become the sole subject with French
writers. This was a great deal owing to Voltaire,

* In most of these pagan plays, whether Roman or Grecian, there
was a particular character, which was acted invariably after a French
fashion, by favourite actors, and known as the " Cavalier Français!" It
fell to a particular actor as of right.

who laid it down formally that love ought to be the ruling principle in every drama. This, it is obvious, putting it at the lowest, is false art, and false as a view of human life, or as a motive of interest. There are other passions and other aims quite as capable of exciting dramatic pleasure, and it would seem more dramatic that the passions should form a sort of republic, where each should have equal power. A certain amount of monotony must result from this constant harping on one subject.

There were some before Dumas who attempted a story quite as stirring as Henri III., after a ponderous, slow moving fashion, that was independent even of the solemn rhymes in which the story lumbered along. But in Dumas there was a novel airiness, as though he had stripped off the tightened tunic and tragic buckram; there was a colour, rapidity of motion, a dash, a nationality, that must have captivated. Above all, there was a surprising knowledge of the stage, of forcible situation, which the most experienced playwright on our side of the water might be proud of, and near which the be-puffed attempts of our new dramatists seem like the floundering exercises of a schoolboy. It will be necessary to bear this in mind when considering the disputed question of Dumas's talent; for Henri III., written with all the earnestness and power that he could command, becomes an excellent gauge of his ability. It shows—his instinct of *arrangement*, his knowledge of effect, his happy power of imparting the true colour by a few touches, which is found in all those novels whose authorship is disputed. Skilful, dramatic arrangement and pointed style, sketchy dialogue, colour—these are the merits of Henri III.; invention alone was wanting. This, his first important work, becomes an exact type of the vast family that followed, in each of which this proportion of contribution was pretty generally followed. There came, indeed, a later era, when Dumas's sole contribution was his name on the title; but it did not augur well that a young fellow, full of enthusiasm and just starting on his career, should have deliberately, and in his first work, have commenced a system of organised literary pillage, for which he afterwards became notorious.

CHAPTER X.

FAME AND PROFIT.

1829.

THE next day the young writer's name was in everyone's mouth. An extraordinary scene had taken place the night before. His friends and admirers had danced a frantic dance of delight in the *foyer* of the theatre to shouts of "Racine done for!" and an engraving was to be put in hand to commemorate the event. Bouquets filled the little room where his mother lay, who knew not what their meaning was. By two o'clock in the afternoon the MS. of the piece had been sold for 240*l.*! Here was fortune indeed! He could not resist showing the notes to M. Deviolaine, who uttered some·of his choicest oaths, but yet exhibited a bearish pleasure. His next duty was to repay his friendly banker.

Everything was going delightfully : but he little knew what was at hand. When he got home he found that the Censors had intervened, and that his piece was forbidden ; one of those stupid unmeaning proceedings which distinguished the ministry of the time. It was conceived, no doubt, that the exhibition of a king and his favourites with their toys and blowpipes, would be considered to be pointed at the reigning monarch. The same judicious guardians were presently to tolerate a tide of scandalous pieces which, for outraging morals, left even the excesses of the Second Empire far behind. This sensitiveness to the slightest political allusion, joined with perfect indifference to decency, is characteristic of the narrowminded and trembling clique who were about the king.

Dumas hurried to the minister and begged some reasonable explanation ; and it would seem, by promise of alteration, succeeded in getting the interdict taken off. At night there was to be a fresh triumph. He was summoned to the Duchess's box, and received her friendly compliments, with an invitation to wait on her next morning and bring news of his mother's health. M. Deviolaine and some other heads of his office were witnesses of this condescension, and were now all smiles and graciousness. But this extraordinary success was sure to raise up enemies and detractors. Envious paragraphs appeared, in one of which it was stated that " this success was not surprising to them, who knew what *jobbing* went on, in every business that had to do with the House of Orleans, one of whose dependents this young fellow is." He felt himself obliged to call the writer to account ; but no meeting took place, owing to the critic's having another account of the same kind to settle, and in which he was wounded. He was presently sent for to the office, and enjoyed the pleasant flattery of being respectfully invited to resume his service in the Duke's employment. He was even offered the post of " reader to the Duchess." He declined this honour, and made his own demand, that of being appointed assistant-librarian to Casimir Delavigne, who was principal. They then proposed that he should be " gentleman of honour " to Madame Adelaide, but he refused to accept anything but the post he demanded ; and this was at last conceded, with a salary of fifty pounds. There is no exaggeration in this story, as it is only in keeping with the politics of the time, which alternated between tyranny and obsequiousness towards everything that showed *power* in literature.

Delavigne, however, did not welcome his assistant very cordially. He had a play accepted at the Français, on the subject of " Marino Faliero," which, though " romantic " enough compared with pieces of the " Marius at Minturnæ " style, yet, by contrast with the new play, was certain to be found tame and stilted. "Henri III." was to be, after all, the piece of the year; and, according to a stage proverb, there can only be one success at a time. Beside, the new play was "to run" for at least three months, then came the leading actress's vacation, and it was found necessary to adjourn "Marino Faliero" to the following year. Greatly mortified at this slight, Delavigne withdrew his piece and transferred it to the Porte St. Martin.

Alexander's success had brought him many friends; but, as may be imagined, almost as many enemies. His picture, by Deveria, was now "stuck in the print-shops"—one of Lofty's tests of notoriety. David of Angers, the famous medalist, struck a medal in his honour. The ill-natured might say that these testimonials were of his own ordering, but his success was incontestable, and is at least established by the opposition and enmity it excited. It brought forth one of the most extraordinary and undignified protests that can be found in stage annals.

With the open disgust which was now evinced for pieces of the old pedantic pattern, the writers who supplied such wares felt, in familiar phrase, that "the bread had been taken out of their mouths." Loss of prestige may be borne, but the sudden destruction of a particular calling, with its

profits, becomes intolerable. The antiquated mono-
polists—the authors of " Sylla," of " Marius at Minturnæ," and five others, addressed a petition to the
king, calling his attention to the extraordinary success
of the new order of plays: " pieces written in imitation of the extravagant compositions to be found on
foreign stages—things which up to this time no one
had ventured to produce even at houses of the lowest
order." The authorities of the great theatre, it
seemed, not only encouraged this corrupt form of
drama, but, by their partiality, were going to vast
expense, with the aim of feasting the eye with dresses,
scenery, and spectacle of the most lavish kind; nay,
the legitimate tragedians and actors were discouraged
in every conceivable way—made to figure in pieces
that were unacceptable, and actually sent away from
the theatre on long *congés.* They were sure that his
Majesty would not allow " the funds, which his
goodness granted to the administrator, to be squandered
in supporting a fancy of this kind, and in degrading
the scene of grand tragic triumphs to the level of the
little houses of the Boulevards."

A serious controversy arose on this singular
demand. But whatever were the merits of the case,
the public were not slow to see the grotesqueness of
the controversy; viz., that these complainants, while

affecting to urge the claims of Racine and Corneille, were in reality pleading for their own pieces, which public taste had left aside. As Dumas and his friends said, it amounted to this : "*We,* sire, are the only true representatives of dramatic art. The public hiss us ; our pieces do not draw ; the actors dislike playing them. Still, sire, give orders that we be played. Let us be hissed rather than be forgotten; for where are the legatees of Racine and Molière ? These new hands are only the bastard offspring of Shakespeare, Goethe, and Schiller."

The King, who did not want wit, extinguished the remonstrants in the well-known reply : " I can do nothing in the matter ; I have only *my place in the pit,* like any other Frenchman."

Yet there was here involved, it will be seen, the whole question of the possibility of directing the public taste by a State institution. Even with such traditions as the " French theatre " possessed, consecrated as it was by the special memory of Racine and Molière, it could hardly be contended that it was to persevere obstinately in presenting ascetic pieces which no one came to see, and which would soon, in spite of Government subsidies, have brought about bankruptcy. As this romantic taste represented the popular taste of the day, the great national theatre was bound to recognise it to a certain extent. The truth is, such an institution should be of an elastic character, combining progressive with conservative tendencies. The present administration of this theatre exemplifies the principle: the old classical pieces being the staple of its entertainment, toge·· ther with a graduated series of the most remarkable pieces of each era between that of Racine and our own. There are sterling and popular plays of some forty or fifty years ago, which, played occasionally, and strictly after the inspiration of the author, have become classical. New pieces of the present time are accepted, provided they are constructed with a certain dignity and solidity. Thus, indeed, a stage becomes ennobled, and a very different thing from a vulgar speculation, opened like a shop, and by every adventurer, to make money. Such a State theatre —and the Français is unique in the world—as a matter of course raises the stage to the dignity of a social department, like law, or that of teaching. With a long and lofty pedigree, it gathers as it goes the choicest of actors, a solidity of practice based on frequent repetition and tradition, and an enormous store of works characteristic of each period. The Théâtre Français was never so thriving as it is at this moment; and though it has no Talma, or Mars, or Clairon, still the presence of such stars is purchased not a little expensively by the dwarfing of other characters, and the choice of plays which shall minister to the triumph of an individual. The comedies which the last twenty years have contributed to its *répertoire* are singularly good and rich in character.

This episode excited a fierce contention in the newspapers. The "Constitutionel" took the side of the Conservatives—and had to record the still triumphal progress of "Henri III." with its receipts of 250*l.* a night. This success was growing steadily; but it excited jealousy, and raised up bitter enemies. The first revelation of this fact caused him not a little surprise, which he expressed naively enough. Arnault, one of the discontented dramatists, and his family, had taken a great fancy to him; so much so, that Dumas found himself regularly welcomed at the Sunday dinner. After the great triumph, he repaired there, expecting a tide of congratulation and sympathy, and to his surprise found only the lady of the house, who, after some conversation, said quietly that "he ought to tell them beforehand when he was coming, as it was very awkward to find himself without anyone to entertain him." He understood the hint, and never came again. Even among the actors he found signs of jealousy and dislike ; for the run of a very successful piece deprived a good many of their opportunities. He had the mortification to overhear one of them say, with great satisfaction, rubbing his hands, " that there was twenty pounds *less* in the house than on the night before "—a highly characteristic trait of the green-room. People grow tired of other people's success quite as much as of " hearing a man called just."

This successful piece was said to have brought him 2,000*l*.,—a vast sum for the humble clerk of Villers-Cotterets.* With these resources he might fairly indulge in a better style of living. He moved his mother to a better apartment in the Rue Madame, where she could enjoy a little garden, and took a bachelor apartment for himself, at the corner of the Rue · de l'Université, which he furnished with great elegance and luxury. He had, however, to repay the ticket-dealer Porcher, and the banker, and with what was intended for a wise prevision, had contracted with a restorateur for a year's dinners and breakfasts at a sum of 70*l*. paid in advance. But, unluckily,

* De Mirecourt, "Alex. Dumas," p. 37. This is probable enough, though there are inaccuracies in the *soi-disant* biographies of the great writer furnished by almost ferocious antagonists. The piece was presented nearly forty times during three months.

a month after the arrangement was made, the *café* was closed, and money and "nourishment" lost. This is his own modest account. But it should be mentioned that others represent him as plunging at once into a course of extravagance. He was seen in rich and fantastic dresses, kept horses, and gave luxurious dinners.* He was greatly sought after, invitations poured in upon him, and, for the rest of the winter, he was the lion of all the evening parties. His natural *esprit* and gaiety gave him the full advantage of these opportunities. He was highly popular with the actors and actresses, and Mademoiselle Mars proved a useful friend. His sketch of the great artist is agreeable enough. She was then nearly fifty, and her powers were somewhat on the wane. For the stage she had a sort of artificial voice—sweet and melodious; but, in private life, it was rough and harsh. She was a thoroughly honest and downright creature—liberal, a "good fellow," with something of the man about her; thus recalling our own English actress, Peg Woffington. She had a dressing-room of great size allotted to her, in which her friends were allowed to visit her during the performance, and where, with a native simplicity, she effected the

* De Lomenie, "Galerie."

necessary changes of her toilette in their presence.* She gave pleasant suppers after the play, when she "took off," with great vivacity and skill, the peculiarities of her fellow-players ; but this was done without ill-nature. Nothing is better or more dramatic than the picture of this curious woman at rehearsal. Though she threw herself into the part during the performance, and honestly contributed all her powers, during rehearsals she was singularly " crotchetty," and harassed the author with difficulties and suggestions. Some such scene as the following took place frequently when a play of Victor Hugo's was in progress. In the midst of the full tide of declamation she would suddenly stop, and, advancing to the edge of the stage, affect to look down into the orchestra, for the place of the author. " Is M. Hugo there ?" she would ask. The author would stand up and answer. With some apologies she would propose her difficulty. She had to say—

" Thou art *my Lion*, proud and generous ! "

" Now, are you satisfied with that, M. Hugo ? It seems so droll calling Firmin here my Lion." "That's the way I have written it, madame. Of course, if you look

* " She had an art, even as she chatted," says the candid Dumas, " of changing her chemise, without letting more *than the tip of her finger* be seen."

at it as Mademoiselle Mars, it is another matter. I put it in the mouth of a Spanish hidalgo." "Oh, quite right," said she, "if you are satisfied, I am. It is down here in the part 'my Lion,' and 'my Lion' I shall say. us go on." But the next day she would advance to the edge of the stage, and peering into the dark orchestra as before, ask, "Was M. Hugo there? Had he turned over what she had said yesterday as to 'my Lion?' She had now an emendation to propose. What would he say to 'my Lord' instead?

" Thou art *my Lord,* so proud and generous ! "

This she would debate in precisely the same fashion, finishing by saying that it was no matter, that it was his look-out, and, as it was down in the part, she would say "my Lion." At last she wore out the patience of the author, who could only bring her to reason by asking her to give up the part altogether. However, on the night of performance she had her way, and said "my Lord," instead of "my Lion."

CHAPTER XI.

" HERNANI."

1830.

MEANWHILE this brilliant example stimulated others. The "romantic school"—which indeed was a strange name for a school of matter-of-fact violence, and brutality—was present in every department of art. Victor Hugo's "Odes and Ballads" had been received with as frantic an enthusiasm as a play was on the stage. De Vigny's novel "Cinq Mars" was welcomed in the same fashion; while Gericault's ghastly picture, "The Wreck of the Medusa," which now attracts the tourist's eye in the great salon of the Louvre, exhibited the same "romantic" principles. Yet all this enthusiasm had an unreal basis, and was encouraged by the attempts made to repress it. And the wretched Government of the day, infinitely more blinded than the Tories in England, who were at that moment making their last struggles against Catholic emancipation, tried with a stupid vigour to "put down" all these novelties, whether on stage, on canvas, or on paper; soldiers and police being used in politics. Prosecutions were instituted against newspapers; the publisher of Béranger's marvellous songs was indicted; the Censor, striking right and left, high and low, refused admission to paintings, suppressed books, and forbade plays to be acted. Such a Government must have been intolerable from these petty persecutions.

Hugo, then a young man of brilliant promise, had now written his "Marion Delorme," which, when competed for by a half-a-dozen managers, and put in rehearsal, was forthwith "struck" by the Censor. The Court trembled before this series of pictures of monarchy, no matter how remote, and no doubt regretted that they had tolerated the example of Dumas. An attempt was made to buy Hugo over by trebling his pension, which, however, he had the spirit to refuse.

Nothing daunted he set to work again, and within three weeks had written "Hernani," a piece which, as the work of a poet, must be placed immeasurably higher than "Henri III." Hugo was, after all, the true prophet of the new school. So recently as 1827 he had published a poetical play called "Cromwell," prefixed to which was a programme of his dramatic principles. These were, "all that we see in nature belongs to dramatic art ; the drama itself results from the union of the sublime with the true and familiar, and should at the same time be the expression of modern life and manners." This, it will be seen, is meant to justify the exhibition of all the rude passions and coarse scenes of violence (as being "true") which had hitherto been excluded from the stage.   Hugo applied his principles, but in the true spirit of a poet.   His treatment was general, and independent of the vulgar accessories of the stage ; and the result is that where "Henri III." is now scarcely known, "Hernani" and "Lucrezia Borgia," and "Le Roi s'amuse" are the common property of nations.

The first night of "Hernani" was to be one famous in the annals of the stage.   Irritated at the persistent and malicious efforts of the old conservative party to crush the new school, the hot youth of the city, who were already getting ready for the serious business of revolution, determined to assemble in force, and carry through the piece of their distinguished leader.   The night was that of March 26th, 1830.   Jules Janin, who was present, fondly recalls how they waited in the darkened theatre for six hours before the doors were opened, and talked and whispered like conspirators : how, as each party appeared at the box doors a storm of hissing or applause burst forth, according to the faction which they were known to favour. Through the whole piece the battle was continued; but its incontestable merits and the exertions of friends carried it through.* For forty nights this extraordinary struggle went on. But the battle was won.

Dumas had not disdained to use some singular devices to forward the success of his piece. One was the taking a share in a burlesque upon it, which was to be called "King Dagobert"; but the Censure, which had now but a few more weeks to give annoyance, saw irreverence in the title, and it had to be changed to "King Petard." He was now busy with his "Christine." He had entirely recast it, and, though it was in verse, had made it even more "romantic" in form than "Henri III." It contained a "prologue" and tableaux, things now familiar enough, but then a novelty. These, and the succeeding pieces, verged more and more towards melodrama, *exhibiting* pictures of ferocious passion or suffering, and departing from the

---

* The story has been often told of the enthusiasm of one of Hugo's supporters, whom some one hard of hearing fancied the actor had said, "Vieil as de pique," instead of "Vieillard stupide," and laughed contemptuously. An eager partisan of the author's defended the phrase hotly, saying, with a triumphant air, that "cards were invented then." Dumas "fathers" the story on old Grandmaison and Lassailly; as he says in his agreeable way, "There was nothing to be said to men who attacked or defended in this style."

comparatively spiritual principles which were found even in Victor Hugo's dramas.* To effect this recasting, he found it necessary to make a journey to Havre in the diligence and back again, such conditions being necessary to favourable composition. Staying just time enough to eat oysters, he returned by the same sort of conveyance, and *voilà!* the piece was done. He had withdrawn it from the Français, where fresh difficulties had been made about playing it, and where they had just played another " Christine " with disastrous results, and it had been accepted by Harel, the manager of the Odéon, who had recently played Soulié's " Christine," which had failed also.   But there followed a yet more singular incident.   The manager seriously proposed that Dumas's " Christine " should be at once brought forward, and acted by Georges, the actress who had played the same part in Soulié's play.   Alexander consulted his friend on this curious proposal, the latter made no objection, and the piece was produced.†

* Though Hugo laid down as one of his principles that the reformed drama should deal with subjects of the day his genius was too poetical to conform to it ; all his important dramas being chosen from remote history.

† Soulié's feelings, indeed, could not have been of the amiable kind, for before the success of ".Henri III." he had contemptuously met a proposal of his friend that they should work together on this very subject. At that time he had made his name, and fancied that the young tyro would be of little assistance. When Dumas said that he felt a delicacy in taking up the subject by himself after his friend had chosen it,

" Christine," which now bore the cumbrous titles of
" Stockholm, Fontainebleau, and Rome," was brought
forward eight days after its namesake, on March 30,
and was the occasion of a terrible struggle, which lasted
until two o'clock in the morning. A dozen times the
piece was all but overpowered in these hostile attacks,
but it rallied again and again, was carried through
triumphantly by its own striking situations and the
fine acting of Georges and Lockroy. " O," says its
author, " after all my five and twenty years of struggle,
I can still say with genuine enthusiasm that there is
nothing like this battle of genius against the ill-will of
a crowd and the cabals of enemies, where the opposition is gradually overborne and forced back!" Our
author, however, leaves out an important element which
had aided this glorious repulse, namely, an organised
cabal on his side, his friends having mustered in great
strength, and Soulié sending out a large band of work-
men from a factory. However, these might have
seemed to him purely defensive measures. The piece
is certainly a powerful and picturesque one ; but the
blood of a man stabbed again and again, and dragged
about the stage struggling for his life, must have been

Soulié haughtily bade him have no scruples about the matter, telling
him, plainly, that his small efforts were *not* likely to do *him* any
harm.

as shocking to the audience as the " prison scenes " which were so resented in a late English play, or the burning of Joan of Arc, which caused such a debate. The truth is, such detailed horrors give no *additional dramatic effect* to the situation—agonies of death, the spectacle of suffering, the incidents of a combat, belong to the department of *exhibition*, and to produce the proper excitement must be *real*, as in a bull fight, or the old combats of gladiators. A far deeper interest is caused by simple suggestion; and the spectacle of George Barnwell walking in procession to the gallows, as the curtain comes down, is infinitely more dramatic and suggestive than if the scene exhibited the gallows and the unhappy apprentice swinging in the air.

It was felt, however, that the piece was far too diffuse, and required the most serious concentration. The alteration was effected in the most wholesale and courageous manner. While he gave a supper that night to some twenty of his supporters, two of his friends, Victor Hugo and De Vigny, spent the rest of the night in this friendly task. When it was broad daylight, and the author and his friends were asleep, they left the completed play on the chimney-piece, and went home. The play was improved vastly, the prologue cut away, and the interest drawn closer.* A good deal of this success must, of course, be set down to the fine playing of Georges, and, indeed, through his whole career, Dumas was singularly fortunate in having his pieces interpreted by three of the finest actresses on the French stage, namely, Mars, Georges, and Dorval. The artistes had, besides, a sympathy for the man himself. They were, all three, women of an extraordinary spirit. The history of Georges made part of the history of Napoleon, and she is said to have received the homage of at least two emperors, and three or four kings.†

All through nothing could have been kinder or more sympathetic than the behaviour of the Duke, and it is highly probable that he was not accountable for any of those little acts of severity which Alexander imputed to him. What could have been more hearty than his request for the Legion for his librarian. "The dramatic success of M. Dumas," he said, "emi-

---

* It will be shown, in the proper place, for how much of the play he is indebted to the labours of others.

† The free *laisser-aller* of Mars at her stage toilette has already been mentioned. Dumas, in his own characteristic fashion, supplies some corresponding details as to that of Georges. " Her nicety was proverbial. Before entering her bath, she made some preparatory ablutions, "*afin de ne point salir l'eau,* dans laquelle elle allait rester une heure. There she received her intimates, every now and again fastening up her hair with gold pins, which gave her the opportunity of showing her splendid arms, &c."

nently deserved this favour, and I should be the more pleased that he obtained it because he was for six years working in my office, during which time he was the whole support of his family, and in the most honourable way. I do not know if the 12th of April could be a desirable opportunity for submitting this request to the King, but I wished, by suggesting the idea, to prove the great interest I take in M. Dumas." His conduct was, indeed, all through that of a kind but judicious friend, who had the true interest of his *protégé* at heart. It will be seen how ungratefully that *protégé* could repay these services. The decoration was refused, Dumas believes, owing to the kind office of M. Empis.

He found himself at the grand entertainment given by the Duke of Orleans, on May 31, 1830, to the King of Naples, where it was intended to exhibit to the guest all the historical notabilities of France. Dumas did not receive an invitation, but the young Duke of Chartres rectified the omission. He hesitated as to going, for this King of Naples was " the son of the King who had poisoned his father ; " but still, the fear of " causing grief to the good young man who had procured the invitation " prevailed over filial scruples. When he presented himself, the Duke came up to him. " M. Dumas," he said, " if the King should by any chance address you, you must know you are not to say *Sire* or *Majesty*, but simply *the King.*" *

Dumas does not see that this strange greeting explains the reason of his being omitted from the list of guests. However, he tells it with his usual delightful candour. He imputes it to a distrust of the Duke at the Tuileries; but a writer, whose pieces had been twice laid under censure, and who belonged to a violent party of reformers, could hardly have expected such an honour. The Revolution was, indeed, just at hand, and there were more serious matters to think of. Ministers had hoped to dazzle the disaffected with some military and diplomatic successes; the first of which was the attack on Algiers, which had turned out successfully. This suggested to Dumas a dashing scheme — to set off and visit the newly-acquired country, and, no doubt, bring back some lively "impressions of travel."

He had fixed his departure for Monday the 26th of July, when on that morning his friend Comté came rushing into his room, with a startling piece of news. The famous "Ordinances" were in the papers! Was he now determined to start for Algiers?

* This was the night when M. Salvandy, the minister, laid the foundation of his future fortune with Louis-Philippe by his pleasant *mot,* "This is a regular Neapolitan fête, for we are dancing upon a volcano."

"Joseph," called out our *farçeur* to his servant, "go to the gunmakers for my double-barrelled gun, *and two hundred bullets!*"

It was in connection with this Algerian expedition that he records a diplomatic anecdote, which is illustrative of that blind credulity and self-delusion which characterises the French in all political matters. Lord Stuart, the English ambassador, called on M. d'Haussez, the French Minister of Marine, to ask for an explanation of this Algerian expedition. "If you wish for a diplomatic one, the President of the Council will give it to you; but if a personal one will do, you are welcome to this ——," and then added a low coarse expression familiar to the streets. A hundred stories, as reliable, appear in the French papers. But Dumas declares that he was at Madame du Cayla's in the evening, "when M. d'Haussez related this piece of *heroic brutality*," and he must say that "everyone present, ladies included, applauded!" Alexander, no doubt, believed that he was telling the truth, or believed that the Minister was telling the truth; but it need hardly be said that the incident is a pure fiction. He was particularly anxious to make this tour, though there were some impediments in the way, which he explains with that extraordinary candour, which must be set down either to simplicity, or, what is more probable, to his curious insensibility to propriety.*

* We give this *textuellement:* "Le troisième étage du No. 7 était occupé à cette époque, par une très jolie femme. . . Les lecteurs qui m'ont fait le grace de suivre les différentes phases de ma vie dans ces Mémoires doivent s'être aperçus combien j'ai été avare des détails du genre de ceux que je leur communique en ce moment : mais j'aurai plus d'une fois occasion de revenir sur cette liaison, *dont Dieu a permis que, pour les mauvais jours, il me restait un de ces vivants souvenirs qui changent les tristesses en joie, les larmes en sourire.*"(!)

CHAPTER XII.

ADVENTURE AT SOISSONS.

1830.

Now opened quite a new page in his adventures, and it may be said that his account of certain scenes in the Revolution of July, and of his own exploits, are singularly vivacious, and present a spirited picture of · those exciting days. His friend Janin wrote happily of him that he saw everything about him with dramatic eyes ; with his keen and picturesque sense everything fell into the shape of a scene on the stage. His story was a good deal ridiculed, but it was only his vanity and candour that can be affected by rude laughter, as it will be seen that the facts are in the main correct.

After giving the order for the two hundred bullets he went out in the town with his friend. Everything was still tranquil. He looked in at the Café du Roi, and found the coterie of royalist newspaper editors —those of the *White Flag, The Thunderbolt*—quite confident, and loudly applauding the steps that had been taken. The day passed by in some excitement, but without any act of violence taking place. The editors of the leading Liberal journals, including M. Thiers, had signed a protest against the unconstitutional action of ministers ; and the following day, when Dumas went out with Carrel of the *National*, they witnessed a curious scene that was taking place at the office of the *Temps*. A Commissary of Police, with a party of gendarmes, was preparing to break in, but though locksmith after locksmith was fetched, the crowd contrived to spirit them away. He wandered about all day, and it seemed at last probable that the whole would pass over without disturbance, when, towards seven o'clock, the welcome sounds of firing were heard in the direction of the Palais-Royal. There had been some stone throwing at the soldiers, who had fired and killed a woman. Dumas was well acquainted with a number of the fighting men of this time, and an intimate of his was Stephen Arago, brother of the savant, who took a leading part in the street skirmishing. It was the morning of the 26th, and the time was come for him to act. He took his gun, with some of the "two hundred bullets," and descended into the street. He tells us that he was at once constituted a leader.

He ordered barricades to be made. He was asked
for arms, and pointed, significantly, to three soldiers
in the distance. D'Artagnan or Aramis would have
made the same answer. He led on his men to the
attack of the Hôtel de Ville, was allowed to pass
by an officer who addressed him by his name, and
paid him compliments on "Christine," and with
whom, too, he exchanged compliments of the most
chivalrous kind, promising him tickets for his new
piece (!), and then went on to the attack, which was
repulsed. He reached home safely after this *débât ;*
and, indeed, according to his vivacious account, the
taste for revolution in Paris is easily explained by
the fascination and excitement, the " turning out " of
friends for the sport, and the certain chances they
afford for bringing obscure persons into importance
with very little exertion.

Next day he was awakened to the news that the
famous artillery museum was being attacked, and
he was struck with horror at the notion of this
precious collection being pillaged. When it was
captured he saw it was hopeless to think of
saving it ; all he could do was to plunder for the
nation. So, seizing on some arms that had belonged
to Francis I. and Charles IX., he put the helmet on,
and, carrying the shield and sword, bore them off to

his rooms.* Later, he joined in the attack on the Louvre. The scene was an exciting one, and furnishes quite a dramatic picture. He and his band advanced along the Quai, by the Institute, and from the other side of the river saw the long line of windows of the great gallery of pictures thrown open, with two scarlet Swiss, musket in hand, at each. The balcony of Charles IX. was filled with other Swiss, who had protected themselves with a rampart of mattresses. All along the Quai were lines of Cuirassiers, while on the right, the great colonnade facing St. Germain l'Auxerrois was half hidden in rolling clouds of smoke. The air was thick, seeming to vibrate with distant musketry and the sound of tolling bells, while a fiery sun blazed luridly in the heavens. Dumas witnessed the whole attack, and frankly confesses that he secured a safe ambuscade behind a bronze lion. At times the clouds of smoke enveloped the whole palace; these would break, and disclose glimpses of the scarlet Swiss. Then he saw a regular attack marshalled, and an attempt made, chiefly by young lads, to pass across the bridge, but a cannon

---

* It is impossible to give an idea of the heroic style in which these events are narrated. He adds that he still preserves the Director's letters thanking him for saving these precious articles, and mentions with pride the reward that was given to him, viz., "the right of admission on days when it was *not* free to the public."

which commanded it was discharged, and swept it completely, the grape rattling about his sheltering lion. He found this part too dangerous, and got away as fast as he could. Later, he made his way round to the other side, saw the Tuileries carried; and heard the shouts caused by the spectacle of what seemed an enormous flight of pigeons fluttering from the windows. This was letters of Napoleon, and Louis, and Charles, all torn up and thrown out by the mob. He rushed in with the rest, witnessed the odd scenes that followed, and the naïve astonishment of the populace as they wandered through the rooms.

He takes care to tell that he saw on a work-table in the library of the Duchess of Berry, a copy of "Christine," bound in violet morocco, adorned with her arms, which he secured. Afterwards he reached the Hotel de Ville, where he found Lafayette and many more important personages whom he knew. He chanced to look in the glass, and hardly recognised himself — unwashed, unshaven, for three days, his face blistered by the sun, his clothes torn, and his shoes all daubed with the blood of a poor wretch whom he had helped out of the conflict—as he listened to the excited discussions as to what was to be done. And he describes with the humour of "Rabagas" the proclamations signed by a Provisional

Government whose members no one could find, and the dressed-up generals who could be found, but had no title to the name.

He had heard Lafayette say that if the King were to advance on Paris they would have no powder to fight him with. Alexander conceived a bold scheme. He proposed to the general to set off for Soissons—a town he well knew—and seize on the magazines there. Lafayette laughed at the idea, but consented to give him a letter to General Gérard, to which Dumas coolly added the words, "and we recommend his scheme to you." From Gérard he, with some difficulty, obtained a requisition addressed to the authorities of the town for the powder; and in this he ingeniously interpolated the words "Minister of War"—a rank which no one but himself had conferred on the general. With this official document he returned to Lafayette, and persuaded the old patriot to give him a sort of letter of introduction to the citizens of Soissons, recommending to them " M. Alexandre Dumas, one of our combatants," as a fit and proper person to whom they should hand over their powder. Then our hero— for such he was on this occasion—prepared himself for as spirited and dramatic an adventure as can be found in the books of romance.

It was about three o'clock in the afternoon of the

30th of July.   As he was hurrying away he met a young painter named Bard, who was only nineteen, and asked him to join. The other agreed with alacrity, and Alexander, sending him back for his double-barrelled pistols and horse, set off himself in a cabriolet for Le Bourget, then the first post on the road to Soissons, and which since has obtained such a disastrous notoriety. Arrived there, he exhibited his Lafayette and Gérard letters to the postmaster, and demanded a chaise and horses for his mission. The postmaster was friendly, and even empressé, and supplied him at once with what he asked. He then went out to buy some pieces of calico—red, white, and blue—which were sewn into a tricolor flag fixed to a broomstick, which latter was tied on to the chaise. With this ensign they started, in hopes of getting to Soissons about midnight. The postmaster shook his head, but, as he sagaciously remarked, "so many miracles had been performed during the last three days that it might be possible." As they hurried through the various villages the flag caused great excitement.   His fellow-traveller, delighted, declared that all was going splendidly, "but that they ought to have some cry."

"Shout away," said Dumas, "and while you are shouting I'll take some sleep."

The only difficulty was what was to be the cry, and with some hesitation the now well-worn and tattered Vive la République! was decided on. Accordingly the young painter, his head out of the window, and his flag waving, roared on. On the high road they met a chaise going to Paris, and a traveller of some fifty years old stopped to ask for news.

"The Louvre is taken; the Bourbons fled; Provisional Government established—Vive la République!" the excited painter poured out. The gentleman fifty years old scratched his ear, and continued his journey. During the next stage they had an old postilion, who persisted in going at a steady trot, and who, to every remonstrance, answered doggedly, "Leave it to me. A man ought to know his own business." Dumas at last from the chaise window laid on the backs of the horses with a stick, and made them gallop. In a rage the man pulled up, swore he would unyoke his horses, and actually proceeded to do so. Dumas fired at him with blank cartridge, and so scared him that he rolled on the ground. Alexander then put on the huge posting-boots, and, mounting, galloped on to the next post. They had soon reached the old familiar Villers-Cotterets, his birthplace, the whole town being thrown into intense excitement when it was known that the chaise with the tricolour contained their Alexander Dumas.

Late as it was, every house poured out its inhabitants, who rushed to the post-house. A thousand eager questions were put to him—what did it mean, the flag, the guns? He knew them all, and told the story of the last few days. It was insisted that he should stay a short time, and have something to eat, and he was carried off to the house of an old friend, where a hasty supper was got ready. A number of old companions, who had been boys with him in the little town, gathered round, listening eagerly as their old friend declaimed and recounted between every mouthful. As he dashed in for them, which he could do admirably, vivid sketches of these thrilling scenes, the rustics listened with delight and wonder, but when he came to explain the object of his present expedition— "when I announced that I meant to capture, single-handed, all the powder that was in a military town, containing eight thousand inhabitants, and a garrison of eight hundred men"—they looked at him doubtfully, and thought he was crazed. This was, of course, welcome to Alexander, who always delighted to put himself in a theatrical attitude, and be the centre of a dramatic situation. He turned to his companion Bard :

"What were my words when proposing this expedition to you ?"

"You asked," was the reply, "was I inclined to get myself shot with you."

"But what do you say now?"

"I am ready still."

All were confounded at such gallantry. One of his friends now stepped forward, and offered to get him into Soissons, as he had a friend at the gates. Then Alexander, always anticipating his d'Artagnan, raised his glass, and drank to his own return to them on the next evening. "Have dinner ready," he called to the host, "for twenty people, and it is to be eaten just the same, whether we be alive or dead. Here are two hundred francs." The other answered that he might pay on the morrow. "But if I should be shot?" "Then I shall pay." A shout arose, "Hurrah for Cartier!" Dumas drank off his wine, and, we might add, the act-drop fell. It was now eleven o'clock. The horses were put to, the chaise was waiting, and the bold trio, Dumas, Bard, and Hutin (who was to pass them through the gates), drove away on their daring expedition. By one o'clock they had reached the gates of Soissons, through which they were allowed to pass, "the door-keeper little dreaming," says the great farçeur, "that he was admitting the Revolution!"

They went straight to the house of Hutin's mother,

where their first business was the manufacture of a tricolour flag. She contributed her blue and red curtains, with a tablecloth, and all the women of the household were set to work to sew the pieces together. By daybreak the work was completed. The pole, of course, gave no trouble, as the one from which the Bourbon white flag was floating would answer. "For a flagstaff," as he says, "has no political opinions."

The plan they had arranged was almost quixotic in its extravagance, and indeed seems almost incredible. Making all allowance for Dumas's bombast, it will be seen that at the most he has been only guilty of a novelist's exaggeration ; and though at the time the story of the adventure was all but scouted, it could not be disproved in its facts, which are given with the most minute details of dates, names, and places. It was settled that Bard and Hutin were to take the flag and contrive to get into the cathedral under pretence of seeing the sun rise from the tower. If the sacristan made any resistance he was to be flung over the parapet. Then having dragged down the white flag, and set the tricolour floating from the tower, Bard was to hurry on to lend his aid to Dumas, who would be engaged at the powder magazine. Such was the dashing plan of three men.

They started at daybreak, and Dumas made his way to the Fort St. Jean, where a small pavilion, close to the gateway, was used as the magazine. He dared not attempt the gate, but stealing round, climbed up the wall cautiously, and took a peep into the fort. He saw two soldiers busy hoeing in a little garden at the corner. He let himself down again, and looked over at the distant cathedral. He saw distinctly against the sky a dark outline of some figures; then the white flag tossing about in an extraordinary fashion that could not have been owing to the wind, and finally disappear, while the tricolour took its place. Now was the moment; his companions had done their part He slung his double-barrelled gun about him, and began to climb the wall. When he got to the top he saw the two soldiers staring with wonder at the strange flag on the cathedral,— then, cocking both barrels of his gun, he leaped down and stood before them. One was named Captain Mollard; the other Sergeant Ragon. He advanced on them, presenting his piece, and made them a courteous but hurried speech, explaining who he was, and his errand. He was Monsieur Alexandre Dumas, son of General Dumas, &c. He came in the name of General Gérard to demand the surrender of the powder—there was his order, signed by the general, which he presented with one hand, and holding his cocked gun in the other. The pair were much taken back, and knew not what to do, when the Colonel, d'Orcourt, who was in command, was seen approaching. The matter was explained to him, and after many courteous phrases, a treaty was arranged, by which the three officers promised their neutrality, and engaged to keep within doors. Thus the powder magazine would seem to have been captured by Dumas single-handed. It had the air of a very brilliant achievement, and the picture of the hero alone in the fort, his fingers on the triggers of his gun, courteously but firmly controlling his three opponents, is a most dramatic scene. He forgot, however, that in the official report, furnished to the *Moniteur* twenty-three years before, he had stated that three of his friends were waiting at the gate.

Thus successful, he opened the gate and found his friend Bard. To him he handed over the charge of the magazine, and went away to deal with the " commandant of the Place " Liniers. He found this officer just risen, and discussing the news of the sudden appearance of the flag on the cathedral. Dumas laid down his gun at the door, and introducing himself, made his demand for an order to remove the powder. The other declined to acknowledge General Gérard's order, and said that there was scarcely any powder in the magazine. The commandant seemed, in fact, rather amused, and smiled scornfully when Dumas answered that the party at the magazine were his prisoners. Alexander replied that he would go back at once and bring proof under their hand that the powder was there, made his bow, and retired. He flew back, found that he was right, and returned presently with satisfactory proof that a large quantity of powder was in the magazine. But when he reached the commandant's office he found that the party had been increased during his absence by Lenferna, an officer of gendarmes, and Bonvilliers, colonel of the Engineers, who were in full uniform, and armed. The commandant addressed him in a sort of bantering tone, telling him that he had sent for those officers, who, with him, were in command of the town, in order that they might have the pleasure of hearing M. Dumas explain his mission. The young man saw that boldness was his only resource, and coolly told them that he had been engaged by Lafayette to bring the powder to Paris, or to lose his life, and that he insisted on the commandant handing over the powder to him. The officers passed on Gérard's order from one to the other with a sort of smiling contempt.

"And so," said the commandant; in the same tone

—" so, single-handed, Monsieur Dumas—I think you said that was your name—you propose to force me to do this. You see we are four."

The young man saw that matters were coming to a crisis, and took a prompt resolution. He stepped back, pulled his double-barrelled pistols from his pockets, and presented them at the startled party. " You are four," he said, " gentlemen ; but I am five ! If that order be not signed in five seconds, I give you my word of honour I will blow all your brains out, beginning with the commandant there ! "

He owned he felt a little nervous, but he was determined.

" Take care," he went on ; " I mean what I say. I am going to count ; one—two—three——"

At this critical moment a side door was flung open, and a lady flung herself among them in a paroxysm of alarm.

" Agree ! agree ! " she cried. " Oh, this is another revolt of the negroes ! Think of my poor father and mother, whom they murdered in Saint Domingo ! "

Alexander owned that the lady's mistake was excusable, considering his own natural tint (deepened by violent browning from the sun), and the peculiar character of hair and voice. But we may wonder at the insensibility to ridicule which could prompt him

to set down such a jest at his own expense.*　The
truth was, he was so filled with vanity, that all the
nicer senses became blunted, and he was even unconscious of the roars of laughter which these foolish con-
fidences produced.　The commandant, however, could
not resist the entreaties of his wife. Alexander declared
that he had infinite respect for the lady, but entreated
her husband to send her away, and let men finish the
business.　The poor commandant protested that his
self-respect must be respected.　He could not decently
yield to a single man.　Alexander then offered to sign
a paper, to the effect that the order had been extorted
at "the mouth of the pistol-barrel!"　"Or would you
prefer," he added, "that I should fetch two or three of
my companions, so that you should seem to have
yielded to a more respectable force?"　The commandant accepted this proposal, and Alexander left
him, bluntly declaring that no advantage must be
taken of the delay, or he would return and "blow all
their brains out," and that the whole party must give
their parole of honour that they would remain as they
were.

"Yes, yes," cried the lady.　Alexander made her a
low bow, but declared that it was not her parole that
he wanted.　The commandant gave what was required

* "O, mon ami, cède ! c'est une seconde révolte des nègres."

of him, and Alexander, hurrying away, speedily re-turned with two or three of his men, whom he placed in the court. Opening the window, he called to them, and bade them inform the gentlemen inside that they were ready to fire on them at the first signal; an appeal answered by the significant sound of cocking the guns. The commandant understood, and going to his desk, wrote out a formal order.

After this the rest was comparatively easy. The magazine was broken open, carts procured and loaded, and at about five o'clock they were outside the town. Dumas was so exhausted that he sank down on the grass, under a hedge, and fell fast asleep. Roused up presently, he started on his journey, and by eight o'clock reached Villers-Cotterets, where they found the supper ready which had been ordered the evening before. After a jovial meal they set out once more, and by three o'clock in the morning were close to Paris, at the post-house whence they had started. At nine he had presented himself, with his powder, at the Hotel de Ville, having triumphantly accomplished the daring exploit he had undertaken.

When Alexander told this adventure, there was many a shrug of the shoulders and loud laughter; such a romance as this was not thought worth serious refutation, as coming from this amusing and

notorious gasconader, an uncomplimentary appreciation which he owed to the incurable vanity which
always made him set his own figure in the most
effective and dramatic positions. But the story is
perfectly true, abating some harmless exaggeration.
It is to be found set forth in a modest official report
addressed to Lafayette, published by his direction in
the *Moniteur* of August 9th, 1830, and signed by
Dumas and the friends who assisted him in the expedition. The names of the various officers whom he
forced to submit to him are given at length. When
the memoirs were published in 1853, the son of the
commandant, Liniers, did, indeed, come forward with
an indignant " reclamation," to clear the memory of
his father, who was then dead, but his testimony, for
he was actually present at the scene in the commandant's cabinet, only confirms Dumas's account.
The purport of the son's letter is merely this : the
town was already ripe for revolt before Dumas's arrival, and that when the latter returned with his friends,
these were taken to be the chiefs of the National
Guard, already known to be disaffected. In short,
that the officer yielded, not to Dumas, but to the
overpowering force behind him. His son describes
Dumas parading his pistols, and menacing the commandant, but declares that the presence of the four

officers armed, and intimidated, was a fiction of the
novelist. He admits, however, that he himself and
the secretary—with Madame de Liniers—were present.
On the whole, the adventure, spiritedly told, and interesting to a degree, may be accepted in all faith,
and reflects credit on the great raconteur.

CHAPTER XIII.

THE Revolution was now complete. For Dumas the change in the dynasty, the putting on the throne his friend and patron of the Palais Royal—the personage who had secured the admission of his play to the Français, had made him librarian, and given him other offices—augured the brightest prospects. His fortune might be considered as made.

He was not long in repairing to the Palais Royal, where he found the Duke engaged with Casimir Delavigne and others. The Duke came up and held out his hand, saying, " Dumas, you have just produced your best piece!" This flattering compliment might have been an earnest of greater favour. But our Alexander had already found his suspicions as to the honesty of the Duke awakened. He was amazed at certain symptoms of duplicity in his behaviour, the evidence of which seemed irresistible. Indeed, his portrait of Louis-Philippe during these days is

N

touched in with singular effect, and a vigour that is more than malicious. There are also scenes described in which the present ruler of France figures, and which are characteristic enough to be true. Thiers then belonged to the enthusiastic band of clever young men who wrote fiery articles in the papers, and fiercely attacked the unconstitutional government of the day. When the Revolution came he was acute enough to see the chances of the Duke, and "glided" cleverly into Orleanism, while his companions, not nearly so clever, followed his movements with a bewildered gaze.

This picture of the Duke thus given is disagreeable enough. The ardent mobs who came shouting to the Palais, and who got admission, were regaled with wine by servants in the handsome livery of the host; but it was remarked that the wine was of the cheapest kind. They said they found the liveries splendid but the liquor bad. When they were filled, fresh mobs would arrive under the balcony, roaring for the Duke, and Dumas describes him rushing to the balcony again and again, joining in the Marseillaise, coming down, his wig all awry, his face covered with perspiration. He would wash his hands and face, while he heartily execrated the whole business.

It was after witnessing scenes like this, it seems, that Dumas became so utterly shocked and disgusted, that, casting the dust off his shoes, and sorrowfully renouncing his faithless patron, he quitted the Palais Royal for ever! "The spectacle," he says, "of a prince thus begging a crown like a street beggar," wounded him to the very soul. He renounced, he says, the road to honours. He had merely to go to the Palais Royal, "ask for some mission to Prussia, Russia, or Spain;—but no, I would have nothing to do with them. I had sworn, of my own free will, never to put my foot in the Palais Royal again." In vain did the chief of his office, Oudard, strive to soothe him, "offering to send him to St. Petersburg with M. Athalin, who was just starting as ambassador extraordinary to the Emperor Nicholas; in vain was the proposal of the Cross of the Legion dangled before his eyes; in vain did his mother come to congratulate him "on his fortune being made," and his sister arrive post-haste from the country to solicit his interest and good offices in favour of her husband. He was inflexible. "Poor dear mother! I took care not to let her know that, far from being able to advance others, I considered that my own career was ended for ever." He had told Oudard that he must consider him as no longer being attached to the establishment.

This picture of self-abnegation, and the story of such noble political integrity, must have made those who knew Alexander smile; but, as it stands, it could hardly be accepted even by the ordinary reader. The truth was, the Duke was displeased that one of his dependants should have taken part with the more violent of the revolutionary party, with whom he himself had broken. Dumas's vanity, leading him to fancy himself an important personage, and one of the leaders of the party, had disgusted the Duke, who had coldly refused to acknowledge his pretensions or demands. Stung to fury by this disappointment, he conceived the most bitter hatred to his former patron, which he exhibited, it must be said, in a rather mean and pitiful way. Years after Louis-Philippe's fall in 1848, when he might have thought of former favours and kindnesses, he shows that for more than twenty years he had been brooding over, not the injury, but the disappointment, and does his best to make the Duke appear dishonest and contemptible. The amusing part of the whole is the naïve good faith with which he believes that his halting story will be accepted.

In this mood he took an extraordinary step. He says that he went to La Fayette, and proposed another expedition, which the old general heartily approved. This was a mission into La Vendée,—not of a very

intelligible sort, according to Dumas's own statement.
The old general had had a hard time of it during
these exciting days,—his chief function being that of
appearing at windows, and embracing various personages, to the applause of the mob. "General," said
Dumas, "I come to ask for something." "Bah!" he
said, "I suppose *you want a prefecture?*" The other
said all he asked was to be empowered to travel
through La Vendée and organise a National Guard!
It was, of course, as Royalist as ever, and the King's
friends would be active in trying to excite a reaction;
but by following his plan their intrigues would be
checked. His theory was that a powerful middle
class had grown up who did not hold Royalist views,
and who only wanted rallying and proper organisation. He would cheerfully undertake the task, and
he came to ask a letter from La Fayette. It was
given him, and "this," says Dumas, "was my com-
mission." "You will authorise me," he went on, "to
wear *some description of uniform?*" "By all means,"
said the general, "get them to make you *something
resembling an aid-de-camp's dress.* How much time
do you want?" "Only sufficient to get my uniform made." Many would pass over all this as
mere fooling on the part of this eminent *farçeur*, but
the whole is genuine and sincere, and we must believe

that the uniform *was* present to his mind as an essential part of the transaction. As he was crossing the
Place du Carrousel, he discovered a friend, who was
riding by, in one of the most brilliant though eccentric
costumes that could be conceived—a plume of tricoloured feathers, a tunic of Royal blue, and silver
sash. Dumas was enchanted with the effect, and
rushed after him, to inquire the name of the corps.
It turned out that it was an invention of the wearer's,
who had thought of establishing a sort of fancy corps,
which he called *The Mounted National Guard*, but
which was not yet in being. Alexander obtained the
name of the tailor, and ordered one exactly the same.

Having procured his uniform, he started. No one
could accept, or, indeed, accepted, this story of a
" mission to organise a middle-class party." It seems
only too probable that he was vain enough to suppose
that he could stir up an insurrection against the new
occupant of the throne, or frighten the occupant of the
throne by the boldness of this eccentric expedition.
He was, no doubt, excited by the success of his
attempt on Soissons. All this is pitiful, and more
pitiful is the conceit which led him to suppose he
could hoodwink the public by so childish a story.

He secured a horse and started ; but he remarked,
with some anxiety, that the farther he got from Paris

the nearer he seemed to approach the North Pole of
coolness. Thus, in the outskirts of Paris, the sight of
his uniform aroused due enthusiasm; at Blois, it
aroused merely transient admiration; at Angers, it
became simple curiosity; but at Meurs and other
places farther on, he began to encounter indifference,
and even angry suspicion. At a place called Che-
mille the uniform almost excited a riot, so that later
he thought it advisable to exchange this conspicuous
dress for a shooting coat. But still his progress was
not encouraging. He was on the point of being ar-
rested several times: for people could not understand
—naturally enough—the designs of such a masque-
rader.*

He found, as might be expected, that he could do
nothing, that his scheme was quixotic; so he returned
as speedily as possible as he could to Paris.

On his arrival he was sent for, he tells us, by the

---

* With this fanciful mission he combined a little sight-seeing, and
some of his sketches and recollections are exceedingly picturesque. At
Angers he found a sacrilegious architect busy "restoring" the cathedral,
scraping the sculptured embroidery off the columns, hacking, hewing,
and cleaning wholesale. His reflections on this scene are not without
wit: "It takes five-and-twenty years, alas! to make a man. A Swiss
fires on him and shoots him dead. It takes six or eight hundred years
to give the colour of age to a cathedral; an architect of taste arrives, and
scrapes it from top to bottom. One might almost wish that the Swiss
had shot the architect, or, better still, that the architect had scraped the
Swiss."

King, who wished to hear all about the mission. He
arrayed himself for the occasion in his sky-blue suit, the
proper uniform of the " Mounted National Guard." He
told his friends that it was to be " war to the knife "—
that no attentions on the side of the royal patron, whom
he had renounced for ever, would propitiate him. He was
received graciously, and was asked about his Vendean
travels. He spoke out boldly and fearlessly—he was
even scornful. When the King said that he had no
fears from La Vendée, he answered, laughing, " The
King will, perhaps, excuse my attempting to refute *his*
opinion, but will allow me to retain my own. May
I say what I think ?" " You mean on the state
of La Vendée ?" " Yes ; and also *on your present
policy ?*" " Well, say what you think of both one
and the other." Dumas, seizing the opportunity,
spoke out, and said: " that the critical state of La
Vendée was a capital pretext for putting aside the
notion of a war on the Rhine or in Italy." " I know,"
he added, " that this would be popular ; but the King
is not inclined for it, and is glad to have such an
excuse for avoiding it." " *Ah !*" said the King,
wincing under the thrust. " He bit his lips, for I had
thrust home." The King answered pettishly : " You
had better leave politics to Kings and to Ministers
—you are a poet ; better stick to your poetry."

"Sire," the other answered, "the ancients called the poets *prophets*." The King, unable to endure more of these "bitter thrusts," waved him off impatiently, and terminated the interview.

Alexander came out triumphant, and said to his friend Oudard, who was waiting: "Yesterday we had only half quarrelled, but to-day I have broken with him for ever!" He says he then sat down and wrote the following letter of resignation :—

" SIRE—My *political opinions not being in harmony* with those which your Majesty is entitled to require in the persons who hold office in your Majesty's household, I must ask your Majesty to accept my resignation.

" I have the honour to remain, &c.,

" ALEX. DUMAS."

This grave narrative, the "making the King quail," must now be unhappily characterised as so much *blague*. It might be unfair to describe it as "untruthful," but the writer hardly believed he was imposing on any one, and fancied that he had the privilege of a "Collegien," as the King, according to faithworthy testimony, later christened him. That he had an interview with the King is probable enough, but it seems

almost too certain that it was for the object not of
"bearding" his patron, but of obsequiously pressing
his claims. It is these extraordinary and elaborate
impostures, which deceive no one, that makes this
book of personal history unique.

He was at once enrolled by his friend Bixio ; this we
may presume to be the Bixio who later became so
well known, in the artillery of the National Guard.
Here, again, he cannot conceal his delight in the *uniform*. Yet he found that with little trouble the fancy
dress of the " Mounted National Guard " could be
cleverly adapted to that of the new corps. Even the
colour was the same. " It was only necessary to sew
on a red stripe down the leg in place of the silver one,
and exchange the silver epaulettes for ones of red
worsted." He was proud of the corps, of its divisions,
one of which went by the name of the *Murderers*,
owing to the number of doctors it contained. He was
on duty when the Polignac ministry was being tried,
and describes dramatically all the street scenes that
attended this crisis. He was presently elected second
captain of his battery, a promotion thus described :
" Within twenty-four hours my stripes, epaulettes,
and cords of red worsted were exchanged for stripes,
epaulettes, and cords of gold. On the 27th of De-
cember I commanded the parade clad in the insignia

of my new rank."   But he was presently led, he says, to make what he candidly calls a most ridiculous exhibition of himself.   New Year's Day was now at hand, and the officers of the corps had decided that they were to go with the other officials and pay the customary visit of congratulation to the King at the palace.   Dumas slept till very late that morning, and hurriedly dressing himself posted away to the Palais Royal.   On the stairs and in the reception rooms he was puzzled at not meeting any of his own officers in the crowd of uniforms, and he noted also that every one was scanning with curious glances himself and his dress.   Just as he was making his way through the crowd the King happened to advance, and Alexander to his own surprise found himself suddenly isolated, as though he had become infected by the cholera.   He fancied that this sudden desertion was owing to a fear of being seen in company with a member of a corps whose opinions were so radical as those of the artillery company, and he accordingly drew himself up with additional pride.   But he noticed that he was the only officer whom the King condescended to notice.   He was surveying him from head to foot, while the others were laughing significantly.   Greatly puzzled, he passed before the King, who was good enough to say— "Ah, Dumas! how are you?   This is you all over!"

He then laughed, and the courtiers round laughed, and the unhappy Dumas, as much bewildered as was the hero of Lever's novel, when he presented himself on parade, having forgotten to wash off the black from his face after the performance of "Othello," retired to be saluted with fresh roars by a crowd of friends in the other room.

"Well, you *have* brass," said one.

"I don't know what you mean."

"O, that's good! I suppose you haven't seen the King's order?"

"What order?"

Amid fresh roars he was told that the artillery corps had been dissolved by royal decree the night before! It was in all the morning papers. It had, of course, the air of a piece of bravado, if not of an insult to the King. But then it was "so like what that Dumas would do"; and so, as indeed he seems to convey, not worth noticing. The candour that prompted him to such a confession really amounted to what the French call *niaiserie;* but his visit to the King showed that he was still eager to win back the royal favour. He now combined this obsequiousness with a petty system of annoyance, by which he hoped to prove that he could be dangerous, and might be well worth conciliating.

One of the steps he took to this end was the writing
of a piece called "Napoleon," meant, of course, to
work up the hostile Bonapartist feeling of the country.
Harel, the manager of the Odéon, he says, had proposed this task to him during the Revolution, but had
since allowed the matter to drop. He invited Dumas
to a sumptuous supper, to which Janin, and Georges,
the famous actress, were also invited. They did not
break up until three in the morning, when the manager
led Dumas through several apartments until they found
themselves in a bedroom, handsomely furnished, and
which was to be the scene of one of the usual "Monte
Christo" surprises. "Here is a pretty room," said Alexander, "one could sleep or work here right well." "Glad
you think so," said the manager, "for it is yours, and
out of it you do not stir until you have finished my
'Napoleon.'" "Oh, no, nonsense," replied the other,
who takes care he shall have this violence done to him
in the most flattering way. "But I have not so much
as an idea ready for your 'Napoleon.'" "Recollect
you told me that you rewrote 'Christine' in a single
night." "Well, but I want books; 'Bourrienne,'
'Norvins,' 'The Victories and Conquests.'" "Here
they all are." Everything had been thought of, even
to his *pantalons à pied*, which had been sent for.
The author yielded. "Good," he said, loftily, "in

eight days you shall have your piece." The manager
was ready to lay out four thousand pounds on it, and
the piece was to begin with Toulon and end with the
" five years' agony at St. Helena." " That very morning I lighted on the part of the Spy ; *the part of* the
Spy once found the whole drama was found. The
day following I began to write. As each tableau was
finished I passed it on to Georges, who passed them
on to Harel, who gave them *to a charming young
fellow named Verteuil*, who is now secretary to the
French Theatre. In eight days it was all finished ; it
consisted of twenty-four tableaux, and comprised nine
thousand lines. It thus had three times the corpulency
of an ordinary piece, *five times the length of*
' Iphigenia,' *six times that of* ' Mérope.' "

The single part of Lemaitre, who played Napoleon,
contained four thousand lines, "about as long as all the
characters put together in the ' Marriage of Figaro.' "
What is here implied is truly characteristic, though
even his complacent vanity must be gratified by a
suppression of the truth. For he was assisted by
collaborators. It proved, however, a wretched piece,
and had but little success. After this proceeding,
which could only be called effrontery, the utmost he
could expect was tolerance or contempt. He had
gone to La Vendée, not "to excite Republican

feeling," but, as he allowed to slip out later, " to feel the pulsations of the Royalist heart." Now he had been trying to " feel the pulsations of the Napoleonic heart." When he returned from that expedition he found the odious persons who had been about the anterooms " all with *fresh offices, and enjoying double salaries.*" He was at once pressed by the manager to write this piece, but, he says, " it seemed unsuitable to attempt such a thing" *without high authority.* He attempted again and again to see his Majesty. He " did antechamber," as it is called, until he was weary. They would ask him, as though he was a *mere stranger*, what was his business with the King. He refused to say unless to the King himself, who was to declare whether " he wished the Napoleon scheme to be carried out" or did not. Still no notice was taken. That decided him. He then wrote and produced his piece.

All this is infinitely amusing. To give the whole in detail would be even more so, but would take too long. In Dumas's character what is so delightful is to find his genuine thoughts invariably revealed, even through his most far-fetched and ingenious exculpations. " People," he said, " called out ' how ungrateful !' people *who had asked and got everything for themselves. I had neither asked nor got anything.* Ah!

I am wrong. I *had* asked pardon for a wretched malefactor condemned to the galleys for life, and the King granted it. It was a happy moment for his family and for me."

Still he was indisposed to break finally with his late patron. The play, like the expedition to La Vendée, was only intended as a warning, a hint of his power and resources, a proof that he was a person worth conciliating. On any return of royal favour, or on some substantial recognition, he would be found to be the most devoted of adherents. What takes all these tricks out of the category of sheer dishonesty is the man's candour and seeming unconsciousness of there being anything discreditable in his manœuvres, and what is really amusing is, his belief that the public will dismiss any previous explanation as lightly as he does himself, and accept the last and most convenient one. He never gave himself the trouble to see whether his last defence was consistent with the one he had given before, and set down what the rage or impulse of the moment prompted. This is deliciously illustrated in his difference with the King. When he was writing his "Memoirs," Louis-Philippe had been driven out of France, the chances of the dynasty were all over. There was nothing to be hoped for in that direction ; he therefore gives way without restraint to all his bitterness, disappointment and dislike. He then could write: "As I owe an explanation to many who have been surprised at the opposition which in my capacity of politician, and later of literary man, I have constantly made to Louis-Philippe's government, I shall continue to enumerate the reasons of the political repugnance, *which compelled me to renounce him at a time when my own interest*, if, indeed, my interest could for a single instant overpower my conscience, ought to have made me attach myself to his royal fortunes." This seemed very noble and self-denying. But besides the mystification of the truth which has been already pointed out, he had forgotten that he had already some twenty years before given a wholly different account of the transaction. In his preface to his play of "Napoleon" he had addressed the King in a solemn strain that is infinitely amusing.

It is indeed almost impossible to follow the shifts and turns of this incomparable being. He had sent in his haughty letter of resignation. Three weeks passed by, and no notice had been taken of it. Dumas says it never reached the King. He expected a request that he was by no means to think of doing such a thing. The King could not afford to lose such a brilliant ornament. A mortifying silence, however, was the only result. The persevering Dumas seeing that, in vulgar phrase, the game was almost up, fancied that he had hardly spoken strongly enough, and determined on another appeal, in which he should make a fresh bid and speak out. He "resigned" a second time in this fashion.*

> "13*th February*, 1831.

"SIRE,—Three weeks ago I had the honour of begging an interview with your Majesty, with the view of personally offering the resignation of my post to your Majesty. I wished to explain that in so doing I was neither ungrateful nor capricious.

" Long ago, Sire, I wrote and printed that according to my ideas *the man of letters was only the preface to the man of politics.*

"The time of life when I can belong to a reformed Chamber of Deputies is approaching.

" *So surely as the sun rises, by the time I am thirty years old,* I shall *be a member.* I am now twenty-eight.

" It is miserable to see how the people, looking up

* He was so flighty and careless in everything that concerned his writings, that it is possible that, when writing his personal memoirs, he may have forgotten that he had already furnished his readers with a etter of resignation, for which perhaps he had drawn on his imagination. But the explanation given in the text may be accepted as the true one.

from below and from a distance, is unable to distinguish between the intentions of the King and the acts of his ministers, which latter are arbitrary and destructive of liberty.

"Among the men who depend upon your Majesty, and tell you every day that they admire and love you, there is not, perhaps, a single one who loves you more than I do. The difference is they say so but do not think so, *whereas I think so, but do not say so.*"

The purport of this communication was unmistakeable. Louis-Philippe must have laughed over this persevering audacity.

But Dumas went farther. When he published his play words of significant menace preceded it. "Creation belongs to the poet. *Kings, citizens, all are equal* before him, and in his hand, *as in that of God*, weigh exactly the same. He snatches the mask from the faces of the living, opens the coffins of the dead. *His pen is now a lash, now a redhot iron.* Woe to those whom he lashes ; shame and misfortune to those whom he brands. So long as he puts his name to what he writes, he answers for all. I have signed mine." How devoutly he must hereafter have wished that he had never done so indiscreet a thing, or added that still more unmeaning declaration, "If I ever profess different principles, let any one smite my cheek with this preface."

Such was the little episode marked by our author's characteristic insolence, petty spite, and stupidity. It entailed on him nearly eighteen years of cringing self-abasement, while he made the most humiliating advances to the King and his family to be forgiven. The King always showed a sort of good-humoured contempt for him, but would never restore him to his favour. This additional humiliation Alexander was able to revenge at the second revolution by publishing the private household books of the King showing his little economies, which Dumas picked up at the Tuileries.

CHAPTER XIV.

" ANTONY."

1831.

"Antony," then, written after these triumphs, had been accepted at the Français, and Mars and Firmin had received the two leading characters. This outrageous piece, which is all violence, brutality, and coarse passion, did not please these two artists. Dumas describes them gradually pruning away this and that extravagance out of mere whim, but the truth was, such cultivated players saw that they could make but little of the raw and inartistic characters offered for their interpretation. As the day drew near, for the performance, both frankly confessed that they " could not see it." In a sort of pet, he abruptly withdrew his play, of course to the consternation of all parties concerned, and at once carried it to the director of the Porte St. Martin, who received it cordially. He read it to Dorval, when, as of course, some such scene as the following must take place :

" I began to read, but she had not patience to remain

in the chair. She came behind me, and read over my shoulder. At the end of the first act she kissed me on the forehead. As I went on I felt the chest of the great actress beating against my shoulder. At the scene between Antony and Adèle *a tear dropped upon the paper, then a second, and then a third.* I raised my face to kiss her.

"'How teasing you are,' she said, 'interrupting me in the midst of my pleasure.'

"I continue to read, and she to *weep*. At the end of the act, it will be remembered, Adèle rushes away.

"'Ah!' said Dorval, sobbing hysterically, 'there's a noble woman. I couldn't have saved myself in that way.'

"'You are a love,' was my answer. I then went on to the third act. She listened, all shuddering. At the fourth she seized my neck with both her hands. *It was no longer her bosom that rose and sank; it was her heart that beat against my shoulder.* I felt it swelling under her dress.

"'Sacré nom d'un chien ?—Why do you stop ?' she cried.

"'Because you are choking me.'

"'Ah ! so I am. But you never hear of such things on the stage. It's *too* naturally absurd. It stifles one.'"

The last act, however, she thought, wanted power,

and wished to have it rewritten. He agreed ; but of course this change could only be done in a melodramatic way. It must be done that night. There was a room ready usually occupied by another gentleman, but who was fortunately absent.

"We shall bring you tea. During the night I will come *and visit you, to see how you are getting on,* and in the morning you will read to me."

She then went over her part with extraordinary animation and power, seizing all the points exactly in the way the author desired.

" O noble organisation, that death fancied it levelled, but *which I took an oath should not succumb to death.* I told you I would make you live again. Be easy ; at each wave of my pen you shall burst from the tomb, *palpitating* with nature—with all the weaknesses that made you woman, &c."

This absurd rhapsody was, we may assume, one of his enchanter's " waves of his pen," but it does little towards ensuring the lady her promised immortality. At eleven o'clock he set to work on his fifth act. It was finished by three in the morning.

It was to be produced in April, but the times were troubled, and the air was charged with storms. Abroad, a war with Austria had nearly come about,*

* Alexander thus speaks—after his own special fashion—of the French

while at home there was fierce discontent on the part of the Republicans, and the feeling of having been deceived by the cunning " attorney " who was on the throne. Just before the general rehearsals of "Antony" began, the order of the " Cross of July " had been established, but with a motto and ribbon that was found highly distasteful. Alexander and some of his friends wished that the colours of the latter had been blue and black, to signify " the blood shed and mourning worn," instead of blue and red, the colours prescribed. He and his friends, however, wore the ribbon they preferred, and ostentatiously lingered in groups about the Tuileries, to provoke the authorities there into a dispute. No notice was taken of these grown-up children, but Alexander records that he had the satisfaction of attending the rehearsals with his ribbon on.

He was rather desponding as to the success of his play, but the actors—Dorval, who played Adèle, and Bocage, who played the hero,—were full of enthusiasm. To the last general rehearsal he refused to admit any of his friends ; who, he says sensibly, on the first night of the performance interfere with the

ambassador to Austria :—" I knew Marshal Maison well, and, in spite of the difference between our ages, with a sort of intimacy. *A fascinating woman, who to me was only a friend, and to him no more than a friend,* was the link between the young poet and the old soldier."

interest of the piece by talking to their neighbours, and wishing to show that they know what is coming. As for giving advice, it is then too late to make alterations; and he truly adds, that the scene-shifters and supernumeraries who stand at the wing, bending forward their necks to catch a few passages, are better judges of what will take than all the doctors and academicians put together.

It was, as we have seen, to be produced at the Porte St. Martin theatre,—a house associated, even in the memory of English playgoers, with some of the most thrilling and romantic sensations; for there was found the art of combining the extreme of spectacular pageantry, processions, crowds, armies, and sumptuous dresses, with some exciting story, and, above all, with a fervid and passionate acting. Whatever defects of exaggeration may belong to this school, the stranger owns that he looks back to these long Porte St. Martin nights with interest and pleasure. Some of the most famous pieces that have found their way to every theatre in Europe have been produced at this house, which was put up in a few weeks' time, to do duty as a temporary structure until a more substantial theatre should be built. It was, however, found so convenient, and so enduring, that it was not thought worth while to disturb it, and thus it flourished for some thirty or forty years, one of the most prosperous theatres in Paris, until the fury of the Commune left a small patch of ground covered with rubbish, as the only memorial of its glories.

The night of performance came round. There was a crowded and excited house. The piece was certainly novel in its daring and almost outrageous situations, which were now, almost for the first time, combined with the ordinary dress and character of every day life. There were moments when the audience paused irresolutely, so startled were they by the extravagant violence and " brutality " of the situation. But the dramatic skill of the author, and the interest, which, to do him justice, he had always had a knack of exciting, turned the balance, and extorted tumultuous bursts of applause.*   His nervousness and excitement

---

* One of these situations which closed an act, and made even those ridiculous agents in the success of a drama, " the clappers," hesitate, was that of a married lady flying from a persistent lover, and arriving at a lonely inn.   Dorval was admirable for the *feminine* naïveté and natural terror she threw into the part.   She said, as no one ever said, or ever will say again, these two simple speeches :—" This door does not shut close."—" Are you sure that nothing unfortunate has ever occurred at your hotel ? "   As soon as the landlady retires, she withdraws hesitatingly into an inner room.   She has barely disappeared, when a pane of glass is shattered into fragments, a hand is put through, and the window opened.   The two suddenly appear, the one at the window, the other in the doorway.   The rest of the scene was full of *an appalling naïveté.*   Adèle had uttered a cry, and to prevent its repetition Antony presses a handkerchief in her mouth, drags her to the door of the cabinet, and the moment they pass the threshold, the curtain

were so great that he could not remain in the theatre, and, with his friend Bixio, hurried out to pace the Boulevards. " If any one had said to the passers-by : ' Look at that cracked fellow down there ! that's the author of the piece now playing at the Porte St. Martin ! ' they would have been amazingly taken aback." When he returned, the audience, actors—all, were in a tumult of excitement. The very air of the theatre was charged with emotions. He had already discovered and valued the ingredient in dramatic success, almost invariably neglected by our moderns— the necessity of short intervals between the acts on first nights. The applause was still continuing in front of the curtain, when he cried to the scene-shifters, " A hundred francs, if you can get the curtain up before they have done applauding ! "—a stimulant which actually had the effect intended. The last act certainly did not want for effect, from the extra- ordinary surprise with which the play closed. The guilty lovers are pursued and overtaken by the in- furiated husband, who bursts open the door to find the lady stabbed to the heart. Her honour, however, is saved, for the lover flings the dagger at the feet of

falls. This " brutal " situation has been copied in the notorious scene in M. Sardou's "Nos Intimes," a delightful comedy, marred towards its close, even in an artistic sense, by a too inharmonious grossness.

the husband, saying, "Elle me resistait ; je l'ai assassiné." As the curtain fell on this extraordinary *dénoûment*, shouts of terror and grief burst from the audience ; they called for the author " with cries of fury." The whole house was stupefied and confounded by what, it must be admitted, was a most original and ingenious situation. An ovation awaited the author behind the scenes. His young friends, " pale, agitated, panting," flung themselves upon him. " I was dragged to the right and to the left. I had on a *green suit*, buttoned from top to bottom, which was torn in pieces. " No wonder that he often looked back fondly to this night of bewildering triumph. With these successes of hot youth, the riper efforts of mature age seem tame and cold.*

* There are few better theatrical stories than one told by Dumas, and no one could tell a story better, which is connected with this piece. The same performers were playing it several years later at the Palais Royal on some benefit night, where the prompter, from his experience of conventional finales, naturally assumed that the piece terminated with the stabbing of the lady and entry of the husband. He accordingly " rang down " the curtain, or, as is the practice on the French stage, called out " au rideau ! " The audience expected what was indeed the key of the whole : " She resisted me, so I stabbed her ! " and in a fury at being disappointed, shouted for " the dénoûment." The prompter, in despair, determined the " situation " should be gone through again, and Dorval good-humouredly sat down in the chair, but no persuasion could get Bocage to appear. The curtain went up and discovered the lady lying back, after receiving the mortal stroke, but there were no signs of the lover. After a long wait, the actress suddenly lifted her head, slowly rose, and advancing to the footlights, said in a calm and measured voice, " Ladies and gentlemen, I resisted him, and so he stabbed me."

CHAPTER XV.

DRAMATIC MORALITY.

THE account given by Dumas himself of the extraordinary effect produced by this piece, is not in the least exaggerated. Those cries " of terror and grief" which filled the theatre on the first night, were but an anticipation of the morbid excitement it was destined to produce through Parisian society, when everybody was presently to be rushing to the house, to enjoy the luxury of having their feelings " harrowed up," and have the passions presented to them under the most " raw" and violent conditions conceivable. Hitherto homage to the conventional code of society, to say nothing of dramatic propriety, required that actual violation of nuptial ties might hover in the background, indistinct and undefined; but it was reserved for Dumas to present guilt itself in concrete shape upon the stage. After this it is almost amusing to turn back to the grave scruples of an English audience on the score of Mrs. Haller, or as to the propriety of the forgiveness extended to that erring lady at the close of the play.

"Antony" was, perhaps, the most conspicuous, if not the earliest, of the long line of plays which have since obtained so strong a hold upon the French stage, a class, that might be described, without exaggeration, as being "base, bloody, and brutal." The reproach of extravagant realism has been made against modern pieces—of placing on the stage ordinary material objects, such as carriages, and railway stations, and under such conditions might be considered to have reached the profoundest depth. But it was reserved for the French writer to find a depth yet deeper—the *realism* of brutal crime and passion. There is something far more gross and *material* in the exhibition of such phenomena than even in the cheap prodigies of scene painters and carpenters, that is in the naked spectacle of revolting crimes, and of gross human passions let loose. The mere display of a collection of murders, adulteries, rapes, ingeniously complicated, are wholly outside the domain of dramatic art and interest. To Dumas belongs the distinction of having boldly carried this revolting system as far as it could possibly go, and in a series of dramas that began with "Antony," was followed by "Richard Darlington," "Angéle,"

" Térésa," and others, he inaugurated that corruption, not only of the French stage, but of Parisian manners, which has since obtained. A single reflection, which might not strike us at first sight, will show from what a low depth must be fetched the secret of entertainment that is supposed to be found in such things, for it might be imagined that a civilised community would turn away its eyes from such horrors, which could shock rather than entertain. It will indeed be found that only the most degraded taste can find pleasure in the exhibition of scenes where human torture or agony is presented. Bull-baitings, public executions, and the like, can have no attraction save for brutish souls; though it may be admitted that one may at least conceive of there being a certain fascination in such spectacles. Advancing a stage higher, it can be conceded that there is a diseased taste which finds a pleasure in reports of trials and *causes célèbres;* while there is a vast mass of the population, in every country, which literally feeds itself on journals of crime, set off, as in our own country, with coarse illustrations. This is, perhaps, the lowest species of human entertainment known, which, like the exhibitions of material objects on the stage, requires each successive dose to be more highly spiced than the preceding. The stock of interest or excitement to be obtained from such things is, after the first surprise, of the most meagre kind. After the first original combination of a murder with an adultery or incest, the end of the tether has been reached; repetition only remains. For a brandy drinker or opium eater nothing more exciting remains than to multiply the doses.

It is curious, too, to note what an advance this was on the character of pieces like " Henry III.," which, though it contained the germ of the monstrosities that were to come later, was still redeemed by a certain romance and chivalry. Such elements as unlawful love, murder, combats, abductions, executions, jealousy, and hatred, by being placed in a remote age, were more or less in keeping with the historical instincts of the audience, and those whose taste was tolerably chastened might accept what they saw as an over-drawn picture of a scene from French history. But now they were plunged into a tide of atrocities, which were not merely false in their dramatic arrangement, but false as a picture of existing manners, or, at least, could only be accepted as *possibly* true by the more degraded classes, whose sympathies went with such horrors. From that time the 'French theatre was inundated with a bloody flood of slaughterings, stranglings, incests, adulteries, violations, secret accouchements, represented with literal accuracy. The mixture of these revolting elements, to cause any emotion, had to be seasoned with an extravagance that was ludicrous, and the most far-fetched criminal situations had to be devised to support the interest. The soiled mantle which Dumas had worn with such effrontery has now fallen on the shoulders of diligent successors, who, finding that the spectacle of the grossest crime, in its material shape, had ceased to shock or interest, imparted something of real dramatic interest, by working with the *passions* only, starting, of course, from a basis as immoral as their master could have desired. The result is as gross, but the complications of unlawful passions are highly ingenious, not so realistic, and, therefore, more dramatic. It is curious, indeed, to note the changes on the French stage within so short a space as fifty years. The dull but decent extracts from the Roman history came with the Restoration, not as a consequence of strict Bourbon manners or censorship, but because they were the only form of drama to hand, and the tradition easiest to recover. Then the elegant but mild romance found in Casimir Delavigne, who was the "Girondin" of the dramatic revolution; later the tumultuous extravagance of Dumas and Hugo, which, of course, represented a corresponding ferment in the community, though the singular spectacle was thus presented of a dramatic terrorism being in favour with the plain bourgeois society of Louis-Philippe. After twenty years of this fiery dram-drinking, a reaction came once more ; the refined sensuality of the Second Empire developed a taste for elegant comedy, duly spiced with elements which, on analysis, would be found almost as revolting as the old complicated immorality of " Antony," but which were disguised by wit, keen observation of life and manners, and agreeable ridicule of the follies. The younger Dumas is the high-priest of this form, and has made his reputation by the ingenious combination.

A clever critic, M. Granier de Cassagnac, boldly analysed with great severity the false principles of the new formed " romantic drama," which, by the way, was neither new nor " romantic," being rude and matter-of-fact to extremity.* It all turned on the exhibition of crude emotions, and on exciting situations. In other words passion and curiosity were appealed to. Now curiosity is the poorest, most egotistical, and lowering of all cravings ; it is a stupid desire to know for knowing's sake. And the mere exhibition of emotional passions, as of a person under the influence of furious love, or rage and hate as furious, is in

* See *Journal des Débats*, 1833.

itself nothing dramatic, Each may be the material for what is dramatic. "The true question," says this excellent critic—and the reasoning applies to the system of our day—"is this: Are we to see in it man according to the best conditions of his state, using passion and character as the means, while curiosity—*i.e.*, interest—links all together? Is man to be shown, then, elevated and ennobled, furnishing an example that will be useful, or is he merely *as an occasion for exciting a nervous irritation in an audience. Are we to throw a great and crowded hall into convulsions of agitation at the expense of all that is good and improving, sending them away a pale and fluttered herd, who seemed to have been dosed with ether or opium? Are the personages on the stage to be poets or to be gladiators?"* This question could not be more happily summed up than in the well chosen words.

But in justification of this offence against public decency, Dumas vehemently urged the classic precedents of the old Greek drama, where shocking and revolting excesses are made the subject of the play. It has been urged with plausibility that it is the age, not the writer, that is accountable. The age furnishes the materials, and if these be corrupt, the drama, to be faithful, must exhibit this corruption.

On this principle, as the manners of the time are lax, and as lax subjects are bound up with the conversation, discussions, newspapers, &c., of society, a piece affecting to reflect society could not ignore such subjects. Thus ladies of easy manners, their villas, dresses, &c., &c., were legitimately introduced. But an answer to this view can be found in an illustration taken from the kindred art of painting, the same, in fact, that was given to the modern pre-Raphaelites, when these were setting forth for admiration elaborately wrought "patches of brick-wall," "satin dresses," "bits of carpet," and the like. The imitation of such objects is of no value, while, if there *be* any interest in such things, the originals are superior and sufficiently, accessible. So with the incidents of "fast life." It should be remembered that the aim of painting is to supply what delights and enchants ; those rare and poetical elements of expression, either in the countenance or in landscape, which escape ordinary observers, which persons search for eagerly and rarely find. Both in painting as well as in the drama, the source of *pleasure* and entertainment is found in this principle—viz., in something which we have not the instinct or skill of discovering for ourselves, and which the genius of painter or of the dramatist sets before us. In the case of ordinary events of life, or of ordinary objects transferred to the stage, the sensation is at best only that of curiosity or of mild surprise. The brutal results, therefore, of violent passions, or mere *crimes* brought forward on the stage, are only like the minute imitation of decayed vegetable matter which these modern pre-Raphaelites were so fond of presenting : they are pieces of morbid anatomy, professedly unpleasant dissections of human character. Such are merely things to look at, to appreciate with eyes and ears ; but there is nothing *dramatic* about them. Again, there is no precedent to be drawn from the dreadful plots of Æschylus, for here there is the awful presence of *Fate,* against which the victims struggle, and which furnishes the most impressively dramatic element conceivable. Finally, these grossly complicated scenes of guilt, as given by Dumas and his school, are undramatic, because improbable and false to nature. As one of his critics said justly of this piece : " Such a conception no more bears the scrutiny of honest instinct than a crime tried at the assizes would the investigation of a jury. The author, in choosing to place himself within the range of frantic passions, which is purely exceptional, mad passions which are not to be meddled with but at the price of blood and tears, has withdrawn himself from all literary jurisdiction. The piece is simply a monstrosity." *

There is here precisely the difference that we see in real life, when a corrupt man tells a story of guilt or wickedness, or a good man. By the former it is told with a certain *sympathy* which he can hardly avoid, and which will produce a corresponding sympathy in some of his hearers. In the case of a man who feels a repulsion to such things it will assume a different aspect, and he will inspire his hearers with a feeling as of something odious and revolting. When, therefore, Dumas and his followers try to justify themselves for exhibiting scenes of guilt and brutal passion by the example of Æschylus and the monstrous crimes of Atreus, they wholly forget this distinction. *There* the result is not sympathy but awe, a sense of warning, and the workings of passion are not exhibited, but its evil results. In other words, in a play like " Antony," the spectator himself is brought on the stage in the

* The revolt against decency and propriety, led by Dumas, might dismay even an enthusiast in such matters. A critic took the trouble of examining ten plays of Dumas and Victor Hugo, with the following pleasing results :—Eight of the characters were adulteresses ; five were common "professional" ladies ; six were seduced ; two were confined almost in presence of the audience ; four mothers were in love with their sons or sons-in-law ; eleven persons were murdered ; and in no less than six of these pieces the leading character was either a foundling or a bastard.

shape of the actor, who, he feels, is artfully put forward as a representative of the frail part of human nature; whereas, from guilt and passion, as put before him by the classical writer, he turns·away with dread, thankful that there is a gulf between him and such a spectacle.

But there is another altogether different view as to the *propriety* of exhibiting such scenes on the stage, and whether a serious outrage on public morality is not perpetrated. Ordinary readers would consider this question settled beyond dispute; but it has been urged with some specious argument, that the indirect result of such exhibitions is wholesome, and that, as the stage must find its materials in the manners of the time, it is only acting the part of a faithful looking-glass. This view was put forward some years ago, on the occasion of the production of "La Traviata," and becomes far more serious where the question of state subsidy is involved. In this shape the discussion was raised some forty years ago, on the occasion of the revival of "Antony." It seems ludicrous to think of the Paris public being scandalised at anything offending against a delicate sense of morality; but the Empire had not yet lifted the sewer gates, and allowed the impure stream to flow.

Strange as it may seem to those who have witnessed·
pieces like " Paul Forestier " at the Français, the idea
of introducing perilous stuff like " Antony " into the
course of what was a state school, and applying state
money to set forth and adorn such a specimen of
morality was felt to be an extreme step. That very
day appeared in the *Constitutionnel* a masterly denun-
ciation of the new policy, which in forcible and almost
vehement language sums up all that could be urged
against this abuse of public patronage. The theatre,
it said, received eight thousand a year from the nation.
Such a sum, together with the prestige of its being a
state institution, must lend it an enormous influence for better or for worse. " It ought not to be
degraded from the high position to which the genius
of the great French masters have raised it, to those
grotesque and scandalous exhibitions which are the
shame of our time, shock public modesty, and inflict a
mortal wound on society. There are literally no
bounds now to the excesses of the stage, to the absence
of all decency. Adultery, murder, incest, rape, crime
in its most revolting shapes, these are the elements
of this boasted dramatic era which affects to despise
the true masters of the art, and takes an infernal
pleasure in poisoning every generous sentiment, and
spreading corruption among the people. The great

artists of this theatre should not be forced to lend the aid of their talents to these pernicious works, whose tendency is to degrade public morals, for which the state is responsible. Who would credit that at such a theatre the performance of 'Antony' is announced, the most daringly obscene piece that has appeared in even these days of obscenity, a piece which made a decent father of a family declare, 'For some time we have not been able to bring our daughters to the theatre, now we cannot take our wives!' On a stage hallowed by the memory of Corneille, Racine, Molière, and Voltaire, we are now to see a woman dragged into an alcove with a handkerchief over her mouth.' . . . . The very day for this performance is announced. Here is a proper spectacle with which to school our youth, who will presently acknowledge no restraint! There is no country in the world in which this deliberate corruption by the state would be tolerated.

"All that we ask is, that in this universal decay of manners a single decent theatre be left to which we can take our families. To M. Thiers we make this appeal, in the hope that he will try and save our youth from destruction, already greedy of all kinds of pleasure, soon satiated and weary of life. This appalling phenomenon is really owing to these shocking and exciting spectacles, when the wildest passions are shown in all their unbridled nakedness."

This appeal, admirably reasoned, seemed prophetic in its terms; and when the great "French theatre" began to admit these pieces of a diseased and morbid immorality into its repertoire, such high sanction had their worst effects.

But the result of this vigorous impeachment was instantaneous, and "Antony," revived after three years' interval, was forbidden that very evening in a notice signed "Thiers."

CHAPTER XVI.

"RICHARD DARLINGTON."

1832.

DUMAS would have us believe that "Antony" is a portrait of himself, and of his own emotions at the time. The object of his passion was a lady whose husband was an officer absent on service. "One day she received a letter from him announcing his return. I thought I should go mad. I rushed to one of my friends, who was employed at the War Office. *Three times the officer's leave of absence, duly signed and ready to be sent off, was torn up or burnt by this friend.*" This may be a piece of romance: but that such an idea should suggest itself shows how lamentably confused were the writer's notions of honour and morality. To French audiences such would appear a commendable dramatic incident; and possibly sympathy would be excited for the "beau jeune homme" whom events had driven to such straits, and whose

ardent passion ought to be the excuse for everything.
Indeed the favourite rôle of the young lovers of the
French stage is one of the most discreditable and
treacherous kind, as indeed is well illustrated in the
hero of "Nos Intimes." And this confession of
Dumas shows how social life and the drama act and
react on each other; for here a personal experience,
and which ought at least to have been kept for a
shameful privacy, is transferred to the stage, and in
that enlarged sphere suggests and teaches, fortified by
all the histrionic arts.

The success of Dumas's pieces was so marked that
Thiers, when minister, and whose fierce republican
opinions, foaming through the columns of an opposition
newspaper, office had wonderfully controlled, proposed
that his friend's services should be transferred to the
National Theatre. He addressed him as "my dear
Poet;" the other replying with "my dear Historian."
It is curious to see how the now famous President
exhibited the same busy, active qualities which distinguish him at present. He saw that the theatre
was languishing and old-fashioned, and seemed to
agree with Dumas, who declared the fate of an old
ship of war was in store for it, viz., to become "a
hulk." Dumas must write a new play, and have two
hundred pounds, while Dorval and Bocage should be

engaged to play in " Antony." This was probably due to the importunity of Dumas, and perhaps Thiers hoped that it might conciliate a troublesome member of a party with whom he had been so intimately connected. Otherwise, the idea of saving the Français from becoming an " old hulk," by such a monstrous concatenation of horrors as " Antony," was absurd. The arrangement was concluded, and the play announced for April 28, 1834, only, however, to be forbidden.

On hearing that his play was suspended, Dumas flew to Thiers, who told him that he was forced to take that step by the Chamber, who would not have passed the Budget. He offered a handsome compensation, which Alexander refused to touch, declaring he would appeal to the Courts. However desirable it might be that such pieces should not be represented, there were two awkward incidents connected with this new-born zeal of the Chamber in the cause of morality. The *Constitutionnel* was ridiculed in the piece, while the reporter of the Budget happened to be M. Jay, writer of the bitter Philippic in that journal against the piece. Within two months the cause came on before the Tribunal of Commerce, and the director of the theatre and Dumas himself were invited to explain their case in person to the Court. Dumas related his story—how M. Thiers declared that he was not acquainted with " Antony," though it had been acted some eighty times, but that " Christine" had given him a great deal of pleasure, so much so that he had written a critique of it. Dumas complained bitterly of the injury done to him, and with some justice, for the " run" of his piece had been suddenly stopped, and the play transferred to another house only to be interdicted. " If M. Thiers did not intend making an agreement he should not have sent for me some twelve or fifteen times. *He should not have entered on all these minute matters of detail*, which, in a minister, could only be ridiculous."

It was elicited that the ministry, notwithstanding the subvention, had no right of legal control over the theatre, and this fact seemed to have influenced the judgment of the Court, which was to the effect that the manager's act was mere complaisance to the higher powers which he was under no obligation to extend, and that M. Thiers's interference in the matter was not warranted. It condemned the manager to pay Dumas a sum of 400*l*. by way of compensation, and to see that the play was performed within a limited time. This was a signal victory; and the incident is interesting as showing us that M. Thiers of forty years ago was the same eager, bustling man of business that the President of to-day is—planning everything for himself, and full of ardent schemes.

Those days, however, were not very favourable to the appreciation of dramatic works. There was a fierce turbulence abroad, prosecutions for speeches and banquets, in which Dumas took his part, with some characteristic caution however. His friends still comprised that earnest band of agitators, among whom were to be found Stephen Arago, Garnier Pagès, Godfrey Cavaignac, and Doctor Raspail, names which have since obtained more notoriety. Some of these, who belonged to the dissolved artillery corps, were put on their trial for joining in a daring plot to seize on the Chamber when the members were sitting ; and Dumas naïvely owns that he ought to have been placed at the dock with the rest, instead of being permitted to superintend the rehearsals of his plays. The accused parties were acquitted triumphantly, a victory which was duly celebrated by a banquet. Various toasts of a rebellious character were given, and Dumas was presently called on for a " sentiment." " I never like," he says, " to speak in public, unless under the influence of some exciting passion." Still, on this occasion, he confesses that what he proposed was of rather a colourless kind. " I give you Art ! May both pen and pencil join as efficaciously in that regeneration of society as the sword and musket have done—a regeneration to which we have consecrated our lives, and for which we are ready to lay them down." This had a fierce and uncompromising sound ("nous avons voué notre vie et pour laquelle nous sommes prêts a mourir!") yet it was one which his late royal patron might have drunk without the least compromise of principle. But later in the evening a less careful speaker produced a dagger and mentioned the name of " Louis-Philippe," which produced some sounds of hissing. This disturbed our hero, who frankly confessed that " this went a good deal beyond the limits of my republican theories; and in obedience to a touch from my neighbour, who was one of the actors of the Royal Theatre, I rose and jumped out of the window into the garden. I went home much troubled in mind, for it was plain that the business would have awkward consequences." Relieved by finding that no notice was taken of his part of the transaction, he betook himself to a little mild agitation in reference to the great question of the " Cross of July," the colour of its ribbon, where he was on safe ground. The distribution of this decoration was in the hands of a sort of republican committee, and the history even of this trifling matter gives a strikingly graphic picture of the selfish and imbecile government which at that time oppressed France. These recollections of Dumas help prodigiously in filling in the colours of this ignoble era, and are more effective than an official narrative. He reports one little incident which gives an excellent idea of the feeble counsels which directed the "citizen king." He sent to this committee of the decoration, asking that it might be awarded to him, and had the mortification to receive a refusal, on the ground that he had taken no part in the "glorious days." The aide-de-camp, thus despatched, had to take back a plain refusal. In delight at being able to inflict such a rebuff, they called a meeting of all the *décorés,* who proceeded to elect a committee of fourteen, and Alexander found himself fourteenth and last on the list. A report was adopted, repudiating all inter-ference on the part of the King or of any one else. Although a long discussion took place on the important question of the colour of the ribbon, Alexander, as we might prophesy beforehand, took a prominent part in the settlement of a matter so directly con-nected with *clothes ;* and it is amusingly characteristic to find him urging and carrying a gracious concession on this point. He perhaps fancied it was as important in the King's eyes as in his own. The colour men-tioned in the royal decree was adopted with much opposition, and Alexander " clinched " the matter by a clever ruse, which showed that he knew a good deal of life.   He had brought with him a number of yards of the ribbon, which he drew from his pocket, and with which he proceeded to " decorate" the button-holes of those nearest.   The immediate possession of some inches of gay ribbon was a bait too tempting to be resisted, even at the expense of a principle.   He adds, that " as soon as twenty or so were seen to be thus decorated, an eager desire seized on every one to be thus adorned."   Messengers were sent to procure larger pieces of the ribbon, and within a short time the whole crowd had issued forth wearing the ribbon.   This may be something of the feeling which makes the audience at a conjuror's performance rise up frantically to secure pieces of the pudding which he has " made in a hat," or the bouquets and crackers which he tosses among them ; but it might in truth be accepted as a parable highly significant of the character of the French, who have been so often unable to resist the bit of coloured ribbon which their leaders have dazzled before their eyes.

All this political excitement was unfavourable for literature.   The result was that where 240*l.* had been offered by his booksellers for " Henry III.," and nearly 500*l.* for " Christine," no one would give him a farthing for " Antony."   These riots, he owned, swallowed up too much of his time and money, and he determined to quit Paris, and make a little excursion to the country in search of ideas, as well as of economy. He took with him the hazy conception of a new drama, founded on incidents in the reign of Charles VII. He determined to halt at Trouville, then a little fishing village, and put up at a little inn on the shore, where he was boarded and lodged for one and eightpence a day. His little picture of this retired spot, as it appeared at that time, before the lines of ambitious villas and stately hotels had been built, is charming. In sketching such impressions Dumas is always at his best; and he has an art of touching those delicate though trivial emotions with which many a traveller has been inspired at some unimportant spot, but which seem too trifling to be worth recording. Such airy and careless sketching is more welcome than the sober and official accounts of better-known places. Here he fell in with a friend, who consulted him on an idea for a drama, and proposed that he should take a share in the composition with him and a .third writer, named Gobeaux. The result was "Richard Darlington." "Charles VII." was completed in a few weeks, and he then returned to Paris.

He had now moved from his rooms in the Rue de l'Université, and had taken a third story in the Square d'Orléans, a handsome mansion, in which several of his intimate friends were living. Almost as soon as he arrived, he made an appointment with Gobeaux to talk over the new play; and it may be found interesting to see how the manufacture of a joint stock piece was carried on in the hands of so experienced a playwright. At Trouville, Beudin, the third partner, had come to him with the following sketch :—A man masked and duly mysterious, attended by a lady, arrives at a roadside inn on his way to Dover, and then calls for a doctor to attend the lady, who has been suddenly taken ill : without removing his mask, he confides to the doctor that he is flying with the lady from an angry father, who is in pursuit. This doctor, who is one of those grave, sagacious, and benevolent practitioners found chiefly on the stage, discovers that an accouchement is at hand, and presently has to announce the birth of a boy. The author was diffident as to the effect of this " situation " on an audience, and submitted his doubts to Alexander, who reassured him by the great precedent of Terence, quoting the original Latin.* At this critical moment the father

---

* *Beudin :* " Il y a cela dans Terence ?"
Alex. : " Parfaitement."
Beudin : " Alors nous sommes sauvés."
Alex. : " Je crois bien, c'est du pur classique."
There is something inexpressibly absurd in this trifling, as well as in the idea of two men gravely reassuring each other as to the propriety of a situation, and its fitness for a modern audience, by applying to the authority of Terence.

arrives in hot pursuit. An excited scene follows. The " accouchée " rushes (!) from the adjoining room, and, flinging herself at his feet, protests she will not be separated from her lover. Then the father drags the mask from the latter's face, and bids her stay with him if she will—for he is the common executioner! Such is the prologue ; and the next act, after an interval of five-and-twenty years, exhibits the offspring of this connection grown up, and married to the doctor's daughter. Beyond this Beudin admitted that he had not been able to travel, and Dumas very naturally remarked, that this was little more than the beginning of a play.

In the interval between the consultation and his return to Paris, Alexander had thrown this prologue into shape, and furnished suitable dialogue. The whole of this singular prologue was not indeed original; and the English reader will recognise one of the most effective scenes in the " Chronicles of the Canongate." But this, on Dumas's theory of "dramatic instinct," *viz.*, that the discovery or " prospecting " what is fit for the stage is equivalent to creation, makes very little difference.

The story, however, had not much advanced. The young man, grown up and married to the doctor's daughter, was to become ambitious, and, seduced by

the prospect of an aristocratic alliance, was to plot
how he was to get rid of his lawful wife. Still this
was not making much progress. " As Gobeaux made his
various suggestions, I was busy picking up and winding
together the various threads, and within the hour I had
a plot roughly blocked out."   This "blocking out"
was done after Dumas's own peculiar way, *i. e.*, by
diligent turning over the leaves of the pocket dramatic
dictionary which he carried in his brain. " A divorce
scene between Richard and his wife struck my fancy
prodigiously." Why ? Because there was a scene in
Schiller, between Philip II. and Elizabeth, on the same
subject, which could be cleverly worked into the situation. There were the same relations and motives ; it
was treated by a great tragic master, and was then
ready to be transferred bodily. A further difficulty
was then started. How was the wife to be disposed
of ? Poisoned ? Alexander objected that this would
not answer, as the deed was to be done at a moment
of desperation, when there was no time for a deliberately planned scheme. The dagger would not do, as
it would be too like " Antony." Dumas allowed his
friend to exhaust himself in devices, and then revealed
the only natural mode of murder which flowed from
the situation, *viz.*, to fling her out of the window.

The other laughed at the idea. Dumas bade him

wait until he had worked out the plan. Let him see; this was Monday: on Thursday they would dine together, and the whole would be finished.* "I went home, running all the way. I went to bed. At this time I always wrote my plays in bed." He had before explained how this practice of composition might, perhaps, be considered accountable for the "brutality" which characterised his works. But when he came to write the critical passage where the lady was flung out of the window, he had to stop. He could get no further than the speech of Richard to her: "Hush! Silence! (*clapping his hand on her mouth*) Do you hear them? They are coming upstairs. If they find a woman here——" It was impossible to get on. The man would have to drag his wife to the window; she would struggle. Then how to get her over the balcony? Her feet would be exposed, and the galleries titter. He tried it in every way, and could find

---

* Dumas glorifies his own powers of composition after his own characteristic way :—

Friend : "What! going already?"

Dumas : "I must begin to work. There is not much time to spare between this and Thursday."

Friend : "You won't forget the character of Thompson?"

Dumas : "Don't be afraid. I have him down. When we get to the scene where Mawbray kills him, we shall furnish him with a death worthy of Shakspeare."

Friend : "What! Mawbray is to kill him?"

Dumas : "You have no objection? Then he is a dead man."

no issue ; spent fifteen days in the fruitless task, until he was reduced to despair. His friend persecuted him with letters and requests, urging the completion of the task ; but no solution of the difficulty appeared. At last, one night, he leaped out of bed with the cry of " Eureka !"—lit a candle, and hurriedly wrote. " By Jove," he said, when he had done, " it was as simple as Columbus's egg. There was no struggle—no risk of the lady's exhibiting her garters, while her husband was still to fling her from the window. After the words, ' If they find a woman here,' Richard rushes to the door and fastens it : his wife runs out on the balcony and cries for help ; he pursues and seizes her ; a noise is heard at the door, when he suddenly closes to the two leaves of the window, thus shutting himself out from the view of the audience. A shriek is then heard, and, in a moment, Richard bursts open the window with a blow, and is seen standing there— pale, wiping his brow, and alone !" This device, com- pared with the mode originally suggested, is not a bad illustration of the difference between what is dramatic and the contrary.* He sat up all night : by eight

* It indeed furnishes a key to that singular controversy which was carried on a year or two ago in reference to Mr. Tom Taylor's " Joan of Arc," as to the propriety of the heroine being " burnt before the audience." It was contended with justice that there was *no gain* of dramatic effect by exhibiting physical suffering or actual death before

o clock in the morning the whole was written ; and by nine he was with his friend, who admitted the perfect success of the alteration.*

Pieces of this "brutal" kind, so long as the novelty lasted, were like so much dram-drinking for the Parisians. The old academical school, which repaired for subjects to the Greek and Roman history, were still making a frantic struggle to retain possession of the stage of the "Théâtre Français," and the Government, associating the "brutal" subjects with radical doctrines, took their side. These correct pieces were still being forced on the "Français," and Arnault,*

---

spectators. Here the exhibition of a man dragging a woman to a balcony and flinging her over would add no horror to the situation. There would be the possibility of her being saved, as the height might not have been excessive; and even if the flights from above were actually witnessed, just as the monk is thrown from the tower in "Nôtre Dame," we cannot help thinking of the cleverness of the actor who has taken the leap, and of the means supplied below to break the fall. But Dumas' "Eureka" showed how superior is the effect when the purely dramatic is relied on. That reappearance *alone* after the opening of the window, left all to the imagination of the audience, which supplied a descent infinitely more effective than a hundred sensation "headers."

* This veteran champion of legitimacy was alive in 1867, and thus wrote to the editor of "Le Grand Journal:"—" I send you my shilling for four numbers of your magazine, and shall continue to do so if my nerves allow me. Your *enfants terribles* chafe them dreadfully by their blasphemies against Racine and the great age ; by their attacks on the Academy, and their admiration for the execrable verses of the New School. I would give all they have manufactured during these forty years for a single scene] of 'Athalie,' or even for the fourth act of 'Mahomet.' But who knows how to make a verse now ? Certainly not the public, ninety-nine hundredths of the public know nothing about it."

Dumas's old enemy in the "Constitutionnel," was very fortunate in having such productions as "The Guelphs and the Ghibelines" and "Pertinax," accorded the honours of a performance, though not of a hearing. We can hardly be surprised at an audience of forty years ago receiving a work on the subject of "Pertinax" with coldness, if not with positive hostility; while "The Guelphs and the Ghibelines" were a disastrous failure, which would not be worth alluding to, but for an amusing exhibition of vexation on the part of the author. He chose to attribute the failure to the neglect of Firmin, the leading actor, who had not studied his part; and this complaint he set forth in a preface to the published piece, dedicated "to the prompter." To him, he says, was owing the existence of the piece. "You, sir, were the real performer in 'The Guelphs,' and each night you played M. Firmin's part. Declaiming while he gesticulated, you may have, indeed, transferred from the 'Shows on the Boulevards' an imitation of that grotesque performance, where an invisible speaker and a silent gesticulator combine their exertions in one part. But still nothing could vanquish the sluggish nature of the actor, which affected the whole performance. When a number of vessels sail in a convoy, their speed must be regulated by the powers of the slowest."

It will be seen that this gentleman had some wit, and the only wonder is that he did not spare a little for his pieces. Yet, after this admitted failure, another piece, by the same "eminent hand," was at once brought forward, as some consolation. This was "Pertinax" (which some persisted in calling "Le Père Tignace"), and in which the Emperor "Commode" and his secretary, &c., figured. Alexander and his friends were present on the first night, and one may imagine, he says, the "gaiety" of the house, as these ancient characters passed before them—a gaiety to which Alexander himself contributed. When the Emperor "Commode" called for his "secrétaire," Alexander could not resist saying to an enthusiastic partisan of the author's who was before him, "Secrétaire! Commode! this seems to be a *chest-of-drawers* kind of piece." No notice was taken of this sally; but, at the end of the piece, the partisan led off some vociferous cries for the author, in which, however, no one seemed inclined to join him. A regular struggle arose between the friends and enemies of the piece, in which the latter were having the advantage, when the gentleman to whom Alexander had communicated his jest turned round, and denounced him as the instigator of the tumult. There was probably some justice in this charge, as Dumas owns that the author

had " cut " him, jealous of the success of " Henri III."
His presence, therefore, at " Le Père Tignace " could
scarcely have been accounted for by a disinterested
love of the drama. A violent altercation ensued, and
the following day the newspapers described this scene,
dwelling, he says, " with their usual impartiality,
truth, and good-nature " on his share in the transaction. He addressed a reply to the " Journal de
Paris," which begins with the account of a " firm
resolution " he had made " never to take any notice
of what the papers said of him. It was probably
the last time he would have to do so." This amusing declaration was to be expected from one of the
most inveterate letter-writers of the day.* He explained how the matter was, appealing in corrobora-
tion of his statement to Victor Hugo, who sat beside
him. He then went back to a long and minute
account of the way *he* had been treated in reference
to his " Henri III.," and, in conclusion, declared that
he merely attended these " first nights " in quality of
a " student of art ; " yet that he was always having
quarrels of this kind fastened on him,—he had had
no less than three on hand lately ; so he asked respect-

---

* The absurdity of such an announcement struck him ; but his justification is as amusing. " *Like Bonaparte* on the 15thVendémiaire, I little
foresaw the destiny before me."

fully, what was he to do? The newspaper strongly advised him, as a sure remedy, not to "offer any provocations that would challenge attack." It then, ironically, congratulated the young author on his modesty and retiring disposition, and counselled him, if, in spite of such dispositions, "natural, no doubt, to his character," people persisted in picking quarrels with him, there was still one course open—"to refrain from attending ' first performances.' " But this advice, Alexander confesses, it was impossible to follow. " I was too young, my heart too near my head, and I had too much curiosity to deny myself the pleasure of attending on these first nights. I have since got over this little malady, but it took time; moreover, it was not time that cured me, but *the first nights themselves.*" Any true playgoer will, indeed, sympathise with this early relish for the excitement of a "first night," and still more with the exquisite enjoyment to be found when some solemn and earnest platitude, meant to be serious, only produces merriment.*

There was another "first night," which, during later

---

* One of these victims, Latouche, had written a piece on the strange subject of Charles II. of Spain "not having an heir," and which caused unbounded amusement. The author published his piece, with "defence," and with notes of the following character:—"At this passage there were sounds of coughing;" "Here there were murmurs;" "Loud laughter;" "'Oh! oh's!' kept up for a long time. Interruptions;" "Here the sentence was divided by a disgusting remark."

years, Dumas could not bring himself to attend—that
of his own pieces.   He had not yet adopted the
custom, for he had not made enough enemies to make
the probation disagreeable, and his pieces were sure of
success.   He would wait at home, and rely for bulle-
tins on the kindness of friends.

"Richard Darlington" was fixed for the 10th De-
cember, 1832, and was performed to a house crowded
to the roof.   "The last scene," says Alexander, mo-
destly, "was one of the most terrible things I have
ever seen on the stage.   When his wife asked him
what he was about to do, and he answered, 'I know
not,—but say your prayers at once,' a great shudder
passed over the audience, and a murmur of fear issu-
ing from every bosom became worked up into a
regular cry of terror."   He, however, affected to repudiate all responsibility as to the authorship, taking his
seat among the audience as "a mere stranger."   The
manager, as the excitement increased, implored him
to let his name be announced, and later on came
again, accompanied by the two authors, with notes
for 120*l.* in his hands, the two authors adding that
he had written it all.   But Dumas was inflexible.
"I embraced them, but refused.   I had tears in my
eyes."   When the curtain fell to frenzied applause,
he rushed behind the scenes to greet the actors, meet-

ing on his way Alfred de Musset, who was, of course,
" very pale " and agitated. "What ails you, my dear
poet ? " "Nothing ; *I am only choking,*" was the
reply. " This was," adds Dumas, " the very highest
praise he could give it, for the play *is* really a choking
one." Still, though congratulating the artists, he did
not feel the same emotion as he did in the case of the
other artists—Bocage and Dorval. " Between me and
Mademoiselle Noblet," who played the heroine, " pretty,
attractive, as she was at this time, there existed merely
relations based upon art; she only interested me
as a young and pretty person, with a hopeful career
before her." This handsome acknowledgment is most
entertaining, and it may be imagined what a source of
amusement a person of such candour must have been
during a long life to the sharp observers of Parisian
society.

CHAPTER XVII.

REVUE DES DEUX MONDES.

THOUGH Dumas had been so far successful in his works for the stage, he felt that this was but a precarious means of support. Dramatic composition had not yet been raised into a certain and opulent means of support ; and the brilliant example of Scribe, who is, perhaps, the unique instance of enormous and unflagging production, combined with an even excellence that never failed, had not given certainty and recognition to the author's profits. But the writer of grand tragedies and romantic melodramas has few opportunities compared with the producer of comedies and light vaudevilles ; and Dumas naturally thought he might find some success in the direction where so many of his friends had tried their powers, *viz.*, writing romance or history.

About this time, Alexander was about twenty-nine, " ardent in pleasure, ardent in love, ardent in

life, ardent in everything but hatred." In this department he could be tolerably "ardent" also. He, indeed, says that he may have exhibited dislike in his
writings, but it was only directed against those " who
in art opposed what was noble, and in politics what
was progress." These fine words, "art and progress,"
might be taken without ill nature to mean the art and
personal progress of Alexander Dumas ; and it is exactly where these are interfered with that his hostility
always breaks out. He had, as we have seen, published a volume of short stories, of which six copies
were sold. One of those, he says, fell into the hands
of one Buloz, who saw in it evidence of some talent,
and thus, as it will be seen, the venture which cost
him, or rather his poor mother, so much was not
thrown away.

This Buloz was a remarkable man, and his name
will be known to those who are familiar with even the
cover of the most literary journal in Europe. He had
been a common printer, was silent and rough in his
manners, but one of those plain men of business who
without knowledge of literature can still administer
it.* A languishing review, which had been started by
Dumas's friend Adolphe de Leuven, had been purchased

* The reader will find some characteristic anecdotes of Buloz in the
Grand Journal of 1867.

by him and two or three others, and, the title changed, was forthwith issued as the now famous " REVUE DES DEUX MONDES."   When it is considered that this miscellany, containing a store of the profoundest criticism, historical research, graceful romance, with a review of public affairs, of music, the drama, and literature, has been issued in a substantial form every fortnight, with only a single interruption ; that it is distinguished by surprising candour, a judicial fairness, which even in England has never been approached ; that it has trained a school of thinkers and elegant writers, historians, political economists, and novelists ; that it has produced observers like Esquiros and Maxime de Camp, publicists like De Broglie and Forcade de la Roquette, critics like Montegut, Scudo and Fiorentino ; that romance writers of the class of About and George Sand are its diligent contributors—with such high claims it may fairly be considered the leading literary journal of Europe.   It is truly cosmopolitan, it is read in every corner of the globe ; its pink wrapper imparts colour to the strewn tables of statesmen and literary men all the world over. Its existence, supported with very little effort, is the best evidence of the high state of culture in France.   In England an attempt was made to launch such an undertaking, and under fair auspices, but the strain was found too great, and it was ·proved that the light touch or abundant variety necessary to keep such an undertaking afloat was wanting.

The proprietor offered Dumas a place in his journal, and the latter then furnished an account of his travels in La Vendée. This led him to the subject of the history of Burgundy; the heroes and heroines of which, at least such glimpses as he could obtain of them, seemed to have extraordinary interest. "The figures of the haughty and guilty Isabella of Bavaria, and the blasé face of Louis of Orleans, the terrible figure of Jean of Burgundy, the pale and poetical one of Charles VII., Ile Adam with his sword, Tanneguy Duchatel and his axe, De Giac and his horse, Bois Bourdon and his gold-laced jerkin, Perinet Le Colere and his keys," all this rose before him; that is to say, he saw them on the stage, with the footlights flaring on their faces, and the "wings" at either side. It was this curious theatrical instinct that led him to the dusty folios of history, which, as he would have us believe, he consulted, but which he troubled as little as he did the painted volumes in a library scene on the stage. Light personal memoirs of the more scandalous sort were the authorities which he relished and consulted. It was thus that he conceived the idea of presenting the whole history of France in this theatrical shape—the figures, dresses, and conversation, an idea that he carried out later himself, or by deputy. He had the example of Walter Scott always before him, but owned, that as yet, he did not feel strong enough to give historical romances like that master of fiction. But he had formed his plan of giving what was neither romance nor pure history, but something between. This he later attempted on a large scale. Such a system of presenting the dresses and scenery of history, however entertaining for the moment, is found to be but a poor substitute for real historical inquiry.

Turning his thoughts, then, to the history of Burgundy, he furnished to the *Revue* some scenes in the life of Isabel of Bavaria, which, he says, was one of the first articles that attracted attention to the journal. It was while he was writing these pages that he pleasantly confessed to the discovery that he possessed "gaiety of style" and wit. At the same time this style of composition revealed to him that he had some other gifts—viz., that of dialogue and narrative. "These qualities," he says, "and all the world knows with what careless candour I speak of myself, I possess in a remarkable degree." There is no vanity in this little confession, for in these qualities he is really unsurpassed ; and it is most natural that this sort of historical commentary, and what is called in the slang of our day " word painting," should have developed in him of a sudden an agreeable fluency and gaiety of remark. Indeed, his little analysis shows that he had a very fair knowledge of character. " Generally people are gay because they are well, have a good stomach, and nothing to grieve about. But I have that sort of steady gaiety which can override not so much grief as little annoyances and even small dangers. Again, a man who is gay by nature and full of spirit is often dull and heavy when he sits down to his desk. Now hard work only stimulates me, and my brightest fancies have often originated in my cloudiest days." He frankly owns that about this time he was *posèing* after Byron and Goethe, and that he affected a sort of fasionable gloom. His friend Oudard had received a letter from him asking him to help Lassailly, an intimate friend of Dumas. The appeal was meant to be serious, but a sort of gaiety pervaded it. The client read it. " How funny," he said, " why, my dear boy, I *declare you have wit !*" This compliment put Dumas on a discovery which was of vast service to him ; and his gossiping " Impressions " was the first thing that let the public into the secret.

CHAPTER XVIII.

THE TOWER OF NESLE.

1832.

In the year 1832, it will be remembered, the cholera made its terrible progress over Europe. Paris had been watching its progress with much uneasiness, and fondly hoped that it would pass by the City of Pleasure. When it reached London they might fairly tremble. Dumas remembered the morning when the news went round that it had arrived. It was a lovely day; the sun shining, the sky of a sapphire-like blue. Never did the Tuileries gardens look more beautiful; and, what seemed to Dumas a higher charm than the attractions of nature, it was literally enamelled with lovely women. There was a lull in the political riots, and the theatres were once more begining to excite interest.

"Suddenly, a cry arose—a cry that recalled the terrible voices read of in the Scriptures — 'The cholera! A man has just died in the Rue Chauchat!'

At once everything was changed; the gay loungers were seen hurrying through the streets, flying home to shut themselves up, cying, 'The cholera! the cholera!' just as they used to cry, 'The Cossacks!'"

It is characteristic of the nation that this terrible scourge could not be accepted as other nations accepted it—without its being made use of for wretched political ends. It was given out, on placards affixed to the walls, that the Government had poisoned not merely the fountains but the meat in the butchers' shops and the wine sold in the public-houses. The Government were glad to lay the concoction of these odious charges to the account of the "enemies of order"—that is, of the opponents of Government. These miserable accusations were fiercely bandied to and fro, and unfortunate men were hunted through the city and torn to pieces as poisoners, by people stimulated by these indecent placards. "Who could ever forget Paris at this time, with its steady blue sky, its mocking sun, its deserted Boulevards. The theatres seemed like huge vaults." Few cared to go to the play, twelve or fourteen pounds being often all that was "in the house."* The lively Harel, finding his

* Once, indeed, at the "Odéon," the audience consisted of a single spectator, who refused to take back his money, and insisted on the play going on. The actors were obliged, by the law, to act, but it may be guessed they "did their worst," and the audience hissed. The

house deserted, and the new piece " Ten Years in the Life of a Woman," neglected, put the following singular advertisement in the papers :—

" It has been noticed, with much astonishment, that the theatres are literally the only places—no matter how crowded—*where not a single case of cholera has appeared.* We leave this fact—and we defy contradiction—to the investigation of the scientific."

At this time the affairs of our hero were scarcely flourishing. The grand receipts of " Henri III." had ceased to flow in ; or rather his extravagance had drained his purse. He speaks of a modest little ordinary, where he would meet his friends and dine for a few sous. He still lived in the Orleans Square, and every day saw some fifty or sixty funerals trailing by to the burying-ground of Montmartre. Yet with this cheerful diurnal prospect, he could write what is in truth the gayest of all his pieces, " The Widow's Husband," (" Le Mari de la Veuve,") full of delightfully-humorous little situations, set off, not with epigrammatic, but with lively and witty dialogue.

A clever young actress, Dupont, belonging to the Français, came to call on him, and as it so chanced, on

manager, a man of wit, gave him in charge to the police " for disturbing the performance," which his single note of disapproval would do.

the very day, March 29, that news that the cholera was in the city got abroad. Her benefit night was fixed, and she came with a request for a little original scene for the occasion. This was Saturday, and the benefit was to be on the Tuesday or Wednesday following; so there was not much time to spare. He promised, if she could give him an entire week, to furnish her with what she required. He set to work on the following day, and had got to the third or fourth scene, when the maid came rushing in with the fatal news of the arrival of the cholera. The man in the Rue Chauchat who had been seized was dead only an hour, yet was already as black as a negro.* He wrote at once to the actress, who, however, wished him to proceed.

The great Mars was to take the leading character; but when it was performed the cholera had begun to rage—as our author says, " was competing with them." There were not five hundred persons present. As one of the reports described it: " No theatre ever presented such a disastrous aspect as the Français did on the occasion of the benefit. The whole city was in a panic; there was confusion in the streets, and the drums were

---

* It has been noticed how Dumas was always coming back to this favourite allusion. It seems to have a fascination for him. He was, indeed, furnished with so little delicacy, that he probably fancied that by this broad allusion he was diverting attention from a favourite topic of raillery.

actually beating as the doors opened. It may be imagined few playgoers were courageous enough to inhale camphor and chloride in such a desert." The author was not named—merely designated as " M. * * *," though it was well known to be the work of Dumas.

He could on this occasion put his principles in practice, and be as gay as possible; and he was to live to find the piece thus coldly received become a stock piece at the Français. Whenever that inimitable company wishes to recreate its audience with something diverting and elegantly gay, it brings forth some such piece as this. Dumas did not allow his spirits to flag, and gathered his friends about him at his rooms, striving to keep away the thought of the dreadful scourge raging outside. There came Hugo, Boulanger, and Listz, who thumped away at a wretched piano, while Hugo occasionally recited his verses. Thus they laughed and sang, and supped together, and agreed that, with reasonable precaution they must escape the cholera; five hundred deaths a day out of a million was only a small percentage; &c. But one night, when he was lighting his friends down, after calling to them from the top of the stairs, "Au revoir!" he felt a curious trembling in his legs, and had to catch the bannister to support himself. His servant met him as he entered : " Lord, sir ! how pale you are." "Nonsense, Catherine." "Look in the glass, sir." He did, and was astonished to find his face of a ghastly white. He was quivering all over. "How odd, Catherine," he said, "I feel like ice." "That's the way it comes on, sir," she answered. "What comes on?" "The cholera!" "Run, then; don't lose a moment; get a lump of sugar and some ether." He had just strength to totter to his bed, where he was presently lying trembling and shaking, while the girl ran out crying, " The cholera! Heavens, he has got the cholera!" In her fright she brought him a whole tumbler of ether, which he swallowed at a gulp. "The effect was," he says, "as though he had swallowed the sword of the destroying angel."

Dumas's "gaiety," like that of his countrymen, at times expends itself in a sort of reckless profanity. When the doctor was trying to restore warmth by hot vapour steaming, the patient's comment is "*Je ne sais ce quil adviendra de moi en enfer*, mais je n'y serai jamais plus près d'être roti que je ne le fus cette nuit-là." However, he had a strong constitution, was successfully treated, and battled through. When he was getting to be convalescent, he received a visit from his friend, the manager Harel. "What do you say about the cholera, now?" "It has gone away—

didn't make its expenses. Ah! my *dear* friend, now is the time for a good piece; there is a regular reaction in favour of the theatres setting in." He then opened his plans.

A young writer from Tonnerre, called Frederick Gaillardet, had brought him a piece on the subject of the "Tower of Nesle" and Margaret of Navarre. It was a rude and crude production, written without knowledge of the stage; but there was a good idea in the piece, which could be made a good deal of. He had handed it over to Jules Janin, who had re-written some of it, but had grown disgusted, and had returned it. Dumas must take the "idea" and make a "regular drama of the whole in his own spirited style." Ill as he was, the manager was so pressing, and, as Dumas always conveys to us on these occasions, so complimentary, that he at last agreed. The manuscript was sent, and Dumas began to read it. He saw at once that it would never "do," that the idea was there, but that the whole was treated coarsely. He was fascinated by the story, and determined to rewrite this drama himself according to his notions of treatment.

The whole of this Gaillardet incident made a great commotion at the time, and it becomes important to consider it in some detail, as it throws light upon the great "Dumas system." It must be said that his share in the matter will be found to have been scarcely honourable. The attempt to rob a young writer of the reputation and profit from his work could not be justified, but more discreditable was the garbled account which our ingenious author gives of the transaction.

The work was duly finished, and the result was a powerful play, which, as most readers know, turns on a queen giving her many lovers appointments in a gloomy tower, then having them thrown over into the river, until she is baffled by Buridan, a man of determined character, whom she has decoyed into the castle.

One of the most original ideas in dramatic literature is to be found in the " prison scene," and he says it had long been floating on his mind. It is that of a man confined in a cell, for whom there is no hope of being saved from death, and whose enemy comes to insult and taunt him. The prisoner, by sheer *intellectual force*, either by fear, by argument, or wit, overcomes the other, and is set free. Long after, Dumas treated this very situation in his novel " Vingt Ans Après," and it is not too high praise to say there is no more dramatic passage to be found than this scene, in which a mysterious lady tempts the officer who is charged with the duty of guarding her, and who is won over by her seductions, to set her free. In this sort of *mental struggle* and psychological movement, the most absorbing motive of interest in the drama, Dumas is excellent ; and even in his dialogue, where the interest concerned is trifling, he piques curiosity by little surprises of interest and small struggles. When the piece was finished, it was arranged that it should appear under the name of the young author, who was also to enjoy the whole of the author's rights, namely, about two pounds a night, with sixty tickets, which could be sold. These perquisites were not to be divided ; the young man was to have the whole. The self-denying Dumas wrote to the young author a singular letter to tell him of these arrangements. He said that the manager had consulted him in reference to "his play." He had given his views with pleasure, " delighted to introduce to the stage a young *confrère,* whom I have not the pleasure of knowing, but whose success I warmly desire. I have smoothed away all the obstructions that might seriously interfere with the success of a first work, and really, your piece as it now stands seems to me very likely to prove a success. It is hardly necessary for me to say that you are to be the sole author, and that my name is not to be mentioned. This little service you must allow me to offer you, and not to sell you." This letter proves conclusively that Dumas did no more than " correct " the piece and prepare it for the stage, just, in fact, what a clever stage manager would do. But the author did not accept this gracious patronage. Dumas bitterly complains that no notice was taken of his handsome letter. Gaillardet had just arrived in town, and flew straight to the manager. He seems to have been a young man of spirit and determination. He told the manager he would have no help and wanted none. It was *his* piece, and should be played as he wrote it. The manager, a cool, unscrupulous man, told him he was quite right, but that there was no help for it. He *had* been badly treated. He might go to law, and the courts would decide with him ; but the piece was in rehearsal ; they would change the name, and he would be " done." He saw this, and had to submit. It was *then*, though Alexander does not tell us so, that the magnificent letter was written, and Gaillardet found it on his table when he got home, evidently with a view of soothing his irritation.* It is quite plain that the arrangement between the manager and Dumas was to be the same as the one in the case of the " Napoleon," and other pieces. Some poor drudge or raw youth furnished a good piece, which the popular

---

* Neither does Alexander tell us that the young author had written to him before, protesting against this imposed collaboration.

writer was to touch up and manipulate. He was to have the chief profit, and also the credit. There were a crowd of young writers who would be delighted to be allowed to work on such terms; but the scheme in the present instance was frustrated by this impetuous young fellow.

After all, he was to have the profits. Alexander said he hoped to be allowed to offer him this service gratis—not to sell it. But before the piece came out, a new Law had been made regulating authors' profits; awarding to them ten per cent. of the receipts, a sum allotted to Dumas by a private treaty between him and the manager. This would give him twelve or fourteen pounds a night, instead of the miserable two allotted to the real author's share.

The young man, therefore, could be no match for these two *rusé* Parisians. He was helpless, and the piece was nearly ready; so he was forced to accept the situation, being solemnly assured—1st, that Dumas's name was not to appear; 2ndly, that he, Gaillardet, was to be the *sole* author; and 3rdly, that Dumas's aid was to be gratuitous.

The piece, as is well known, caused a *furore* on its first representation. Dumas took all the honours of its paternity. He dined with Odilon Barrot, and brought him and his wife—" then a young and lovely creature, ever witty and full of original wit "—to the theatre. He was on thorns to get away from table.[*] Tableau succeeded tableau ; it was all " terrible, men and women trembling and pale with excitement," as he loves to describe it. " Success was in the very air." " Something of the ancient fatalism of Sophocles was present, mingled with the scenic terrors of Shakspeare." The " great tribune," Odilon Barrot, was " stupefied " to find that emotion could be carried to such a point. The manager saw that there was here a great success for his house, and flew to Dumas to implore him to allow himself to be named. But Dumas was firm. The piece was destined to be played eight hundred times. This prestige and glory he determined to sacrifice. He held firm, and, amid tumultuous applause, M. Frederick Gaillardet was proclaimed the sole author.

The most curious feature in Dumas's character is his want of delicacy, and in his defence on this occasion, his dull insensibility to the real point involved. Looking always to profit, and considering the person who receives the money for a book to be the real

---

[*] " The great tribune, her husband, could not understand any one being so impatient to see a first performance." Dumas is always insinuating these *bonnes fortunes*, even if he dare not do more.

author, he seems to wonder at the discontent of
Gaillardet, and really not to understand why he
should be so anxious for mere prestige. Did he not
obtain his tickets and his two pounds a night ? What
more could he desire ? But now we approach an even
more doubtful stage of the transaction.

There was not an intelligent person in the theatre,
says Dumas, that did not recognise his touch, his
masterly situations at every turn of the drama. But
the agreement with the " young man," as he persisted
in styling him, to the " young man's " annoyance,
was not to be got over. The manager, however, was
far less scrupulous, and he, seeing during the night
what a run was in store for the piece, coolly announced
the piece in the newspapers of the next morning as
" by MM. * * * et Gaillardet." Every one would, of
course, know who the three stars stood for. He went
to the manager to protest. He found him chuckling
over the business. " My dear sir, we shall have a
tremendous success. All we wanted was a little scandal.
Gaillardet will make a noise—there we have it. At
all events, he'll then have *done something to the piece.*"
" Now, Harel "—said the other. " You are delightful,"
continued the manager ; " what ! you think you can
write masterpieces, and then say, ' Not my work ! '
Get along ! All Paris shall know it, whether you like

it or not." At this moment a writ was brought in, summoning the manager to appear before the tribunal to show cause why he should not remove the stars. The manager rubbed his hands in delight. "An action!—the very thing!—I only ask two of them a year for half a dozen years, and my fortune is made! As for you, you'll be brought before the court—the three stars—the MS.—your name—mine—Janin's! My dear friend, I really did not expect a run of a hundred nights. Now I would back myself for two hundred."

There presently appeared a letter of Gaillardet's in the papers, which ran :—

" Sir,—Announced yesterday in the theatre as the sole author of the 'Tower of Nesle,' I find my name in the bills of to-day preceded by a ' Messrs. ' and by three stars. This is a mistake or trick, of which I do not intend being the victim or the dupe. At all events, you will oblige me by announcing what I trust will appear upon the bill of to-morrow, that I am the sole author of the ' Tower of Nesle.' "

The manager at once answered this letter :—

" Sir,—My reply to M. Gaillardet's extraordinary letter is simply this. The piece, in style and composition, certainly for nineteen-twentieth's, is the work of a celebrated writer who, for certain reasons notwithstanding this remarkable success, does not wish his name to appear. Of M. Gaillardet's original work little or nothing is left. A comparison of the piece as played with M. Gaillardet's MS. will prove this."

The answer to this audacious statement was Dumas's own letter, already quoted, and which stated that he had merely " helped," and had smoothed away some rough places. " I confess," says Dumas, " the appearance of this letter astonished me." He at once wrote an answer. All his " delicacy " had been thrown away. But this want of appreciation forced him to tell a secret which would no doubt be highly disagreeable to M. Gaillardet. This was, that he had never even seen M. Gaillardet's MS., and that he had worked entirely without reference to it. In other words, he revealed Janin's share in the matter. But the answer to this was, that Janin's alteration was very slight, consisting chiefly in the language, and this is admitted by Dumas himself. In conclusion, he suggested that the various MSS. should be compared, and then would be seen how they differed. The Court, however, decided at once that the three stars should be removed from their place and put last, Gaillardet receiving the due honours of the authorship. Knowing the fancy of our author for money, this attempt has rather an awkward air; for by this coupling of names, Dumas actually took half of the miserable two pounds a night and the allowance of tickets; this, too, besides his ten per cent. on the receipts. Never was a poor young writer so jockeyed. When the play was to be disposed of to the booksellers, Barba agreed to give twenty pounds for it; of which ten pounds were to be paid then and the rest in six months; each was therefore to receive five pounds in cash. When poor Gaillardet called for his pittance he found that the great man had been there before him, and had carried off all the cash, adjourning him to the *credit* settlement of the transaction. This was trickery, to say the least. Finally, in defiance of all protests, Dumas, when collating his works, inserted this piece (which was played under the author's name) with no name but his own on the title! It would take long to unfold all the shifts that appeared in this business—the statements which the manager and his secretary and friends put forward, and which were shown to be untrue. The young writer published a summary of the chief points and incidents of his piece, and established conclusively his claim to the authorship.

The piece had been running for some two years—

not night after night, according to the modern fashion
—but with judicious intervals, so as not wholly to
shut out those who had seen it from the theatre, and
the dispute between the parties had become em-
bittered.   The indefatigable young author could fight
his own battle with spirit, and actually summoned
Dumas before the "Committee of Authors."   No
less than six decisions were given by the Courts, all
adverse to Dumas.   After two years the public began
to forget the dispute, when it was revived again
by an allusion of Gaillardet's in a periodical.   This
called out angry and recriminating letters on both
sides ; correspondence thus wound up by Gaillardet :—
"Do you know, M. Dumas—you, who affect to
treat me as if I was some *poor devil*—the sort of
answer I ought to make you ?   But I have too much
politeness to tell you."   He then speaks of "disgrace,"
"apostasy," "shame," using other complimentary
words.

This indignant *exposé* of Dumas's behaviour was
so cutting and so damaging that only one sort of reply
could be sent.   This was a challenge ; and a duel
was fixed for October 17, 1834.   Alexander had a
strange objection to pistols in such affairs, but as his
opponent had the choice of weapons, he had no alternative.   By a singular arrangement, it was agreed

that they should draw lots for seconds, and two intimate friends of Dumas's—Soulié and Fontan—found themselves obliged to act for Gaillardet. Dumas, who was pressing that swords should be the weapons employed, wished to prove that this preference was not from feeling himself at any disadvantage, and took the following characteristic mode of doing so. He actually took the two seconds of his adversary—and his own bosom friends—to a shooting-gallery the evening before the duel, to give them a specimen of his skill. "Let me have ten balls, Philip," he said to the boy of the place, and landed four of them in a circle round the little figure in the centre of the target. "With the fifth I smashed the figure itself; the sixth I threw on the ground, and with the seventh sent it spinning. At the same moment a sparrow perched on a chimney, and I killed it. *Fontan and Soulié looked at each other.*" Well they might; for he had, of course, satisfactorily proved that he was a good shot at an *inanimate* target. Being men, however, who had fought duels themselves, they understood how valueless it was as a test of aim in the Bois de Boulogne, and what bad taste it was on the part of their friend to invite them to witness such a proceeding. They might suspect, as others must have done, that he hoped they

would report to their principal what a deadly adversary he would have to encounter, and that he had
better be wise and withdraw, or else adopt swords.
With a young provincial and a skilled swordsman,
such as Dumas was, a few passes, and perhaps a
scratch or two would decide the matter, without
danger to the honour of all concerned; whereas pistols
placed the experienced and inexperienced too dangerously on an equality.   But Gaillardet had shown
that he was not to be trifled with, and this demonstration of shooting had no effect whatever on him.
Dumas evidently thought the matter looking serious,
for he spent the night in writing some twenty letters,
all directed to his mother—a good lady, whom he
seems to have neglected on less romantic occasions.
Like most of his brother Frenchmen, he made effective use of "ma mère" when a theatrical opening
occurred.   It so happened that he, with Fontan, the
second of Gaillardet, was on the eve of starting
for Rouen, whither they were going as a deputation
to represent the dramatic authors on the inauguration
of a statue of Corneille.   His mother knew he was
going on a journey, and her son took the trouble of
composing and dating these twenty letters from
various towns in Italy, so that she might believe he
was alive for some time, and the matter be gradually

broken to her. With a true eye to business, he used this dramatic notion in one of his plays ; for it will be remembered how Chateau Renaud, when forced to fight *his* duel, says to his friend : " Mongiron, write to my mother, and tell her that I have fallen from my horse ; in a week that I am dangerously hurt ; in a fortnight that I am dead, &c."

When his two seconds arrived, they found him asleep. " The business," he said, " was to go on" (*l'affaire tenait toujours*), an odd remark in the challenger, which suggests Bob Acres, and his " we won't iun." They were to breakfast at the Café des Variétés. Englishmen, when duels were in vogue, went out with a quiet composure and seriousness which contrasts with the general flurry of Frenchmen, the breakfasts on their return, &c., and their general bravado. Just as he was leaving the house—and he had the swords with him after all, under his cloak,—he was stopped by a friend with an album, who wished for some verses. Dumas explained his own particular errand, on which the other became only more pressing. " Only think," he said, " how curious it will be for my wife, *should you be killed*, to have the last lines you ever wrote." He yielded, went back, and wrote a few lines.

They reached the ground. Gaillardet arrived in a

regular duelling dress, perfectly black, without a single white speck about him. Decidedly this Gaillardet was a most awkward person for a man of Dumas's disposition to have encountered. Bixio, who attended as surgeon, was condoling with him on this disadvantage, when Dumas seized his arm. "*He has got cotton in his ears*," he said, " I shall hit him in the head." The other congratulated him on his calmness. He again attempted to have swords adopted, then had a franc piece tossed into the air, challenging the other seconds to "call," but no notice was taken of this unbecoming appeal. He insisted on a *procès-verbal* being drawn up of the refusal, which imparted a rather too attorney-like air to the proceedings. The pistol, he says, was then accepted by him as a magnanimous concession. They were placed at fifty paces distance, and at a signal were to advance till within fifteen paces of each other and fire when they pleased. At the signal Gaillardet set off at full speed, and having reached the limit waited there for his opponent, who advanced on him slowly. When the latter had taken a few steps Gaillardet fired and missed. Dumas then made ready, but he found that the other was all cleverly drawn together, his head sheltered behind his pistol and extended arm. Dumas sought in vain for some point, and after some delay fired and missed. He thought that he had hit his enemy, and owns that he felt a spasm of joy at a result, which, at the time, he would have heartily regretted. "Come," he cried, "load again ; let us stay in our places so as to lose no time." But here, he says, the seconds refused to allow the contest to be renewed, on the ground, as stated in the *procès-verbal*, "that they did not think it their duty to forward a struggle that could only end mortally." The parties then left the ground. This extraordinary termination to the affair might seem inexplicable, and there was certainly no reason why the two combatants, who were both willing, should not have been indulged in their wish for another shot. But on reading the *procès-verbal* more carefully, it turns out that there was no objection to this reasonable course, and that M. Dumas had insisted that the combat should *be continued until one or other of the parties should be killed !* The seconds were willing to gratify him with a fair opportunity of shooting, but for so trifling a cause of quarrel they felt that a duel *à mort* was ridiculous. Our grave *farceur*, now clamouring for blood, had protected himself by this ingenious alternative, and it would seem with prospect of success.

It may be imagined what talk, and perhaps laughter, this affair occasioned. Alexander, with the strange vanity that belonged to him, imagined that he had acquitted himself *en héros*, and to the admiration of the public. Soon some other extravagance of the writer caused it to be forgotten. Twenty-five years passed over, a generous mind might have allowed it to be forgotten ; a shrewd and sensible one would wisely have done so. Dumas, however, revived the whole with all the offensive letters, and protesting " that God knew he would not for the world say anything that would rouse the slumbering susceptibilities of M. Gaillardet." He had heard, indeed, that the latter had made a fortune in America, " to my sincere joy," to his still greater joy he had learned that his (Dumas's) books had something to do with that good fortune. Such is *his* retrospect of the affair. Dumas's publishers, however, took care to produce a letter of Gaillardet's, written at a still later period, when the play was being revived. " As you are about reviving the piece," he wrote, to the manager, " I give you full permission, and would ask you at the same time to join with my name that of M. Alexander Dumas, my partner, to whom I am anxious to show that I have forgotten our old disputes, and recollect only our friendly relations of late years, and the important share which his incomparable talent had in the success of ' The Tower of Nesle.' "

These generous words, quite in keeping with his previous behaviour, contrast strangely with the rather shabby behaviour of the other party to the dispute.*

* When Dumas's "Memoirs" were published, the indomitable Gaillardet came forward again, and in an admirable and vigorous letter demolished the pleasant narrative that Dumas had just told. Nearly all the incidents were characteristic of Dumas's "mistakes." Thus the "writ" was served on the manager, not the day after the performance, but nine days later. Gaillardet never wore cotton in his ears in his life. The seconds, Soulié and his friend, voluntarily offered their services to him, and were "not obliged to act for him." He is also able to appeal to the signed depositions of six persons holding important office, who declared that the MS. as read to them and the piece as acted were identically the same.

CHAPTER XIX.

A TOUR.

1832.

BEFORE this dispute was composed, the hot blood of Dumas was to be excited by political troubles. The noisy and turbulent republicans with whom he associated, and whom nothing could satisfy, were eagerly seeking every pretext for a commotion. This was soon found on the occasion of the funeral of Lamarque, an old Bonapartist general. In all disaffected communities the funeral is found to be the most convenient form of protest, and a Government can be harassed more effectually on such an occasion than on any other. This Lamarque had known Dumas's father, had been intimate with the son, and the family had requested the latter to act as director of the solemnities, which gave him a welcome opportunity of again figuring in uniform on a public occasion. The National Guard Artillery had been reorganised on a new footing. All the revolutionary

elements were present in a vast procession, and it
seems to have been arranged that an attempt should
be made at renewing the scenes of July, which had
before been so successful. As the funeral passed
along, it was interrupted by various incidents, which
had nearly led to *émeutes;* but the "commissary" of
the *cortége,* as Alexander dubbed himself, was always
at hand. " I ran forward to find out the cause of the
stoppage. Thanks to my uniform, and to a certain
popularity which always attended me, and, *above all,
to a tricoloured scarf, fringed with gold, which I
wore on my left arm,* the crowd opened before me."
Every moment a murderous riot was on the point
of breaking out. A policeman, in a scuffle with a
man, cut his throat open with his sword, and came
nigh to being torn in pieces ; but he saw Dumas and
his uniform, and rushed to him with the cry, " Oh,
save me ! " and the " commissary," pushing him into
the ranks of the artillery, did save him. When
they got to the bridge where the speech-making was
to commence, Alexander began to feel exhausted and
ready to faint. He had not yet recovered from his
illness, and with some friends he left his duties as
commissary to go and dine at a *café.* While there,
they heard the sounds of musketry, and knew that the
fighting had begun ; then followed the usual street

slaughter, the story of which has been told by Louis Blanc in his "Histoire de Dix Ans." Dumas does not appear to have taken any part, and, indeed, found to his surprise that he had no arms. So he hurried away, not to his own house, or to that of a friend, to procure them, but to the theatre! The director, his friend Harel, wisely refused to supply him with any. But while they were disputing, the mob arrived at the stage door, recollecting the spectacular performance of "Napoleon," and insisted on the stage muskets being distributed. Dumas showed great presence of mind, had thirty of the stage muskets brought down, and by that sacrifice saved the rest of the "properties." He, however, was now anxious to get home to take advantage of the opportunity to exchange his uniform for plain clothes, and contrived to reach his own house. He attended a meeting where was La Fayette and Lafitte, but where, he says, he saw there was nothing to be decided beyond talking. "I passed out," he says, "and this was easy enough, as I was a very unimportant personage and not likely to be missed by any one. My intention was to go to the office of the *National*, but, when I got to the Boulevard, I found that fighting was going on in that direction. Besides, *I was unarmed*, I could hardly stand from weakness, and was burning with fever. I took a cabriolet and was brought home, fainted away on mounting the stair, and was found insensible on the landing. They undressed me and put me to bed." This suggests the constitutional infirmity of Henri Rochefort. After a feverish night he got up, and went out to look for news, "but, not being able to walk, I took a carriage." He went to his friend Arago, who asked him, not unnaturally, "behind what barricade he had passed the night?" "In my bed, unfortunately," was the reply. They then waited the result of a conference, in which it was proposed to send a deputation to the King, either to repudiate the excesses of the night before, or to ask for indulgence now that the riot had collapsed. Alexander and other young men waited in the courtyard to hear the result of the deliberations. He is proud to be able to quote from Louis Blanc, who mentions his share in the proceedings. "When Arago came out from the meeting, he was met by Savary and Alexander Dumas, by a savant and a poet. Both were greatly excited ; and, as soon as they learned what had passed inside, broke out into bitter expostulations, declaring that Paris had only waited for open encouragement to rise, and that the deputies who could thus repudiate the exertions of the people were very guilty in the eyes of their country." This testimonial is satisfactory as to his energetic language ; but it can be seen that his characteristic caution made him unwilling to compromise his interests by joining the violent party. His eyes still fondly wandered to the Court.

As he was sitting at the door of the " Café de Paris," ("I was too weak to stand up," he says), he saw the King go by, shaking the outstretched hands of National Guards, when the following strange reflection occurred to him. "Seeing him pass so calm, and smiling, and indifferent to danger, I felt a sort of bewilderment, and asked myself, if this man, thus greeted so enthusiastically, were not indeed a chosen man, and whether any one had the right to make attempts against a power which God, by ranging Himself on its side, seemed to sanction?" This is significant enough. Still his proceedings had certainly been sufficient to compromise him. One of the newspapers announced that he had been taken fighting in the streets, tried summarily by court-martial, and shot at three o'clock in the morning. He had even given away arms to the mob, and though these were only stage muskets, the authorities would hardly entertain such nice distinctions. He indeed received a warning from an aide-de-camp of the King that the question of his arrest was under discussion, with a friendly hint that he had better travel for a few months until the matter had blown over. This banishment was an awkward result of his inconsiderate and half-hearted meddling with revolt. It was the more awkward as he was busy on a new play for the "Porte St. Martin,"—"Le Fils de l'Emigré,"—which the manager was eager he should finish, promising him 250*l.* for his expenses, if he set seriously to work. Dumas agreed, and sent for his coadjutor, Anicet Bourgeois, " that conscientious labourer and indefatigable searcher." " No one could do his part more handsomely in a joint composition. It was he who had brought me the plan of ' Térésa,' ready made. I supplied him with the idea of ' Angela.' The idea of the ' Fils de l'Emigré ' was his; the execution, especially of the first three acts, was mine. We wrote the last two acts together." * This task accomplished, his eyes turned towards Switzerland, a country he longed to visit. He proposed to a bookseller to write a book of travels, and frankly owns that the bookseller " could not see it." The subject was stale and used up. His doctor, too, declared that his health would be benefited, so that his political and medical advisers enjoined change of scene. He determined to look on the expedition as a sacrifice paid to health,

* Alexander is profuse in these acknowledgments of assistance in his " Memoirs ; " but this was after the *exposé* of his practices.

as time fatally lost so far as pecuniary profit was concerned, and in this frame of mind started on his tour, on July 21, 1832.

His Swiss travels were not very extensive, and he seems to have scarcely left the beaten track. He talked with the guides, saw the *mer de glace*, and related the curious history of the "Bears of Berne," for whose annual support a lady had left a considerable sum. He described the luxury in which these creatures lived, until the French came by during the wars, and carried off the whole sum, which was in specie, and made up of old coins.* He also called on Chateaubriand at Lucerne, and had a very animated conversation with him on politics, which he printed, and saw the great writer feed his poultry. He waited on the ex-Queen—the Duchess of St. Leu, as she was called—at Arenenberg, walked with her in the garden, where he remained for some moments, his face covered up in his hands, while he reflected on the vicissitudes of fortune. These were the principal incidents of his journey. He returned within a few months. His quick instinct saw a new source of profit in this direction. He fancied that he could do

---

* Much ridicule was thrown upon this story of the Berne Bears, but he was able to invoke the testimony of General Dermoncourt, who had actually belonged to the French force that carried off the "Bears' money."

for foreign countries what he had done for the history of his own—viz., *exploiter* them, and present everything that it was desirable to know about them in an agreeable shape, combined with as much of his own personal fancies as could be introduced. Such was the idea of the "Impressions de Voyage," which he developed in his usual fruitful style, and on this principle, he was to treat France, Switzerland, Spain, Italy, Algiers, and the Rhine. These singular mélanges are full of old stories, personal opinions, scraps of history and gossip. Yet, like everything attempted by this strange writer, they are most lively and entertaining.* A statement, often repeated during the publication of these travels, and accepted seriously, was that they were entirely the fruit of his imagination, and that his journeys were no more extensive than those of a brother littérateur, " round his room." But it was notorious that he was an ardent traveller, and had seen many countries; and it was after each journey that the lively account appeared, just as most Frenchmen of letters, when they travel, almost invariably make some money out of their

---

* De Mirecourt states that he never worked on those productions without having some thirty or forty volumes open before him, with all the passages marked for extract. This means a certain industry, and, in this instance at least is opposed to that theory of his vicarious labour which the pamphleteer so insisted upon.

travelling.   Some of his stories are simple bits of buffoonery, meant to " humbug " what he would call " *ce jobard de public ;* " and the latter laughing at him, as a crowd would at some Jack Pudding in the street, if not with him, the end of amusement was attained.   One of these was his story of having enjoyed " some delicious bear steaks " at a Swiss hotel, whose name he gave.*   As might be expected, these tales reveal his vanity in the most effective way, for wherever he came he took care to flourish his name and merits, and described himself as receiving the most flattering honours and compliments.   People are always amazed at finding out that it is the great Dumas they are receiving or entertaining.†

When Dumas taxed Janin, in their famous dispute, with the geographical blunders in his " Voyage in Italy," the other gave the rough and ready retort,

* Later he heard of some friend or friends asking the innkeeper in jest for some of the " bear steaks " Dumas had so enjoyed, and when he was writing his " Memoirs," he worked this up into an amusing scene which is all purely imaginative.   Every traveller that drives up gives the same order : " Waiter, a bear steak !—Not got it ?—Why, M. Dumas says that you gave it to him.   Drive on, then ! "   Until the landlord, driven to fury, cursed the name of Dumas.

† " Dumas seems to travel," says one of his critics (Cherbuliez, " Rev. Crit.," 1836,) " without seeing or learning anything of the country he visits."   " He puts himself on the stage," says another critic, " to make an omelet, or prepare his bed.   He has always a friend, usually Jadin, to sustain the conversation, and, as required, to father the bon mots ; with a dog to act the part of mute, like the notorious ' milord.' "

"That only proves that I don't copy my 'impressions' out of 'The Traveller's Guide through Europe.' In this way I am a more *original* traveller than you will ever be." Notwithstanding which hard hit Dumas's travels, especially those in the "South of France," are entertaining, and a pleasant mixture of information and romance.

When he stopped at Koenigsfelden, he found a copy of the *Constitutionnel*, which contained an account of his piece which had been produced in his absence. To his horror, real or affected, he saw that his name had been given as being joint author. He had latterly, as we have seen, been eager that his share in these new pieces should not be known—an anxiety that contrasts amusingly with the greediness for publicity which was presently to take possession of him, when he claimed every kind of work, and work in which he had not the smallest share. He explains, however, that he was discovering that a very well-known author has to contend not merely with the rivalry of other writers, but with that of his own previous productions; and the public, indulgent and enthusiastic about the work of a new and clever writer, would become severe and hostile should it learn that the same work was from the hand of an old and familiar servant. There is much truth in this

view; but there were other elements in his case. His
behaviour, always aggressive, had made him hosts of
enemies, private and political, who were delighted to
repay him in kind for his diligent attendance on the
first nights, when writers whom *he* disliked were on
their trial.

In this newspaper he read that the play had failed
signally. "As I have always described my successes
with a naïveté which has often been set down to mere
vanity, I do not shrink from chronicling a splendid,
downright failure." He himself frankly owned that it
was a bad piece; but then, like all his bad pieces and
failures, it was the work of others. It can only be
said that it deserved to fail, for a more monstrous,
unnatural, and childish accumulation of horrors could
not be conceived. It would be hard, with anything
like decency, to give an idea of this vile piece; but it
is such an excellent *reductio ad absurdum* of the
principles of the average French drama, that we shall
attempt it as delicately as we can. A certain count
is filled with "a hatred of the people," which he determines to gratify in the most thorough way. He
begins by going to fight against the republicans in
Switzerland, is defeated, and sheltered by an honest
mechanic, who entertains him, and helps him to
escape. The count would naturally be expected to

show some gratitude for this service. " Dear, no !"
wrote the sound critic of the *Constitutionnel*, whose
words could apply to certain pieces of our own time,
" our grand drama of the day is not so childish as to
accustom us to such rustic sentiments as these ; it must
have something else—what is odious, ignoble, and
absurd, before everything." And the count who hates
the people, writes to tell his preserver that he no
doubt thought himself a happy father and husband,
but that the fact was, that he (the count) was the
father of the child with which the mechanic's wife is
about to present him. The mechanic, receiving this
news, was about to kill the woman, when the scene
opens and reveals his wife just after a happy accouchement—the doctor and priest blessing the new-born
infant, &c. (!) The father determines to spare the
wife, but to raise up another son, who will avenge
them all. Twenty years elapse ; the count, now
turned spy, has a secretary, who proves to be the first
child now grown up. Then follows an incredible
mixture of horrors—murder, debauchery, scenes of
police-spies, Magdalen asylums. The count is condemned to the gallies ; his secretary to the scaffold.
Everything is set before the audience with that
disagreeable realism, lately in such vogue. The
discovery of the relationship is made in the

prison. But when it came to the last scene, when the convict was exhibited in his chains, and the condemned man with his head shaved for the guillotine, the whole audience rose up, and, with yells of horror and disgust, hooted the piece from the boards." "This piece," wrote another excellent critic, "reminds us of the drunken slave which the Lacedemonians exhibited to their children to give them a horror of drunkenness. It is simply a mass of disgusting horrors—a number *of scenes as false to nature as they are vile,* and which it revolts us even to hear described." What French critic would now protest so boldly? Yet such protest is to-day not less necessary, though the writers have abandoned these physical horrors, as wanting effect, and have produced moral monstrosities, quite as revolting. That sentence, "false to nature as they are vile," is really a happy condemnation of the whole of this gross system, for such complications of crime are mere exercises of ingenuity, helped by a depraved imagination; and being false to nature and probability, are outside dramatic art.

Nor could it be said, in putting forth compositions of this kind, that he was following the pernicious example of his fellows, or wanted an example of courage and honesty. These qualities he might have found in the conduct of his companion and contemporary, Victor Hugo, who had started on his dramatic career almost at the same time, and whose literary course has been marked by principles almost opposed to those of his friend. It is not too harsh a judgment to pass, to say that Dumas sacrificed everything to money, and to what he thought would win popularity. Without at all approving Hugo's frantic Jacobinism, it is impossible not to respect his uncompromising spirit, as on the occasion when it was proposed to double his pension to soothe him for the interdiction of his " Marion de Larme." His plays and novels are so genuine, so full of poetry and life, that they have become, as it were, part of the sum of human experience, and will always live. It may be said that his subjects are open to the objections made to those of Dumas and other French writers, that they deal with subjects where horrors are exaggerated too painfully, and crime presented too faithfully. But this borrowing from what may be called the moral dissecting-room, is not done for the purpose of exhibiting the bleeding anatomy, but from an earnest purpose that vehemently impels the writer, and fills his soul,—a moral end or vindication, even though we may think it a false one. With Dumas there is no ultimate purpose and no conviction, and the aim is simply to excite curiosity or to horrify. In

"Notre Dame" (virtually a drama) the figures of the monk and Quasimodo will never pass from public memory; the story of the "Le Roi s'amuse" will never be forgotten by those who have read it; "Ruy Blas," and "Les Miserables" full of dramatic situation, are all genuine inspirations of a poet who *saw* the scenes pass as it were before him.

"Le Roi s'amuse," that remarkable piece (and the cry of the deceived jester Triboulet still rings in our ears), was acted for one night, November 22nd, 1833, and on the next, though the censure was considered to be abolished by the charter, was interdicted. This was supposed to be on account of an allusion in one line, which some of the audience chose to apply to royalty, an intention which Hugo, in a manly defence, protested he was entirely innocent of. It was objected that the scope of the piece was immoral, and the audience, or rather Hugo's enemies, affected to be shocked at the fate of the jester's daughter. But it was ludicrous to think that pieces like "Richard Darlington" and "Teresa" should have been tolerated, without interference on the part of the authorities, and that a piece of genuine tragedy like "Le Roi s'amuse" should have been suppressed.* Hugo ap-

* As Hugo himself has shown, there is a distinct moral purpose in this play; for the wretched jester, though from his hatred to the nobles

pealed to the Tribunal. He might justly complain, since his three great pieces, "Marion," "Hernani," and "Le Roi s'amuse," had been interdicted. He pleaded his own cause in a spirited and effective speech, delivered before all the literary and artistic celebrities of Paris ; but where a government was concerned, not much was .to be expected from French judges, who, on this occasion, declared that "the Tribunal had no jurisdiction."

There was another writer whose career had not been less respectable than that of Hugo, and whose example might have profited Dumas. Scribe utilized his dramatic talents on almost commercial principles, a system which was strictly " business-like," yet contrived to make the excellence of his pieces the means, and profit the end. Dumas had, indeed, the same end in view, but was reckless and unscrupulous as to the means. Yet Scribe enriched the literature of Europe with hundreds of elegant pieces, and at the same time amassed an enormous fortune. It is not sufficiently considered how much the French stage is indebted

he encourages the King in his licentious designs, is in the end made the victim of what he had himself advocated. At the same time it must be said that the subjects of his pieces have their share of that morbidness and repulsiveness which is found in Dumas's writings, a taste which culminated in the work of the poet's old age, the revolting " L'Homme qui rit." But as we have seen, these have been the means and not the end.

to Scribe. Before his day, the favourite shape of light piece was a sort of rude farce, roughly put together, in which much was left to be supplied by the actors, and in which some broadly comic idea was exhibited, though it could not be said to be worked out. It was Scribe who furnished those elegantly constructed little intrigues, to which, even when far-fetched, he imparted an air of probability, and which are put together with the ingenuity of a Chinese puzzle. Wit, grace, the rousing and sustaining of curiosity, dilemmas not so far wrought as to become painful, yet sufficiently embarrassing to be amusing, lively dialogue (which is yet inferior to that of Dumas), these are the charms of the thousand and one Scribe dramas. It is again to be regretted that by two such examples Dumas could not have profited.

The mention of the name of Scribe suggests a theory which has been often gravely urged. The English stage has of late years become about as much dependent on French writers for supplies, as foreign countries are on England for supplies of coal and iron and racehorses. Indeed, the arguments to which French patrons of *le sport* have been driven, to secure for their country the full glory of the victories, which horses sent from France have lately begun to score, have a general analogy to those put forward by wholesale trans-

lators, adapters, or "original" writers of French
pieces. It is maintained that, though the horse may
have been born and bred and trained in England,
or ridden to victory by English jockeys, still French
nurture and direction, and some more mysterious
French manipulation, or some exercise of judgment on
the part of the owner, has made it virtually French.
Adaptation from the French in regard of the drama
has become so much a system, and so necessary to the
very existence of our own stage, furnishing bread, also,
to a large and important class of clever men, that it
has become essential to find respectable arguments to
justify the continued appropriation. These, it must
be said, are quite akin to what the French sportsman urges for the honour of the nationality of his
horses. It is curious, too, to see how these theories of
excuse have become gradually more daring, according
as the spoliation became more wholesale and almost
necessary. Marauders, whom a dearth of food has
accustomed to raids on their neighbours, will ingeniously devise a whole code of morals nicely adapted
to their special case, gradually exhibiting more and
more comprehensive principles. But the curious fact
remains, that it is owing to the utter destitution of our
stage during recent times, that English playwrights
have become more noisy in asserting the originality

and legitimacy of their own operations. And it will be
seen how from the wholesale character of their proceedings they have been compelled to shift their
ground, formerly being, as it were, engaged in a
contraband trade, and anxious to escape observation ;
now, when these " runnings " of French pieces may be
engaged in without danger, boldly facing it out, protesting that these are not French goods at all, but of
their own make.   It is now seriously maintained that
there is no such thing as the old-fashioned translation
or adaptation, but that the dramatist helping himself
to a foreigner's play or novel is in truth presenting a
form of original composition.   The fashion in which
this is urged is almost startling, and seems incomprehensible to simple outsiders, accustomed to call things
by their old names.

It might seem at first sight that this scarcely needed
argument ; but it has become necessary to look a little
closely into the principles of the matter.   In other
directions the question of originality is jealously
watched, and an almost detective nicety applied.   A
poet writes a popular line, the germ of which is presently discovered in another poet, though the phrase
be different.   Some of Sir Joshua's most characteristic
attitudes are found to have been suggested by old
prints ; the façades of innumerable buildings of pre-

tence have been furnished by old classical models; it is found that actors and orators borrow a gesture and intonation, while the novelist works up some local tradition, like the "Bride of Lammermoor," or historical character. Above all, the composer is most speedily "run to earth," and even the imitator of the style, though not of the airs of composers like Meyerbeer, Gounod, and Verdi, is at once detected. The joke, even in its new variation, is marked down. In short, the account of indebtedness is vigorously kept and watched, and so much is always placed to the credit of the borrowed element. But with the drama it would seem a wholly different principle must obtain, and it is coolly asserted that the shaping and moulding which the imported piece undergoes to fit it for its new sphere, gives to the shaper and moulder the entire credit of creation or paternity. Later, however, when our stage had sunk into such discreditable mendicancy as to be almost entirely dependent on the French, some ingenious variations of the system were discovered, which became necessary to save the pride of the various clever men engaged in the system. The art of this consisted in seizing on some powerful foreign drama, using it for a couple of acts, and then adding in the bills that "the third act is entirely original;" that "a new conclusion has been given to the piece," and that some entirely new characters have been introduced. This is considered to put the matter of lawful proprietorship, if not of originality, beyond question.

The whole, indeed, is one of the most curious delusions on record ; but when we think of the number of men who have made a reputation and earned a livelihood by this wholesale system of appropriation, the matter becomes a national discredit. It is only in England that this system of dramatic smuggling combined with adulteration is known. In Germany, pieces are honestly translated from the French, and presented as French pieces. And it may be said that this is significant of a healthy and honest public taste. For, as the writer has shown elsewhere, the genuine dramatic productions of a country are " racy " of the soil, as well as of the society, manners, and character of the people among whom the piece is produced ; and any alteration or shaping, so as to fit them to a new society, can only result in something that is unnatural. This will be seen in many an adapted farce where, though the manners are English, the situation is French. The Germans and Italians, more honest and logical, accept no distortions. From a false taste, and also from their not possessing any contemporary national drama, the

English are quite satisfied with these perverted exhibitions ; which suggests the Irish whisky now said to be exported in large quantities to France, and which returns to England in the shape of a so-called brandy. The purchaser gets an honest liquor, and does not suffer much ; but the imposition is in selling whisky *as* brandy. Here is the offence in the case of our band of adapters, in setting off a foreign as a British article, merely on the ground of certain mixings, " finings," and flavourings.

Taken in the most favourable way, the adapter who even rewrites, recasts, or reshapes the whole, is performing a mechanical operation, though an operation which may require great skill and cleverness. We might test this in the instance of a popular writer, whose two best known plays—" The Ticket-of-Leave Man " and " Still Waters Run Deep "—claim to be virtually independent of all foreign aid. There is, indeed, a French piece which has been named as containing the germ of the first ; but this germ could be described in a sentence, which constitutes the whole of what the English author borrowed ; who, starting with this slender stock, worked entirely on his own resources, finding new incidents, new characters, new dialogue. So with " Still Waters," the *idea* of which is found in a novel of

Balzac's, called "Le Gendre," and to which the English author is under little more obligation than he is to the suggestion of the " Ticket-of-Leave Man." Yet even in these extreme cases, we hold that the French writer is the *real* author, and that the Englishman, however skilful his work, deserves no credit but that of being a consummate play-writer.

Without entering here into the study of the nature of the dramatic, it may be said that an original dramatic idea—one that is powerful and distinct— would present itself, as it were, in a flash, and compressed within the limits of a sentence. And every striking play will be found on analysis to turn on some such original notion—the key to the whole. Thus, one well-known play of Sardou's—" Nos Bons Villageois "—could be described as turning on the supposed pastoral virtues of rural life, which in reality exhibits a host of petty vices that cannot be found in town life. Here is the dramatic idea, which, moreover, to be treated in its most effective manner, could only be dealt with in one way, viz., by making a trusting stranger visit some such happy valley full of this firm belief, and being disagreeably and rudely awakened to the truth. This idea is truly dramatic, and no manipulation or dexterous treatment or alterations could overlay it, or make it the property of an adapter. Did we see a second play on the same subject, no matter how differently treated, we should still say, " I have seen something like this before, in another shape." And indeed those who saw M. Sardou's play at once recalled the admirable " Little Pedlington." So with the " Ticket-of-Leave Man," the *idea* of the French piece was the cruel severity of society towards a man who has been convicted unjustly of a crime, showing how all his exertions cannot efface the stigma. So with " Still Waters," whose " idea," as found in De Balzac's story, is that of a husband tyrannized over by a mother-in-law, and contriving to defeat her by quiet tactics. These " ideas " are each, in fact, the whole drama ; such as they suggested themselves to the original writer. When he had secured them he felt that he had got a play, which he had to work out. The adapter takes possession of this core or back-bone, as it were, and clothes and decorates it according to his views. Finally, what disposes of his claim is, that without the foreign piece, no matter how independent he may claim to be of it, *his own would have had no existence at all.*

Are we, then, to be shut out from the enjoyment of these pieces of foreign countries? By no means. But the true and legitimate method of enjoying such pieces is not to adapt, or turn them into indigenous pieces of English manners, but to translate them with due skill and pains, and present them as a picture of their native manners and society. The great success of such a translation of "Nos Intimes," and of "Le Juif Polonais," shows that more interest will be taken in a carefully-prepared English counterpart of a French play, than in a patched and twisted or shaped and trimmed version, which affects, by means of native names, to be of English growth. It is when we see the original of one of these mutilated pieces, after being accustomed to the prepared version, that we see what an amazing difference there is in the spirit and execution; the adaptation bearing the same relation to the original that a schoolgirl's copy has to the water-colour drawing set before her by the master.

As we have seen, we have no flourishing national drama of our own, and must be more or less dependent on the importation of foreign products for home consumption. The late Mr. Robertson, the present Mr. Albery, and other writers, will be mentioned in disproof of this assertion; but their productions are mere pictures of ephemeral manners and customs of the time, and do not reach down to the great moving principles and passions and humours of society. A false delusion makes us suppose that exhibitions of young ladies flirting with officers, of evening parties, and the like, represent the dramatic principles of society sufficiently. We have only to turn to the French stage during the last twenty years to see how, in spite of the enfeeblement of manners produced by the Empire, what a vigour—what a bold masculine system obtained in the writing of plays. If the practice followed on the English stage had been adopted, we ought to have seen the luxurious manners of the new-blown Imperial followers, the dinners, the salons of officials, the hunting parties at Fontainebleau, and such tame spectacles reproduced. Instead, dramatists like young Dumas, Sardou, and Augier, seized on the strong vehement passions and follies of the day, studied how they affected society, and held them up in the broad glare of noon-day, or more lurid flare of gas. The vile worship of money, the fever for speculation, and the vulgarity and corruption of character induced by the sudden rise of speculators into leading positions, furnished the theme of the " Question d'Argent ; " the frantic passion for dress, the " Famille Benoiton ; " the reign of vice, the " Demi-Monde ; " in all of which the exhibition of manners and customs are used merely as decoration, but the leading passion is worked out with extraordinary power and effect. Beside these vigorous and exciting pieces, such plays as " School " and " Apple Blossoms " seem tame indeed ; and make it hardly surprising that the consumers of dramatic food should find it necessary to import the superior foreign produce. This wholesale system of " conveying " then, being found absolutely necessary to the life of our theatres, has gone on merrily, and, strange to say, with but little protest on the part of the French themselves—an indifference which may be set down more, perhaps, to that complacent ignorance of all that goes on in England, than to a dignified indifference to such treatment. The spoliation has, indeed, grown to such a pitch that writers of reputation actually describe their adaptations as " original," and set down what is well known to be a translation as " a new play by ——." Single instances of this kind might be passed over ; but that a great intellectual nation should for years draw profit and amusement from an organised system of depredation as unlawful as smuggling, at the same time clamouring for protection against American robbery, is an unbecoming spectacle. Rich in their own inexhaustible resources, the French have rarely been found borrowing from their neighbours ; and it is certainly not flattering to our reputation that, during the last twenty years, they should not have thought it worth while to entertain more than three or four of our pieces, giving these but a languid reception!* It is curious, then, that, in a country so completely independent, there should be found the most startling instance of wholesale dramatic pillage that the world has yet witnessed, and that one of the most versatile and brilliant of Frenchmen, gifted with a wealth of dramatic power, should have organised a complicated and ingenious system of spoliation, beside which ours seems absolute trifling! This is in itself a phenomenon; and the acceptance of Dumas's monstrous system of robbery by his countrymen can only be accounted for by the skill with which it was carried out, and their ignorance of foreign literature.

Dumas's part in this nefarious traffic is but little known. The public were aware, indeed, of his keeping a sort of workshop, where skilled hands laboured, under his direction, at innumerable stories, on whose title-pages was to appear his own name. They also knew that he had a skilful "collaborator" like Maquet, with whose powers he joined his own, and to which was owing a good deal of the effective portions of the "Monte Christo" and "Memoirs of a Physician."

---

* Mr. Dickens's "L'Abîme," and "Jean la Poste," by Mr. Boucicault, are the most conspicuous examples. These, however, were entirely successful.

But not so well known is the strange and elaborate course he pursued when he worked .alone, and which, from the very hour of his first success, he carried out on system. In the flush and enthusiasm of youth, his western blood warming in his veins, his own original sallies did not seem to him so precious as those passages in other writers which he deliberately noted and copied, to be made useful as the occasion served; and thus there resulted the strange phenomenon that works, with the air of undoubted originality, and stamped with genius, such as was " Henry III.," were found, on examination, to be no more than pieces of mosaic work, made up of fragments of a dozen writers. Here was the genius of the man, and here he stands alone; for, though a copyist, he was original; and it must be said there is a good deal of speciousness, if not of truth, in his defence of his practice, but it is a defence that could only apply to himself. This we shall understand when we presently come to consider the gigantic system of spoliation on which a European reputation was built, and which has no parallel in the history of letters.

We have .already spoken of the honourable and loyal system pursued by Scribe, whose practice is indeed no more than what every really great writer or

painter has pursued.　A character is suggested, a
peculiar expression or scene is noticed which furnishes
writer or painter with stuff that he works up after his
own fashion.　This is a species of collaboration, and
it is at the bottom of all " original " composition ; for
genius works on what it observes, or has been suggested to it.　Men like Dickens or De Balzac repro-
duce what is thus offered to them in a shape that is
unrecognisable, and has no likeness to the original,
while inferior writers of fiction can testify from their
own experience how the suggestion or observation of a
particular character has opened to them the delinea-
tion of a new one wholly different.　Scribe's practice
illustrates this excellently.　In the year 1830 a M.
Cornu waited on him with a drama which he was asked
to leave.　He did so, wrote other plays, acquired a
name, and after two or three years bethought himself
of his play and M. Scribe.　The latter had forgotten
him, but turning to his classified list took out a M.S.
which he asked the visitor to hear him read.　This
proved to be the graceful little piece known as the
" Chanoinesse."　The other listened, was delighted,
and heartily applauded, then returning to the object
of his visit, asked for his piece.　" You have just heard
it," said Scribe.　" The truth is, *your play contained
an idea*, and I used it after my own fashion."

The piece was not in the least like Cornu's in plot or characters, but, as he read it, suggested to the skilful Scribe an idea for a piece of his own. With scrupulous honour he named Cornu as joint author, and shared the profits with him. Such loyalty did no harm to one who might perhaps be considered the most successful writer of the century. On another occasion Mazères happened to tell him some story of Turenne and the coiners, saying that something could be made of it. Scribe said he had heard the anecdote, and it had never occurred to him to think of it in reference to dramatic purposes. Years afterwards, when called on for a libretto he wrote " Le Serment," and allowed the claim of Mazères to be considered as joint author. Here, however, came in one of the nice distinctions of collaboration. Mazères admitted that he had had no actual share in the composition, and could not therefore be " named." He appeared, therefore, under the disguise of * * *. This was to secure his place on the register, as well as his legal share of profit. Again, when the Marquis de Saint-Georges once brought him a play on the subject of a game at lansquenet, Scribe shook his head. Any light piece, he said, founded on a game that was not in fashion, would never do. Ecarté would have been better. A little story could be easily made out of such a game, and, his imagination kindling, he proceeded to sketch a lively piece. When later "Ecarté, or a Corner in the Drawing-room" was given at the Gymnase, Saint Georges was "named," though he had done no more than excite the invention of the dramatist.* The French courts would seem to have supported this view of indirect obligation; as where a dramatist took the subject of his piece from an old and little known writer of memoirs, it was decreed that another dramatist, who had gone to the same source for a piece, was infringing the rights of the first dramatist, who was to be at least "original" in the discovery. But the variations of this singular system became most elaborate. Some were named "joint author," for a consideration, merely to secure their right of entry behind the scenes. A successful dramatist owed money, and in his next piece named the creditor as joint author, who had thus an official title to a share in the receipts. Maquet is thus registered as having had a share in the composition of the following plays by Dumas: "Intrigue el L'amour," "Hamlet," "Le Comte Hermann," "La Chasse au Chastre," "Le Capitaine Lajonquière," and "La Barrière Clichy." "I have not written a line in them," he told Goizet, "but I receive my 'droits d'auteur' as payment for

---

* Goizet, "Hist. de la Collaboration."

moneys lent." There was, therefore, a singular complication in this arrangement. The great Dumas himself could not be called the author of any of these, —nearly all of which were translations executed for him,—but was named as the author. The following curious confession was the result. A person to whom he owed money was also credited with a share in the composition : the actual translators or arrangers were not named : while the original writers of all, beings like Shakspeare, Schiller, or Iffland, were not mentioned at all.

END OF VOL. I.

BRADBURY, EVANS, AND CO., PRINTERS, WHITEFRIARS.